Christopher Kenworthy was born in Preston in 1968, but has lived all over the UK. His short-story collection *Will You Hold Me?* was published in 1996 by The Do-Not Press. He has written more than forty stories for *Interzone, The Third Alternative, The Time Out Book of Paris Stories, Year's Best Horror* and many others. He now lives by the Swan River in Western Australia. *The Winter Inside* is his first novel.

The Winter Inside

Christopher Kenworthy

Library of Congress Catalog Card Number: 99-069159

A catalogue record for this book is available from
the British Library on request

First published 2000 by Serpent's Tail,
4 Blackstock Mews,
London N4 2BT
website: www.serpentstail.com

Typeset by Avon Dataset Ltd, Bidford on Avon, B50 4JH

Printed in Italy by Chromo Litho Ltd

10 9 8 7 6 5 4 3 2 1

To Mum and Dad

Special thanks to Chantal Bourgault du Coudray for helping me to move on with my life and my work.

Thanks to all those who kept an eye on me, during the creation of this novel. Your warmth is appreciated.

Prologue

When he woke, Sarah was taking up most of the bed, cramming him against the wall. In sleep, her dry mouth was open, each tooth dented with the molten black of a filling. Moving to the foot of the bed, Nick opened the window, and heat rose from the radiator mingling with cold air from outside. The narrow street of labs and offices was made colourless by the weather, the cars armoured with snow. Tree trunks had turned glossy black, their branches and twigs holding impossibly thick ledges of white. Even the icicles hanging from gutters were opaque with a roughening of flakes. There were no sounds of dogs or traffic, no car doors or footsteps. All he could hear was snow falling on snow, like the sound of blinking.

Lying down again he kissed Sarah's back and neck, a habit of giving her attention. Her hair smelt of smoke, making his guts wrench. She yawned, her breath pungent with last night's beer, and when her eyes opened she stared as though drunk and put a palm on her forehead.

'Fucked,' she muttered, holding her tongue out to show him how stale it was. He passed her the water and she gulped at it, wincing. She looked better now the expression was returning to her face, but her skin was an unpleasant mix of pale and blush. She sat up to be near the window, breathing the fresh air, eyes closed. Her hair looked darker than usual, the ends wet with the sweat on her shoulders. The heating in his flat was on automatic, being dormant except for three burning hours in the early morning. It could have been designed to exacerbate a hangover, drying you out and thinning the air.

That was more of a problem during November, because it was impossible to get out and do much when the weather was bad. They'd spent more nights in, cooking, drinking and watching TV, than they had going out. It took an act of determination to get further than the shops on the next road. The night before, the footpaths had been so thick with packed snow they'd effectively had to skate into the centre of Leicester for the pubs. He couldn't remember much after last orders, except being mad at her when she said he was 'getting embarrassing'. There were vague memories of the walk home, the snow bright with orange streetlight. He remembered a fall by the park gates, stinging skin as he tried to get up, her sodden mitten gripping his hand. They'd been laughing at one point. From what he could remember they went to bed happy, if only for the warmth they gained from each other.

He went closer to kiss her, but she turned her cheek to him. 'Not until I've brushed my teeth,' she said. It was the sort of comment he'd have jumped on once, saying it was a veiled criticism, meaning he should brush his teeth first. He let them go these days, tried not to get mad when she turned away. It was the one habit she still had that bothered him, though. She used to do it all the time, refusing to look at him when he talked, turning when he tried to kiss her. The more he tried to make eye contact, the more she'd stare off elsewhere. If he complained, she'd say something like, 'Are you so insecure that I have to look at you all the time?' Worst of all was when they were walking and he felt he had to lean round, head on an angle towards her face, struggling for a response. He'd found the best way to deal with it wasn't to move in eagerly, or to seek her approval, but to trail off quietly, act as though he didn't mind whether she listened. As a result she hardly ever did it any more. And when she wanted to be kissed, she made it clear.

Sarah reached out to the windowsill, collecting a pinch of snow, rubbing the melt of it across her forehead. There was nothing for breakfast except a green apple, which they shared. Sarah got back into bed and said that because it was Sunday she didn't intend to move. He knew then that he should ask her to leave. They'd agreed months ago never to spend time together out of obligation, but only when they genuinely wanted. It was easy to spot when she was growing tired of him, but he was only just learning to recognise his own limits. If he started finding her body distasteful, that was the sign they should spend time apart. It wasn't healthy, resenting the way she looked; in a relationship you make a commitment to look for the appeal in somebody even when it isn't obvious. Seeing her flaws was unfair, and a good reason to get away from her.

He remembered something he'd said to Dave the morning after he'd met Sarah. 'She's everything I dislike. Dark hair, brown eyes, big tits. And still a teenager.' It was something Dave had reminded him of frequently during the past eighteen months. Sarah was twenty-one now, and whatever Dave said, Nick was convinced she'd matured. The twelve-year age gap was barely noticeable these days.

In truth, he could enjoy her body in the right mood. It didn't matter that he'd once preferred a different sort of person. It was ridiculous to insist on a specific set of preferences in somebody. So long as she was capable of moving him, of arousing him, it didn't matter that she wasn't what he'd been looking for. It's like people who write personal ads, he thought. The wording is so specific they narrow their options down to nothing. It's because they've refused to trust chance that they resort to advertising. There's nothing wrong with being picky, getting what you want, but preconceptions like that are too limiting. If somebody unexpected makes you happy, that should be enough.

But despite all this, if he spent more than a few days with Sarah, he found himself resenting the way her breasts slid around her ribs when she lay back. He fixated on every blue vein in her chest, knowing they would get darker with each year. He would even get close to her face, just to look at the shadow of pores in her sallow skin. The worst thing about it was that it made him feel shallow. If she knew, if anybody knew about these thoughts, he wouldn't be able to defend them. And holding in the resentment could only do more damage. That's why it was best to get rid of her as soon as the feeling arose, so he could look forward to seeing her again.

He was trying to think of a way to make her leave when the phone rang.

'Ignore it,' Sarah said, putting her arms around his waist, pressing her face into his neck. He'd have laughed, except that she hadn't shown much interest in being near him until the phone had rung. 'It's Sunday morning,' she said, as he pulled away.

In the hallway, still naked, he crouched to answer the phone.

'Nick? It's me,' the voice said.

Sarah sat up in bed, her mouth a quizzical pout as she leaned round to look down the hall. Nick pushed the phone closer to his ear and turned away. It was the first time he'd heard Wendy's voice in three years, but he could only say, 'Oh, hello.'

'Can I see you?' She was shivering, and from the quality of the line she must have been in a phone box.

'Yes, all right.'

'Your voice sounds different. Are you with somebody?'

'I'm afraid so.'

'Can you get rid of her, Nick? I need to see you now.' She said it as forcefully as she could, but it still sounded like a question. He heard another coin drop as she waited for him to speak.

'Are you in Leicester?' he asked.

'Yes, by the park, at the end of your road. Can I come round?'

'I'll meet you there as soon as I can.'

Walking back to the bedroom, he had three seconds to think of a way to make Sarah leave. Hints and suggestions would fall flat, because she'd stay as long as he was there. Whenever they were at her place and he tried to go home, she was even worse. She'd crouch on all fours over him, grinning, insisting that he stay. If he refused, she'd lie on her back, showing her stern profile, folding the duvet around herself like a shroud. He'd find himself making excuses, saying sorry as he left. To avoid another scene like that, he took the direct approach.

'You have to leave, Sarah,' he said. 'Now.'

'I don't think so.' She grabbed at the duvet as though it could hold her in.

'Yes, you do. I have a friend who's in trouble.' On the floor, her knickers were coiled around her mud-smeared jeans. He parted them and threw them on to the bed. 'Get dressed. Please, for once, Sarah, let me get on with my day.'

'Who is she?'

'She's an old friend.'

'Girlfriend?'

'Yes, but so what? You have no right to be cross.'

'Which one is she?'

'Please, get dressed.'

'I'll wait here for you,' she said, as though nothing was happening, her last attempt at being happy before she switched to anger. When he didn't answer she said, 'You're not bringing her here.'

'Just get dressed. I'm *not* going to argue with you.'

'I'll tell you something, Nick . . .' she snapped, rummaging to get her knickers on under the covers. For once, she was stuck for something to say. She got out of bed, rushing her last clothes on faster than him. He felt giddy with the relief of getting rid of her. She put her coat on and set off down the stairs without another word.

The park was nothing more than a square of snowed-over grass, bordered with trees and benches. Behind those, main roads and houses, their curtains left open to reveal lamplight and early Christmas trees. It was nine o'clock, but still like twilight, the snow and sky a dim morning blue.

Wendy had cleared the snow from a bench and sat leaning forward, rubbing her gloveless hands together, blowing into them. The ends of her blonde hair mixed with the snow on her shoulders. When she saw him, she looked as though she was sorry for something; there was no smile left in her face. She stood, brushing the snow from her long coat. He'd forgotten how much taller he was than her, so that when she hugged him his face was pressed against her scalp. Her hair smelt like it had been rained on, not quite dry. The way she pressed her face into his jumper, he expected her hug to be tight, but she felt too tired to put in much effort. When she moved back, he saw that the whites of her eyes were so webbed with red she must have been crying.

The first thing he said was, 'Are you all right?'

'I just wanted to see you.'

He was already concerned that they'd been unable to have an ordinary greeting, simply to say hello, and be pleased to see each other. It would have been good to meet up without having to think about the past, but it must have been bothering her.

When her eyes closed, he expected her to lean on him again, but she lowered her head into her hands and sobbed, the breath of vapour passing from her fingers. Behind her, a blackbird left its branch, snow breaking free beneath it.

'Has something happened?'

She shook her head, pushing her face into her hands again, then quickly pulled it away. 'I'm all right. But I missed you.'

'It's been three years, Wendy. I didn't think you wanted to see me again.'

'I don't know what to do.'

'About what?'

She looked past him, towards his house.

'I'm so cold,' she said calmly. 'You seemed to take for ever. I was worried you weren't coming.'

'I said I'd come. Should we get inside, somewhere, get some coffee?'

'I need something warm.' She explained that her trains had been variously delayed and cancelled, so that she'd had to spend the night at Crewe station, too cold to sleep in the waiting-room. And then the heater on the train wasn't working.

His feet were already frozen, so he tried to speed her up, suggested they get some breakfast at a café. Wendy nodded towards Regent Road.

'Can't we just go to yours?'

'I've nothing in to eat.'

'I can't really face being in public any longer,' she said. It struck him as a strange thing to say, because there were so few people about. She'd never been one for crowded places such as pubs, but he'd hoped the thought of a café would cheer her. She used to like nothing more than buying food out in the mornings, when the cafés were quiet. He offered to pay, in case that was the problem.

'I just want to feel at home somewhere.'

He doubted that was possible, because even as they walked it was difficult to speak. Their questions and answers were no more intimate than those passed between strangers, listing the facts of their recent existence. She sounded less desperate now, much further from crying, but he found it difficult to believe they were the same people who were once so close. They'd reached a point in their relationship, years ago, where they knew the other's needs and thoughts before they were ever voiced. But unlike some couples who reach that stage, they hadn't taken the risk of giving up on conversation. For a while at least, they'd put in the effort.

Now, though, it was a different kind of effort, struggling to find anything to talk about. Their speech was clumsy and filled with silence, then comments on the cold. Their responses to each other's statements were toned with an overt sincerity that made them sound false. Until they talked about the past directly that was unlikely to change, but he didn't feel up to tackling it yet, and from the way Wendy looked neither did she.

It was a relief to get to the corner shop, even though it was overheated and stuffy, the light a vile fluorescent that made it difficult to focus. When they left with a bag of bread and fruit, they were so close to his house that they managed the whole walk without speaking at all.

As he unlocked the door, he wished he hadn't been so curt

with Sarah. He wouldn't blame her if she ended it over this. No matter what he said about Wendy's needs, Sarah would say he'd treated *her* like shit. It wasn't the way he'd done it that bothered him, but that he could prioritise somebody who wasn't part of his life any more. It had been years since he'd done this; jumping to, when Wendy showed up. During their on-and-off period, she'd shown a remarkable ability to distance herself from him, until he got into a new relationship. And then she knew all she had to do was ring up for them to get back together. He'd earned a reputation as a prize bastard with a certain group of women for dumping a girlfriend the second Wendy called.

Inside he put the kettle on and slid in some toast. Wendy was in the middle of the front room, taking off her coat, weighing up the place.

'Has it changed much?'

'Not that much. Can I have a bath?'

He said she could, before moving further into the kitchen to hide his expression. Twenty minutes ago she was virtually a stranger, and now she wanted to be in his bath. She was going to be naked again, in the building where they'd begun their relationship.

'It still feels like home,' she called through, 'whatever you think about me.'

Unable to leave that hanging, he went through to her.

'I'm not sure what you want from me,' he said, but she looked so shocked he felt as though he'd told her to get out. 'I'm glad to see you, but I don't know what you're expecting. I'm in a relationship with somebody. And although I'm really pleased to see you, I can't threaten that.'

Her face hardened for a second, so that he thought she might get mad, but then she sat down, her teeth chewing softly on her bottom lip.

'I'm sorry, turning up like this.'

'That's OK. I am glad to see you.'

'I'm not going to cause trouble, but I wanted to see you again. It's such a long time since we spent time together, without all that.'

'Well, that's good, then.'

She ran the bath while he finished making breakfast, and when everything was on the tray he heard the taps stop. He knocked and told her it was ready.

'I'm already undressed,' she said through the door. 'Hang on.'

She opened the door, hiding behind it rather than covering herself with a towel, and asked him to push it through. Once he'd taken his own share of breakfast off the tray, he slid it into the steamy room, clear of the door.

'Thanks. Stay and talk.'

She closed the door, and he heard her get into the water.

'I can't talk to you through the door,' he said, surprised, because he hoped she'd ask him to open it. He felt angry with himself, but he wanted to catch a glimpse of her, or at least be near her while she was warm and naked. It was peculiar, but seeing her look so frail made him desire her more than if she'd turned up looking her best. It wasn't that her fragility attracted him, but seeing her so cold in the park made him yearn to see her as she had been. In the bath, she'd always been at her most relaxed, speculating happily, proposing futures. It was the only time she seemed pleasantly idle, willing to let time pass without worrying or striving. When she'd lived in London, they did most of their talking while she was in the bath. People usually prefer to be alone in the bathroom, but she always called him in, chatting freely, completely unfazed by his presence as she washed, shaved and soaked. Mostly he'd sit with his back to the wall, a distance from her so she didn't feel pestered. Before she got out, she'd let him wash her hair, and that was when his touch was most gentle.

She didn't answer though, so he took his food through to the front room and turned on the radio to cover the noise of her washing.

It was almost certain that he'd have to send her away if she didn't leave soon. He couldn't risk letting her stay, because even if nothing happened, he couldn't explain it to Sarah, and wasn't willing to lie. There was no way he could let go of everything he'd worked for with Sarah, just because Wendy was having a brief change of heart, or a period of need. Although he felt desire, it wasn't something he wanted to follow up. Finding her attractive was almost a reaction to her presence, a habit that had grown to annoy him. It was as though their bodies remembered each other. He was sure they could have been better friends if there hadn't been that persistent hunger for each other. It was something they'd both voiced displeasure at, especially towards the end; but every time they met, spoke or wrote, it had come back. Whenever they were alone, it was impossible for them to avoid touching. It would be stupid, though, to give into that now, because he would spoil everything with Sarah for something that had no future. If it could ever have worked with Wendy, it would have done by now.

It was better to send her away before the day was over, he thought. He should be kind but clear and honest. Even tell her that the desire was a problem, so there would be no flirting or build-up. Nothing would be worse than succumbing and then sending her away. If he once touched her in the state she was in, he'd feel obliged to let her stay as long as she wanted.

He heard the water run out of the bath and was surprised

when, a few minutes later, she came through dressed. He'd expected her to emerge in a towel.

'You look better,' he said.

'Thanks. You always help me feel better.'

That wasn't true, and it was strange that she could remember things that way. It was good to be appreciated though, and he knew that he could make her trip across country worthwhile. That might go some way to making up for the problems they'd shared.

'Is this your girlfriend?' she asked, pointing to a framed photograph of Sarah, taken at a mutual friend's wedding.

'Yes, that's her. She's not usually so dressed up, or as flushed.'

'She looks nice.'

'Nice?'

Wendy shrugged. 'What do you like about her?'

'She makes me laugh. We get on well. She's intelligent enough.' He knew that sounded defensive, so he added, 'She's grown on me.'

'That doesn't sound like you.'

'It's how I am now, and it's working. You're still with Ian?'

'Yes. Still in Newtown,' she said, sitting on the floor, against the armchair. 'That's partly why I came away now. It's so snowed up there I thought I was going to freeze to death. We can't afford to heat the place properly. We spend most of the time collecting wood. And there's nothing else to do anyway.'

'But you're OK with each other?'

She didn't answer that directly but said that neither of them were working so things were getting a bit claustrophobic.

'I feel like I have to do something other than exist with him. I've wasted so much time.'

'And Ian?'

She said he was still intent on signing on for life. He frequently referred to the legend of a local man who'd been declared unfit to work because of his mental condition. It was something Ian aspired to.

'Then what are you doing staying with him?'

'Where else would I go?'

'What about your mum's?'

'I doubt it.'

'But come on, that's not like you, sticking to something you don't want. If you need to, get out.'

'I've run out of energy,' she said.

'Then what made you come here?'

Wendy shook her head, ran her fingers back through her hair, and left her hand resting on her neck. She looked down at her knees, and he saw tears.

'I missed you. You're the only one who ever gave me any encouragement. I just need a bit of that, to get going again. I can't face it.'

He told her she wasn't being clear, but she didn't want to elaborate.

'It would help just to hear what you've been up to,' she said.

They talked until lunch, and then he cooked them both some soup. She ate it so eagerly that he wondered if she'd been eating enough. It started going dark at about three in the afternoon, and he expected them to sit in the gloaming, talking as it turned to night outside. That was something they used to do all the time. Being so interested in each other, they wouldn't notice time go by. They'd often cited it as a sign of how good their relationship was. But before the streetlights lit up Wendy turned his lights on – both lamps and the overhead – then closed the curtains.

'All we need's a real fire,' she said, then: 'I suppose I'd better check the train times.'

He got her the number for train enquiries, but while she dialled he felt guilty. The last time they'd parted had been less than friendly, but at the time it had seemed necessary. Now, what was the point in being so harsh? It took about five minutes for anyone to answer the phone, and in all that time they didn't speak or move.

After a brief discussion Wendy said, 'That's that then.'

It had snowed for so long that all the trains had been cancelled. They could have found a way around that somehow, looked up a place for her to stay, but it would be artificial to pretend to be so distant. Sarah had left, without calling back, so there was no harm in letting a friend stay. With that commitment made, they were able to enjoy the evening more. During dinner, they swapped memories of their time together and laughed at some of the stories.

'I miss all that,' she said when they'd finished eating. 'I really miss it.'

They talked until the early hours, both sensing that this might be the only time they'd have together, unwilling for it to be over. When she suggested they go to bed, it wasn't because of fatigue, she said, but cold.

'We can still talk. We don't have to go to sleep yet.'

That meant she assumed they were going to be in the same bed. It was a scene they'd played out many times before, with her stopping over after they'd split up, sharing a bed. Beneath the sheets there would be a slight brush of contact, their legs touching, then a held hand; a kind comment would lead to a kiss. It was a contrived and obvious game that had always annoyed him, so in the bedroom he said, 'I'm still with Sarah, so nothing can happen.'

'I don't want it to, Nick,' she said, sounding disappointed that he'd felt the need to bring it up.

It was strange watching her undress down to her T-shirt, and she looked deep in thought; her eyes were dark and her brow furrowed. She turned out the light and climbed in next to him. Rather than excitement, he almost felt at peace, and before either of them spoke again he fell asleep.

The heat of the radiators woke him at dawn. Outside, the unlit bulb of a streetlamp was illumined by the rising sun, and there was a sound of dripping. It wasn't much of a thaw, but probably enough for Wendy to get home. In sleep, her face was more familiar than it had been yesterday. He would have to ask her to leave as soon as she awoke. Keeping still, he watched her sleeping, one hand on her stomach, rising and falling with the waves of her breathing.

Part One

Chapter One

When I met Wendy she was nineteen, still living with her parents and trying to come to terms with the fact that she hadn't gone to university. She'd wanted to study art but hadn't got as far as a foundation course. Her dad wanted her to find something more secure, and his idea of a compromise was to let her do what she wanted so long as she paid her way. She could have left home and supported herself, but that would have eaten into her money, delaying her further. So for the past year she'd been working in Waterstone's, trying to save up. 'And now I don't even paint much,' she said, 'so what's the point?' It was strange for a first conversation to be so doubtful; people are usually keen to show you how well their life is going.

It was the coldest January I'd known in Leicester, perhaps made worse because the tail end of 1991 had been mild. I was living in a shared house, next to the football ground. With only a few weeks to go until my twenty-seventh birthday, I was keen to move out alone. During winter my room was in shadow even on clear days, because only the sun's white corona cleared the stadium. The house was centrally heated, but my room was on the top floor at the end of the radiator chain. Jutting out over the garage, it didn't even gain heat from the rest of the house. There was only one window, looking out over the road, its glass dusted with fine rain or frost.

My housemates thought I was an obsessive worker, because I was hardly ever home. It was preferable to eat out on my own than go back there early. Teaching at the university, I virtually lived in my office, using one corner as a studio space. Designing book covers and occasional magazine illustrations was more than a supplement to my income; it allowed me to feel I'd never given up my interest in art. Even though uni took up most of the time, it was preferable to believe I was more than a casual artist. It was probably this minor artistic dabbling that interested Wendy in the first place. It didn't matter that it was illustration, rather than oils and canvas; I was doing something she still hadn't got round to. Despite the doubts she voiced, I knew it was something she dreamed of. Even on that first night, I couldn't resist encouraging her.

That had been a problem with my last few relationships. Although I was only a part-time illustrator, it apparently made me that bit more attractive to women who wanted to be artists. I'd come to enjoy the role of pseudo-mentor, and had the pleasure of feeling I was making a difference, watching successive girlfriends explore their creative interests. It didn't occur to me at the time that anybody who's going to persist with their work doesn't need encouragement.

It was only when my mate Dave pointed out that each new girlfriend was around the nineteen mark, no matter how I aged, that it became clear what was going on. I believed I was attracting people who were going to be inspired, but the opposite was true. I was attracting people who were just about to give up on their dreams. It was as though they could touch the world they'd longed for through me, without making sacrifices or putting in effort. It was enough to sate their interest and allow them to move on. They weren't consciously using me but touching a lifestyle they idolised without having to live it. In every case it took only a few months until they got a proper job. *Just until I have enough money*, they said, and I believed it every time. But they always stayed in those jobs, and then, months later, when I tried to encourage them to get back to their work, I was told not to interfere. *We can't all sit around being an artist, you know.* I'd forgotten what it was like to end a relationship, because I was always the one being dumped.

From the outset, Dave insisted that Wendy was the same. *Another failed artist sapping off your mediocre success* was the way he put it. When I said she was different, he just said *for now*. Dave's attempts to annoy me were so familiar that I didn't take this comment seriously. I consoled myself with the fact that Dave hadn't even met Wendy. At that point, I'd only been with her a week, but we'd seen each other most nights.

We met on a Saturday so cold I woke up before dawn. The cloud was low, almost like fog, but the air was rushing with an icy wind. It never got fully light, and when I went outside that afternoon the stadium floodlights were haloed with sleety rain. My feet were wet before I reached the town centre. I went into Waterstone's for warmth and to see if any of my book covers were on show. It wasn't vanity, but a way of checking whether publishers should have sent my complimentary copies.

The lowest level in Waterstone's is always quieter, more like a library; the sound of traffic and rain is distant, you can hear pages being turned. Wendy was sitting in front of a shelf, leaning on one arm, filing art manuals into place. I'd seen her before, on the till, but I rarely bought new books, so we'd never made eye contact. She looked up at me and smiled so directly I thought she must have mistaken me for somebody else. I wasn't able to smile back before she looked away.

She was wearing a black jumper, a long floral skirt and leggings. It was almost a uniform in Waterstone's, but she looked so at ease with herself that it didn't bother me. Guessing her age was difficult; her skin and smile put her at eighteen. She was small enough to appear childlike, except for the way she moved. It would be crass to call it graceful; she moved as though she enjoyed everything she touched. She'd lost the angular uneasiness that lingers in some women well into their twenties. She looked so relaxed, sliding books into place, I could imagine her in a warm living-room, by her own bookshelf, with a glass of wine and a cat.

'Am I in your way?' she asked.

'Not at all.'

I wanted to speak again but couldn't think of anything to say, so tilted my head to one side, pretending to read titles. Now would be a good time to find a book with my work in it, hoping she'd ask what I was looking at, giving me a chance to show off.

She stood up, saw that I was looking at the section on oil technique, and said, 'Do you paint?'

'I do some illustration. Bits of things for books. A few covers.'

'Oh, that's great. God, you're so lucky. Is it hard work?'

'It takes time. Getting the first few sales is the tricky bit.'

I felt insincere, because I'd been through this exact nonchalant conversation many times when meeting people and at the beginning of relationships. Wendy was talking so rapidly, and blushing, I could tell it was something that mattered to her. She wasn't impressed by me, but I reminded her of what she wanted.

'Do *you* paint?' I asked.

'I'm meant to,' she said, and when I smiled she added: 'Not as much as I should.'

A pale man behind the main counter called her name, waving a book.

'Hang on a minute,' she said, as though it was obvious we were going to carry on talking. She was gone longer than I expected, so that it was unreasonable for me to stay in the art section the whole time. I moved toward politics, already wondering what hers were. By the time you reach your mid-twenties you worry about people's preferences before you begin to hope. When you're younger, you feel something for a stranger, believe in it, and hope you'll get along. That instinct often proves to be correct, for a while. After a few disasters, though, you begin to weigh people up before you allow yourself to feel anything. The way Wendy had talked to me would have dropped me in love when I was eighteen. As it was, I was wondering about her age, where she lived, what she believed in. You know the odds of being disappointed are fairly high, so you hold back until there's more information.

There are ways around some differences. I'd even been out with a girl who agreed with fox-hunting once; we managed not to talk about it, although when we split up we kept repeating the phrase *just too different* to each other.

I pulled out a Ken Livingstone book; it was one of his more obscure efforts, about the politics of biology. If she were a Tory, she'd see what I'd chosen and that would be that.

'Gynaecology,' Wendy said when she returned, as though that made it clear what the delay had been. Then she said, 'What's your name?'

'Nick.'

'OK.'

'And you're Wendy?'

'Yes. Are you going to buy that? It's not his best.'

We spoke about his books, briefly, and then she looked worried that she'd bored me. If I was distracted, it was because I was preparing myself.

I asked her out, and she said 'yes' as though she meant *of course.*

When you ask somebody out, there's usually a brief competition over social obligations. *I can't come out tonight, or this weekend, but I'm free next Wednesday.* You're meant to be impressed by how busy and loved they are.

'Can you come out tonight?' Wendy asked. It was a direct request, and I was touched. She didn't appear overeager, or desperate, but was letting me know what she wanted. As it was, I hadn't arranged anything, except a vague plan to see Dave for a drink. I wasn't cynical enough to turn her down, so I said, 'Tonight's great.'

The rain had gradually set, landing in gluey blobs through the afternoon, pausing for an hour, then returning as snow. I knew this because I sat in my room, watching, waiting for evening. The ground was nowhere near frozen, but as I left the house snow was beginning to stick.

The doors to Waterstone's were locked, so I stood beneath a vent in the wall; hot air blew out, making little strands of filth on the grille shiver.

Wendy came out, saw my wet hair and apologised for being late.

'I didn't have time to get changed. You don't mind, do you?'

I said that I didn't, so long as she'd be warm enough. Her black woollen coat was too big for her shoulders, and she looked colder than I was. We set off walking before we'd talked about where to go. I'd spent hours trying to decide the best combination of food, drink and film for our initial meeting, knowing that women generally hate it if you say, *I don't mind what we do.* Before I could voice this Wendy told me that she didn't want to go to pubs or for food. She asked me to drive her into the surrounding countryside.

'Just for the ride,' she said.

My car was in one of the lab car-parks, five minutes away, and on the walk over, dodging pedestrians and slush, we found it difficult to talk. There was an eager politeness, wanting to get on, but the conversation laboured. It wasn't that we had nothing to say, I hoped, but that we needed more privacy before we could start talking properly.

I let her into the Mazda and was about to wipe the back window when she leaned out and said, 'Get in first.'

It was dark in the car, the windows mottled with snow. We closed our doors and the snow eased down, wrinkling, cracks of streetlight coming through.

'I can't believe how still it is in here,' she said, her voice sounding loud because the noise from outside was dampened by snow.

I put the wipers on, and the windscreen went so clear it looked shiny.

'Look at that,' Wendy said. 'It's so orange.'

The car-park glared with streetlight, the snow-rounded cars, the ledges and paths, all the same harsh orange. When I put the headlights on, fans of white snow appeared in front of us. Wendy said, 'Beautiful.' Most people wouldn't have noticed or, if they had, would have kept it to themselves. I didn't care whether she painted or not, but it pleased me that she was impressed by what she saw.

The only relationship I'd ended on holiday was with Jo

Thatcher, who picked her nails as we drove, instead of looking at the scenery. I'd been patient, until we drove over the Kirkstone Pass, when I'd said, 'Look at that view', and Jo had replied, 'Oh, yes, more hills'.

I headed out of town and, when the engine was warm, put the heater on so loud we had to raise our voices. Once we left the salted roads I had to drive slowly, and there wasn't much to see apart from white hedges and tyre tracks until we reached higher ground. I parked by the reservoir, and with the headlights off the landscape brightened. The sky was clearing, the moon appearing at odd moments, lighting up the snowy hills, its wide shimmer spread on the water.

I wanted to get out and walk, but Wendy said it was too cold, so we stayed in the car until the windows had steamed up. She made me smile and I talked more than usual. It didn't feel like the usual discovery and dissection of a personality, but was more like going out with a friend. She wasn't trying to look good and didn't put any effort into pretending things were going well. When she told me about her parents, her regrets about uni and her art, she wasn't whining but honestly letting me know that she'd fucked up. She even seemed embarrassed by the word *art*, and referred to her work as drawing.

'But you do paint?'

'I used to.'

It was past midnight when she finally told me she was cold. We'd both been blowing into our hands for hours, but she meant it was time to go.

Driving back, we were quiet, my lips feeling rough, as though we'd been kissing. I hadn't eaten since mid-afternoon, and it was probably hunger that made my sense of smell so acute. I could smell Wendy's skin and hair, as though I were lying next to her. It made the tiredness seem pleasant, and if she'd offered I'd have stayed up with her all night.

During those first weeks, we spent all our time in the car, parked in lay-bys, eating at service stations, driving down winding roads. Wendy spent so much time working in town that she cherished getting out. I'd tidied my room and kept it neat since the day we met, but she never got to see it. If I invited her back, it would either be too late or she'd say *later* until the time ran out. For a while I thought she might just want to be friends. We didn't go to a single pub or restaurant or to see a film; she was happy to sit in the car with me and talk. It suited me because she made me laugh and never bored me. I got the feeling this was a delaying tactic, a way of getting to know me before we slipped into a more normal relationship.

On a still night, when we parked at Bradgate Park, we were talking about previous relationships, and she used the phrase *other girlfriends*. We hadn't even kissed, so I said something light about her being my girlfriend. The word excited me; it's more friendly than lover or partner. She didn't speak, and lowered her head, so her face was hidden by her hair. I moved it aside and, leaving my hand on her cheek, kissed her. She put her arms around me, gently at first, then holding me so tight I had to draw her face into my neck. I breathed into her hair for so long it became damp. I felt her ribs through her jumper, but given the cold I didn't want to put my hands directly against her skin. We didn't speak for the next hour, because we kissed until our mouths were sore.

By mid-March a thaw had set in, and I moved to a larger flat on Regent Road, the whole top floor to myself. The bedroom looked out on the university buildings, where nearly every window framed a Labour poster for the coming election.

I never knew why, but the move seemed to make a difference to Wendy. As soon as I'd moved in she said, 'Aren't you going to invite me over?'

I met her at work, and it was raining so much that we stopped off at a gaudy pub near Leicester's train station. Frequented mostly by businessmen, it was empty when we arrived, with almost too much space for us to be intimate, but soon filled up as it went dark outside. She held my hand and said that she loved me.

Later, in my room, with the sound of heavy rain falling on to the pavement outside, we undressed each other. I felt it was going to be unrushed, but she made a noise almost like crying when I put my hand between her legs. She was so wet when I entered her, and I was so close to coming, that I imagined it ending in apologies. I was hypnotised by the noises she made, almost musical, until she paused, holding her breath, before releasing it like she'd been winded.

We didn't talk, but I pulled the covers over and held her, breathing at her rhythm so she wouldn't wake.

In the morning we drove down the M1 to get breakfast at the Forest East service station. Wearing yesterday's clothes, we looked unwashed and tired. Instead of sitting opposite me to talk, Wendy shuffled in next to me, her hands between her legs, blowing on her coffee. It was cold outside, but the windows made the sunshine feel hot. I worried out loud that she might be pregnant.

'A baby,' she said. 'Imagine that.' She looked puzzled rather than worried, as though the thought of such a change could excite her.

I rambled on about responsibility, and how many lives it

wrecked, and how she had to pursue her own life first. Wendy nodded solemnly.

'I know I couldn't really cope.'

'And if you're not pregnant?' I was hinting about contraception, but she missed the point.

'I need an outlet,' she said, though it wasn't clear for what.

She wanted me to meet her parents, because they were anxious about her spending so much time out without knowing who I was. It was a reasonable request, but I'd resisted for weeks.

'If you'd gone to uni, you wouldn't have to tell them where you were.'

'Please don't get at me for that. Please.'

'I'm not. But if you'd left home, they'd get used to not knowing. It frees you up.'

Meeting parents is never easy, because whatever your age, you greet them with a tone of apology in your voice. I didn't admit it at the time, but I was afraid of Laurence Paige before I met him. It was seeing the effect he had on Wendy that made me wary. Even just talking about him, she would look anxious. It bothered me, because Wendy wouldn't let me get away with anything thoughtless but was too afraid to answer back to this man. When he was angry, she preferred to back down.

The Paiges' house was well out from the centre of Leicester, with enough space for a bare garden and what remained of a willow that had suffered at the hands of an overzealous tree surgeon. The front hall had thick red carpets, which made for a disturbing hush, the sort that is usually filled by a ticking clock. The ornaments were all evenly spaced, well dusted, and the wallpaper was like thin velvet. It was the sort of house that made you whisper.

Her dad was leaning over the kitchen counter staring at an

estate agent's card. He was short and bald, with a downy swathe of blonde hair around his skull. The fluorescent light made him look sickly. He didn't shake hands or even straighten up but grinned with all his teeth showing. He looked pleased to see me, eager and pleasant, not at all what I'd expected. Wendy had gone on about how successful a businessman he was, so I hadn't expected him to be wearing a light blue pullover and a cheap gold watch.

'Hiya, Wendy.' It sounded like *Hoya Windy*, a strong Birmingham accent. 'Hiya, Nick. Eh, Wendy, look at this.' He started showing her the house on the card. 'Near Stratford. Four bedrooms. How about that, eh? Look at this, Nick.'

'Oh, yes, lovely.'

'I think we might have that.' He grinned again. He seemed incapable of smiling, so I wondered how he'd look when angry.

Wendy's mother came through from the washroom carrying a basket stuffed with damp laundry. It had the lemony smell I associated with Wendy, only wetter. She spoke excitedly. 'Hi, hi. Oh, it's good to meet you. At last.' Linda looked to be early thirties, her orange T-shirt tucked tight into her jeans. She was closer to forty, but next to Laurence she looked like his daughter, except she was taller than him. It was difficult to believe she was Wendy's real mother, because her hair was black and her skin a deep tan. The only betrayal of her age was the make-up, two charcoal lines around her eyes, lashes stiff with mascara. She reminded me of a pop star who'd aged well. 'Sorry about this. Just doing my chores.' She laughed at herself.

I'd heard so many stories of Laurence bullying her I'd imagined a prim, sad woman in a print dress with brittle hair and a lost expression. It was difficult to picture this woman letting him get away with anything. Laurence looked at her as though he was watching from behind glass, his tongue teasing his lip.

Wendy went to help her mum hang the washing out, and Laurence used the opportunity to talk to me. It went on for longer than I would have liked, but he was reasonably pleasant until he said something about 'those blacks'. I'd been nodding along, hardly listening to him until he said that. I didn't respond but must have looked shocked.

'You're not a nigger-lover, are you?' He looked angry, unblinking, his lips sealed. I thought he'd hit me if I said yes.

I mumbled, 'No, no, but . . .'

I only had one black friend, called Carl. If he knew what I'd just done, he'd have spat in my face.

I took it out on Wendy as we drove away.

'He's a fucking cunt.'

'Don't fall out with my dad. It's not worth it.'

'Why? Will he beat me up?' I mocked, doing such a good job of being annoying that my own mood worsened. 'How *terrifying*.'

'I don't mean that,' she said, sounding as though she was struggling to make me understand rather than arguing. 'But you'd make it difficult for *us*. And he is my dad.'

'You're welcome to love him, but I choose not to.'

'Drop me here then.' She put her hand on the door handle.

I slowed, worried she might open the door while we were still moving. I'd pushed her too far but didn't want to back down.

'What? So I have to love your dad? You're being ridiculous.'

'You're ridiculous if you're threatened by every man you ever meet.'

'I'm not threatened. I'm twenty-seven. I don't have to live in awe of your parents. I'm an adult.'

'You should act like one then.'

I tried to get out of it by saying, 'It's only because he makes you unhappy.'

'You're the one doing that.'

It was the first time I'd heard bitterness in her voice.

Three days later, her period started while we were making love. At first I thought it had embarrassed her because she pulled away from me, but then she stripped the bloody condom from me and threw it aside. She lay on her back, legs spread so widely it looked painful. 'In me, in me,' she said, her eyes tightly closed. Her face remained clenched with wrinkles while we made love. When she came, her jaw opened like somebody shocked by cold water. Her fists drew me into her, and she continued moving until I came. I waited a long time before trying to withdraw, but even then she held me in place. I wanted to say how relieved I was to know that she wasn't pregnant, but whenever she heard me breathe in to speak she shook her head.

When we both had the time, we'd spend whole days in bed. We watched the grey rain sharpen the light on the ivy of the labs outside my window. The clouds pearled and spread, until they revealed the sun when it was low enough to sink into twilight. At night, we'd go out for take-away food, bringing it back to eat in bed, then, too restless to sleep, we'd stay up all night talking.

Even on the night of the general election, we busied ourselves with each other rather than with the news. And then in the morning we were so bewildered by the result that we couldn't face going into work and repeated the process again.

Sometimes our insularity bothered me; we should be getting out, seeing things together, sharing our friends, rather than endlessly analysing ourselves. If I suggested something, she'd claim to be too tired or just say *next week*. When I pushed, she became upset, asking if I was bored.

'Next thing you'll be wanting to watch TV together,' she said. 'I don't want us to be ordinary. I could go out with anyone for that.'

'But while we're locked in here, I might as well be ordinary. You haven't even been to see my studio.'

It was the closest we'd come to an argument for days, but because she sounded so upset I backed down. She'd been so relaxed about being with me when we met that I never imagined she would worry about our future. When we did start arguing it was always after a particularly good day. I'd find myself amazed to hear her driving the conversation to the point where she'd be saying *just end it then*. It was as though she was so afraid of it being over that she wanted to get it over with rather than live with the fear. This confused me because I was happy with her and had no reason to leave. I made that as clear as I could, every time we met, but still the arguments would arise in the same way. She had a way of avoiding eye contact and accusing me of hating her that managed to stir my anger. No matter what I said, she'd insist that I hated her. Only when I'd finally break and say *sod off then*, would she cry, until I told her it was all right. With that pattern established, I understood her better. She wasn't trying to get the break-up over but was gaining reassurance in the most painful way. Attacking our relationship and seeing it survive, despite almost ending, was the only way she could have faith in it.

When she was in a good mood, having cooked me a meal, I asked her why she went from being so casual to worrying all the time. She told me she'd been worried since we met. That first night we went out, she'd been starving, but couldn't eat because she was so nervous. Those nights when we'd sat talking, she'd been longing to kiss me. 'You can't imagine what it was like. I wanted you to touch me. I just wanted you to touch my breasts.'

'Why didn't you say?'

'I didn't want to come across as a typical teenager.'

She had no idea how erotic I found the word. She acted so much older than nineteen that I tended to forget; being reminded was a pleasure. It was less than an eight-year-age gap, but she treated it like more, certain that I thought of her as trivial and shallow. She wasn't obsessed with her body, but slowly convinced herself that I hated it. For a while I found her paranoia amusing. I loved nothing more than watching her in front of the mirror, wearing just socks, holding her breasts, arching her back, looking for faults.

If she had a fear, it would come out as an accusation.

'You hate my nipples, don't you?'

I tried to correct her, but she didn't seem convinced.

'You'd have to be a paedophile to like this,' she said, because her breasts were less than handfuls, with nipples like a boy's. If I told her that was how I liked women, she'd say *what happens when I get older*? Unless I was careful, our conversations turned to her doubts. One of her habits was to question me with bizarre insecurities.

'Would you still love me if I lost a leg? What if I was disabled? Would you still love me if I was disfigured?'

It was a peculiar way to test me, and I didn't like to think about it. Why do we stay with people? At first, it's out of joy, rather than responsibility. She was asking me whether I loved her enough to stay with her, even if doing so was unpleasant. It was like saying, *What if I'm no fun any more, what if I bore you? Will you stay with me if I'm bad-tempered and angry?* I'd joke my way out of it, as far as I could.

'Even if you were a brain in a bottle, I'd stay with you.'

We were in bed, too tired to get supper, but too hungry to sleep, idling through conversations.

'What if I was paralysed? Or burnt?'

'Yes, I suppose so.'

She paused, streetlight gleaming on her pupils.

'What if I was pregnant?'

It took a long time for her to convince me she was joking.

Chapter Two

Whenever things went well for me, Dave's life took a turn for the worse. He came round after midnight, unannounced, throwing stones at my window. I flicked the light on and off to make him wait, then went down to meet him. It was raining, the wind blowing water into my face as I cowered towards his car. Before my door closed, switching off the overhead lamp, I got a glimpse of his face, pale and exhausted. He wanted to go driving. It was a custom we'd developed when we were eighteen, driving ten miles out past Oadby, to his girlfriend's house. Instead of ringing her up to sort out their problems, we'd park within view of her front room. He'd never want to leave until he'd seen her shadow through the curtains, when she got up during the adverts.

We'd driven the same route ever since, even though she'd moved to Wigan years ago. If either of us needed to talk, that's how we'd establish it. It had become a habit to be serious on that drive. Talking on a dark road was more practical than whispering in my room, face to face.

Dave worked in a components warehouse, some nameless job organising the whole place; horrendous hours, high pay, and he got to sack at least one person a week. Our politics were just about opposite, but we both argued so extremely that it never felt personal. When he came round late, his breath always smelt fishy, either from drinking too little, or the tuna sandwiches he lived off. He'd still be in his work shirt, tie pulled loose, but never removed. His stubble was patchy, making him look unwashed rather than rugged.

'Still oppressing the masses?' I asked as we pulled out.

'I wish. Bloody unions.'

'Not for long.'

'Too right. As it should be.'

That was the extent of our preamble. After that I asked him what was up, and before we'd even left my road he began to tell me. It was the same as usual; Rachel had broken up with him.

For the past three years, he'd been trying to establish a relationship with her. We'd known Rachel since sixth form but lost touch for half a decade while she learned to teach sign language at a school in Nottingham. When she'd moved back to Leicester, Dave had tracked her down and asked her out at once. They went out with each other for five months, and managed to have some kind of intimacy without ever sleeping together. Polite about it to the point of being slow, he'd let her continually turn him down. 'It gets pretty horny,' he'd assured me, sounding less than satisfied. Whenever they reached the point where they were about to have sex, Rachel had ended the relationship. It had happened four times, and every time, after a three-month gap, they'd get back together. At New Year she'd said she couldn't see him, because she didn't want to hurt him by changing her mind again. She wanted to be certain first. And then the next day she'd said yes.

'I took that to mean she was certain,' he said. We passed his ex-girlfriend's house, the rain so thick the building was indistinct. Dave wasn't even aware of it. 'And now she's fucked off,' he said.

'Did she give a reason?'

'She doesn't want to give me hope. Which means there's *no* hope.'

'Do you think you frighten her off, being so serious? You've always wanted to be married by the time you were twenty-eight.'

'No, I said not *until* I'm twenty-eight.'

'It comes across the other way. She might think you're desperate.'

'It's not that. But she won't even see me. She dumped me over the phone. She said: "I don't want to see you, because you'll talk me round." And that's the end of it. Just like that. Not even to my face.'

Instead of saying *I'm sorry*, I said, 'It's not on.'

'It's bang out of order.'

When I suggested what he could do he cut me off and said he didn't want plans or advice, so I left him to it.

He was driving slowly, because the roads were narrow and shining with rain. There were no streetlights out there, and for a while no houses, so the view was black, apart from the sky, its low cloud lit by the city.

Once he'd been through it all again, he went quiet for a few miles, so I listened to the strained motor of the wind-screen wipers, kept awake only by the cold. Then he perked up.

'So tell me about this Wendy.'

I'd already described her physically and knew if I said words such as *intelligent, creative, original* he'd laugh his arse off. *Yeah, yeah, course she is*. I'd made similar claims about every previous girlfriend, having to admit later that I'd been kidding myself. When a relationship is under way you ignore aspects of a person that might have put you off, if they'd been spotted before you got together. It's not worth ending it, though, just because somebody doesn't meet every expectation. My downfall had been attracting women much less intelligent than myself, then pretending it didn't bother me. *Course it doesn't matter if you don't have a degree. A-levels aren't really important. Exams only test one kind of thought.* I'd developed a reaction of assuming every girlfriend was intelligent. It was my own fault for refusing to go out with people from the university. I'd only been out with an academic once, and we talked so much bullshit, in public, that it became an embarrassing competition, like writing essays at each other.

'She's a good laugh,' I said. 'It's as good as it could be, at this point.'

'What do you like about her?'

'Little things. The way she talks. Her sense of humour. Her habits. The way she sees things.'

'But she's nineteen?'

'She acts older, except that she isn't cynical. And she couldn't care less about having the right clothes, the right job, the car, the house.'

'Sounds like a nightmare.'

'The last thing I want is another woman telling me I'm selfish because I don't want to set up home.'

'So you go out with a teenager.'

'Fuck off.'

'Does she still play with dolls?'

Instead of letting him wind me up, I played along. 'She stills buys sweets.' He grunted, so I said, 'After sex, she's starving hungry and makes me drive her out to the garage for chocolate.'

'Women and chocolate,' he said vaguely.

'And she's the most generous person I know.'

'Yeah, yeah. Heard it all before.' It was standard practice

for him to lay into my girlfriends, reminding me of previous claims. 'You said Lucy Walker was generous, and look what a cow she turned out to be.'

'That was different. Wendy isn't like that.'

'Course she isn't. Not yet. Is she thick?'

'*No.*'

'Fat?'

'No, she's thin.'

'That's what you said about that blob Samantha. I *told* you she was fat, and you said she was big-boned.'

He laughed so much his eyes narrowed and went teary, and when I tried to speak he laughed louder, doubling up. It wasn't a safe way to drive, especially as we were crossing a bridge over the M1, wind pushing at the car. I could have been annoyed, except it was a relief to see him smiling again. And I knew he was doing more than goading me. It was his way of warning me to open my eyes, take it slowly and assess Wendy before I felt too much. He confirmed this when, out of breath from laughing, he said, 'Just remember the mess you've been in before, caring about people you don't like. Make sure you like her, that's all.'

On nights like that, it usually started with him wanting to talk, but by the end I always got the feeling he was looking out for me.

Wendy's generosity troubled me. Initially, she gave me books, saying she got a staff discount so I needn't feel guilty. She bought me *The Little Prince*, because I'd never read it, and *Island of the Blue Dolphins*, because it was the first novel she'd read. Books are the best presents, but with other women I'd often felt they were using them to impress me; I'd read more Russian novels than was pleasant. Wendy bought on impulse, anything from a book on salamanders – 'I thought you'd like the pictures' – to anthologies of science fiction. She often read them before I did. On each title page, she wrote something to me, usually a quote from the text.

Love Wendy.

Once, I'd have hated that, because I collected books, treating them like antiques. She made me realise the gesture was more important than the object. My only worry was having a shelf full of favourite books, which future girlfriends would feel obliged to hate.

The presents became more inventive, and whenever she turned up with a carrier bag at night I knew there would be something inside for me. She bought me prints and art posters, a ceramic Gandalf, a set of brass dragons, rainbow candles, and josstick holders.

'It's a bit different,' she'd say hopefully. 'Not your usual stuff.'

One evening I was tactless enough to say, 'This place is going to look like a student bedroom.' I wasn't ungrateful and was glad to see my flat lose its spartan look. But it was early in the relationship, and her generosity made it look like she was chasing me, that I needed to be convinced. And I worried about her money, knowing she couldn't be saving much for uni.

In contradiction to all that, I dreaded the time when she'd come round without a present; it would be a sign she was getting used to me. To avoid it I suggested she stop immediately, before it became an obligation.

'I don't want to stop.'

'Why not?'

'You're easy to buy for, and it makes me feel better.'

I agreed, in that it was a good way to start an evening. If I'd been brooding over something she'd said on the phone, or worrying about her being late, the presents stopped me snapping. She probably thought I was naturally even-tempered.

'You should buy yourself some stuff,' I said. 'Paints, pencils. None of it's cheap.'

'I want enough money to buy a load, all at once,' she said, which made it seem like too much of an occasion. She looked worried, so I didn't say what I was thinking. If you're serious about painting, you have to do a bit every day, constantly sketching and experimenting. It should be a reaction to record what you see, rather than an obligation. Making a ceremony of it pushes it into the realm of the unusual, so that you do less and less.

To solve the problem, I blew a month's spare money on art materials for her, to make up for the presents that had accumulated in my flat. The idea was that we could put a lid on present-swapping, and it would help to get her career moving. The gear was all student-quality, and I bought canvas board rather than stretchers, but there was plenty for her to work with. I made sure there were notebooks and sketchpads, everything to set her going. It reminded me of starting my own foundation course, buying so preciously only to spend the first month working with soil, litter and PVA glue.

She was so flustered when I gave the bag to her that I wondered if I'd done the right thing. When she looked inside, her face went sad, as though I'd been unbelievably generous. She drew out every brush, tube and bottle, admiring each, thanking me. I tried to keep smiling, leaving her to it, but I desperately wanted to hold her. It was like watching a child take gifts from a Christmas stocking; she showed me each one as though it would be a surprise to me too.

'I didn't even wrap them up.'

'They're wonderful. Thank you. We should go away, so I can get the most out of them.'

* * *

That week we were meant to spend four nights apart. Wendy's friend Caryn was up from Bath, and they hadn't seen each other for months. Caryn had surprised her the previous Christmas by announcing that she was gay. 'I still think it's a phase,' Wendy said. 'She doesn't even have a girlfriend.' She was joking, but I could tell that it bothered her. 'I was surprised more than anything. And it's difficult knowing what we can talk about now. It's like finding out somebody's ill. I won't know whether or not to mention it.' I didn't hear from her while Caryn was there, so assumed things must have been going well.

She rang me late on Friday night – after Caryn had caught a taxi to her mum's – wanting to come round. She was in the phone box at the end of the road, so I could hardly refuse.

A blast of cold followed her in, and she was out of breath. 'You should have come out with us,' she said loudly in the hallway. I urged her to be quiet.

I'd never seen her drunk. Her hair smelt burnt, and when we kissed she tasted like she'd been eating old fruit. She couldn't remember how much she'd had to drink, but her speech sounded normal, if a little rapid. She was as bright and happy as I'd seen her, none of the usual wistfulness being added to the end of a thought.

'I wish you were like this more often. I should get some bottles in.'

'It's not that, it's Caryn. She cheers me up.'

Wendy was more awake than I was, for a while, then just as I started to liven up she slowed down. By the time I'd taken her shoes and socks off, she was complaining, wanting to sleep in her jeans. I persisted until she helped me undress her.

When I was about to sleep, she told me she felt sick. Not

enough to *be* sick, but enough to prevent her from sleeping. She wanted the light on, because she was dizzy, and sat upright with her eyes open. We didn't talk, but grew hot, so the bed was slick, the sheets sticking to our feet. Resigned to a restless night, I allowed myself to wake up properly.

'You left your stuff, you know,' I said, pointing out the Sketchers bag in the corner.

'No. I took a sketchbook and two soft pencils. I drew our house, but my dad saw it. He said he ought to give me a lesson in perspective.'

'He said that?'

She nodded.

'Bastard.'

'It wasn't that good.'

'But he's got no right.'

'He isn't happy at all. He gives me shit all the time.'

'About me?'

'*No*. About me.'

She wanted to leave the materials at my house, so they'd feel special. If they were associated with her home, they'd feel ordinary. Or, she suggested, her dad would throw them out. He'd done this with books and clothes he'd disapproved of: a long black skirt because it was 'for hippies', a multicoloured waistcoat, even a hat she'd bought for summer. If he got his way, she'd be wearing office clothes all day.

'You're nineteen. It's up to you what you wear.'

'Not while I'm in his house.'

'Then leave. Get your own place.'

Unexpectedly, she started crying. She assured me it wasn't because of me, but said, 'Don't be mad. Look after me. Please.'

Her choice of words struck me as drunken melodrama, but I knew that if she was crying I should take her seriously.

She didn't want to talk, so I put my arms around her until she was still. From what I can remember, that was the first time I held her all night, even in sleep.

At what point did she stop being just another girlfriend? I often said it was from the beginning, because there was so little pretence. But the truth is that something changed when we went on holiday to Arnside. After that, whatever reservations I had about her age or intensity were put aside.

We set off late, with a sense of relief and urgency, almost like we were running away. It was going dark as we left the M6, driving through countryside that was a mixture of artificial lakes, pasture and quarries.

Beyond Arnside village, a broken concrete road took us over the edge of the beach, the tide having left vast plates of water to reflect what remained of the sky. The road turned back into the woods, where caravans were spread around the lanes that curled between the trees. As the headlights passed over them, their paintwork glittered, somehow crystalline. We found my uncle's caravan and unloaded by torchlight; inside it smelt like a damp cupboard. I held a match to the wall-lamp, turning on its brass tap; the filament, like a thimble of lace, swallowed the flame and burned green-white. Wendy held me, and despite the cold and the sense of mildew she told me it was perfect.

We assembled the bed by dismantling the cushion-seats and left it that way for nine days, eating, drawing, reading, playing Scrabble and making love there.

Each morning, I'd wake first, going out to the tap for water, making her tea before she awoke. During the day we'd drive out to the southern Lakes, looking for things to draw. I always looked for the borderline between technology and nature; a rust-rotten oil drum embedded in soil; a burnt-out barn, its black wood greening; inexplicable metal rods in the side of a tree. I was cautious at first, because other girlfriends had seen these excursions to draw as delays. It made me feel selfish, but with Wendy I needn't have worried. Never once did she say *I'll wait here*, or fold her arms impatiently. I never had to point things out to her, because I knew she'd already seen them. Before long, she was the one urging me to stop, because she'd seen a peculiar effect of light. She was obsessed with the weather and the time of day, wanting to revisit places, to see how a change of light had affected them.

When it rained, she wasn't put out but delighted by the grey darkness that came over us in the car. We parked at the top of the Hardknot Pass, wiping the windows as they steamed, watching the ground around us river, days of dust carried on the new bulges of water. At the horizon, the cloud thinned, its yellow light looking three hours earlier than the storm above. It caught the wet trees below us, making them glare, the only colour in the valley.

On drier days we drew for hours at a time. It was the first time I'd seen what she could do, and I was relieved. Her reluctance had made me doubt her abilities, but she could sketch with realism as quickly as I could draw outlines. After a day, though, she was bored with realism. She stopped taking her equipment out with us, but at night, in the lamplight, she'd paint shapes and colours based on what she remembered. They weren't observations so much as reminders of how she'd felt when she saw those scenes. I adored her work, because although simple it underlined the intensity of her experience. All the time we were together, the feelings were sinking in.

There was an element of frustration in that she felt her paintings were only hinting at the emotion. 'I know what it means, but will anybody else?' I said something lame about the universal being achieved by the personal. At that point it wasn't enough to get her angry.

Each night we walked down the stone path, where it rose over the low grass cliffs, then down through gorse to the beach. The white pebbles were like flat slate eggs, blackened by rags of crisp seaweed where they met the sand. When a train crossed over the estuary viaduct, we could hear its precise rattling.

We'd return to the caravan exhausted, and I'd watch Wendy fall asleep. She wanted the curtains open, and we lay naked on top of the sheets. The light in there was almost green, because the rice-paper skylight was limed with bark stain dripped from the trees. We'd wake again before midnight and stay up until the early hours, talking.

On the last night we sat on the cliffs, looking over the shallow estuary to Grange as the hills blackened, tiny chains of streetlight coming on. Even when the sun had gone, a light aeroplane passed, high enough to be inflamed with sunset.

It was the first time we talked about marriage, both convincing each other we didn't need it. Even if we stayed together. *It's just a piece of paper*, we said. *So long as we make a commitment to each other, it doesn't matter what other people think.*

Neither of us wanted to move, even when it cooled.

Later that night we argued for the first time. It was brief, a dispute about the name of a village, turning into personal attacks. When it was over, we assured each other it didn't have to spoil the holiday. We could forget it. She put her head in my lap, and I held it, finding it hard to believe the person I knew was in there between my hands. I wanted to tell her, but it didn't seem an original thought.

'What are you thinking?'

When I told her, she said, 'You should tell me more things like that. They're important.'

In the morning we bought breakfast out and spent our last money on petrol. I'd left my cash card at home, and the needle was below the red line on the outskirts of Leicester. When we got home we had 2p left. Wendy Blu-Tacked it to my wall, next to the bed.

Laurence developed a curious respect for me. Other boyfriends he'd hated unreservedly, calling them layabouts to their face, but he valued my company. Linda took me to one side and said I was the only person who ever disagreed with him, and he seemed to enjoy it. If Wendy had a problem, or if he was pushing her to do a shorthand course, she'd bring it up with him while I was there. And he'd acquiesce. When she was thinking about making a late application to the polytechnic, for the autumn foundation course, she ran through her reasons to both of us.

'It makes sense, doesn't it?' she said to me.

'Well, it makes sense to do what feels right.'

Laurence agreed readily. 'No doubt about that. Eh, I can just imagine you as an artist.'

When he laughed, it was all in his mouth, never coming from any deeper.

Wendy's relief made the rest of the evening a bit frantic; she talked about nothing else, insisting he'd never have agreed if I hadn't been there.

Wendy left Waterstone's in July, and I rushed through my teaching plans and a few illustrations. It gave us six weeks together. We packed the car and set off to tour Britain. For most of those weeks we lived out of the tent, fortunate that 1992 was a hot summer. A few times we joked that we should just keep going, earn what we could and live like that for ever. Sometimes she looked so determined as we fantasised about it that I thought she meant it. We barely argued, and when we were out, eating on lawns or in pubs, we chattered constantly, never tiring of each other. We laughed secretly at middle-aged couples, who munched through their food with sour faces, refusing to speak. It came to our attention because we were the only ones talking; all the couples would listen to us rather than to each other. It became a game, betting on who would speak the least. The winners were a Welsh pair, at a pub in Devon; the only time he spoke was when he spilt his beer and said, 'Look what you've made me do.' We weren't being smug but grateful, both amazed at how well things were going. I remember waking every morning in the orange light of the tent, pleased she was there. Mostly, I remember driving with the windows down, the air smelling of wheat and Wendy trying to map-read, always turning to the wrong page, always wondering which way was north.

She started her course that September, a rush of enthusiasm dwindling within a week and turning into a dislike of the other students. She'd grown tense as soon as we'd returned to Leicester, our arguments becoming foul in the days before she started college. By October she was jaded, and when we did talk she seemed to feel attacked. If I spoke about the benefits of the course, she thought I was getting at her.

We met most lunchtimes, in a coffee shop on North Street, next door to the college. It was too bright by the windows, so we'd sit at the back, eating rock-hard bagels because they were cheap.

Even when we agreed about something, there'd be tension. Feminism was one of those subjects that made me go on the defensive because no matter how much I agreed with her I felt like one of those tits who says *I'm not like other men*. It's similar to arguing about racism when you're white and middle-class; you can't be all that forceful because you feel partly to blame.

She was complaining about the people on her course, because they were more interested in Nintendo and MTV than politics. 'If I hear one more of those girls say *I'm not a feminist, but* . . . I'll kill them.'

'It's like my dad,' I said. 'He thinks he hates socialism, but he's always ranting on about corporations and low wages. But socialism's a dirty word now. And with feminism, half the problem is that they always drag out those withered, vocal man-haters on TV.'

'There's nothing wrong with being vocal.'

'I didn't say that. I'm saying that they go out of their way to portray it all in the wrong light.'

Already I was feeling a sense of argument, but after a pause she carried on talking, telling me how easily led the other students were.

'They're more interested in that Mars and Venus shit. Which doesn't try to change anything so much as excuse people's shortcomings. But then one of the lads says the word *cunt* and they pounce on him for being sexist. They're twenty years out of date.'

It turned out she'd had an argument that afternoon with a girl called Lucy, who was slagging off one of the Booker nominees for being sexist. The women in the novel supposedly came across as victims.

'I said that for all the backlash pontificating about post-feminism, men do still bully women. But she wouldn't have it. She said authors should portray women as strong and striving. I know that's important, but it's not the whole story. Role models are all very well, but it's no good pretending everything's all right when it clearly isn't. If some women are victims of men, that's a valid story to be told.'

I tried to agree, but she was angry with me, perhaps because I pointed out that she hadn't even read the book in question.

Encouraging her to forget about the social side, I asked about the course itself, but she seemed unable to discuss the work without mentioning the other students.

'They talk such crap.'

'That's all part of it. You have to pass through student thinking.'

'They're so pretentious. I don't know, Nick. I really am thinking about leaving.'

'Isn't that a backward step?'

'The course seems backwards. I know what I want to do. I know what to paint, and they're limiting it with these *exercises*. It's beneath me.' This didn't sound like arrogance but embarrassment. 'You're the one always telling me to do what I want, to follow my dreams. I feel like I'm being wasted here.'

'But if you leave, you'll *not* do as much work. You say you will, but you won't, and then all those students you hate will be above you. You'll be stuck in Waterstone's again when they're selling paintings.'

She looked like somebody first sensing they're going to be sick. After two short breaths, she said, 'You have no idea how much you hurt me.' Her face was a mixture of wanting me to be kind and anger.

I like to look back on that afternoon in terms of me trying to help, and Wendy being unreasonably reactive, but I should have listened. She was frustrated and confused, in need of my support, and I was telling her off.

She told me our relationship was over, but even as I said

come on, I knew she meant it. She had calmed down, so it was too late for me to reach out and touch her.

After she left, I sat in the same position, trying to drink my tea, wondering why it had gone cold. When I went outside, it was like leaving a pub when you're drunk in the afternoon; my skin was hot, the air too bright. I knew exactly where I was, but couldn't help feeling lost.

Chapter Three

When I went round three days later, Wendy was out, which put me in a fury of jealousy and confusion. It was after nine at night, so there was no way she could be at college. I'd gone round hoping we'd talk and that she would change her mind. After other arguments, it took only one smile for us to get together again. It was unbelievable that she could be somewhere, with other people, enjoying herself.

Linda saw my distress and invited me in, offering a cup of tea. We began talking at once, sitting on opposite sides of the kitchen counter, and she never got to boil the kettle. She said Wendy had gone out with friends from college, to see the fireworks at Abbey Park.

'You could stay until she gets back, except Laurence will probably be home by then. He thinks she's with you.'

'Doesn't he know we split up?'

'Wendy doesn't talk to him much, except when you're there. She hasn't told him.' It was the first time I'd spoken to Linda without Laurence being present, and as I'd expected she acted more as if she was my age. It was like talking to a female friend rather than the mother of my ex-girlfriend. I was livid, though, to find out Wendy was using me as a cover for going out with other people.

'I'm so sorry about you two. I was sure it would work out.'

There was nothing I could say, except phrases such as *well, she's only nineteen* or *we only saw each other for nine months*, but they seemed completely irrelevant. It felt like I was getting divorced.

We could hear the fireworks, and Linda urged me into the conservatory to watch. It was cold, our voices sounding breathy and sharp over the thudding noise. Glittered light came through the trees. We didn't speak except to comment on the fireworks, and during the lulls to debate whether or not the display had finished.

When it was over we went back in, but I felt too awkward to sit down again, so I said I'd better leave.

'I'm sorry about Laurence. He doesn't make things easy.'

She wanted to say more, so I stopped halfway down the hall.

'He's not particularly cruel,' she said, 'but thoughtless. Wendy takes it all to heart. He has no idea how much he affects her.'

'It's that bad?'

'She's miserable, Nick.'

'I knew she was bothered by college, but . . .'

'Well, Laurence gets at her *constantly* for that. And when she shows a bit of initiative, he tells her she's wasting her time. She doesn't know what to do to please him.' She gave me a look as though she was weighing me up. Wendy had told me her mum didn't have friends that were hers alone, only those shared with Laurence, and I could tell she didn't get much chance to talk. 'I keep telling Wendy to leave. For her own sake. He treats her like a child.'

'Do you think she will?' I imagined offering her a place at my flat and pictured her settled in the bath while I made us supper.

'She might, but if she does, she won't stay in Leicester.'

Before I could take that in she added, 'If anything, I'm waiting until she's gone, before I leave.'

I wasn't comfortable being taken into her confidence, but I said, 'I think Wendy stays here because she's worried about leaving you on your own. With him.'

'Oh.' She said it with such surprise that I really don't think it had ever occurred to her.

When a relationship is going well, you think it's just a facet of your life. When it's over, it feels like the whole point. My days were filled with unfamiliar space. I pestered Dave to come out more but then cancelled on him in case Wendy called back.

When I was free during the day, I went for long walks, because I couldn't bear to stay at uni. I'd shuffle down the canal path, freezing cold, my feet loud on the cinders. It was like the feeling you get when you've not quite recovered from a cold; your senses are sharp, but you feel worn out.

When I finally got through to her, we hadn't spoken for three weeks and I'd missed her twentieth birthday. Despite this she sounded pleased to hear from me, so I asked why she'd never called.

'I've been busy.'

'You couldn't even afford two minutes to ring me up?' She was quiet so I said, 'Well, I'm glad you're in now, anyway.' I asked her what she'd been up to, but her description was so enthusiastic it made me angry. I told her I'd been having a shit time.

'Don't be cruel,' she said quickly.

'You never went out with me. What's changed that you suddenly want to be out every minute?'

'You've no right to get at me. I'm not with you any more.'

I wanted to be kind but was terrified that if I was polite

and understanding it would make it easy for her to seal off
the past. If she reacted angrily, at least it meant there was still
something unresolved between us.

'How could you say you loved me and then just give up so
easily?' I said. She tried to stop me going on, but I raised my
voice. 'How? One day you say you love me, and then the
next, when something *minor* doesn't please you, it counts for
nothing. Nothing.'

'If you hate me that much, why bother?'

She put down the phone.

It happened almost every time we talked.

On a Saturday morning I drove up to Wigan to see my mum
and dad and broke the news to them. They didn't seem too
bothered, because they immediately told me a story about
the bloke who did their plumbing, then something about an
insurance form. I assumed they just wanted to distract me.
Later, after I'd been out for milk, I found Mum at the sink.
Her back was to me, and although her hands were in the
water she was motionless. The sun wasn't setting as such, but
in coming through thin cloud the light had yellowed, making
the kitchen warm. It caught in Mum's hair, making it look
more blonde than grey. When I asked if she was all right, she
looked down, pretending to busy herself with the pots. Then
she turned to me, hands still in the sink, and shook her head.

'I can't bear the thought of it being over,' she said.

Christmas was a low point. Wendy had moved down to Bath
to share a flat with Caryn; they were both working part-time
in a hotel. Just for the time being. To earn some money. She
hadn't rung me since she'd moved there.

On days off from teaching, I didn't even bother to shave,
but I knew this was partly melodrama. I'd look at myself in

the mirror, wishing Wendy could see me so that I could blame her for my state. But the truth was that I still washed, changed my clothes and kept the place tidy. I was pissed off but playing at being depressed. After all, I never went more than two days without shaving, and only left one day's growth because in truth I wondered if the stubble might just be attractive to other people. I'd expected my desire for other women to be reduced, but it grew. Wendy's absence made me desperate to sleep with somebody else. It wasn't that I wanted to purge myself of her, or move on, but I was sick of wanking with cold hands into a freezing sink. It doesn't matter how many articles you read that say masturbation is normal, or how openly people joke about it these days; you feel like shit after coming into your palm. I know where the Victorians got all those ideas about wasting vital fluids. Afterwards you feel the same shakiness and weakness that comes over you after a bad argument. You feel like you've wasted yourself, and although your aim was satisfaction you feel anything but satisfied. Washing the webs of semen from between my fingers, I'd be livid with myself, wondering what she'd think if she could see me.

After a while my ability to come was reduced, and wanking became almost as frustrating as not doing. The fantasies that normally brought me off in a matter of minutes couldn't even keep me erect. I'd never pictured Wendy while wanking, but now it was the only way I could come. I didn't picture any sexual act, but just tried to remember her. In the final seconds as the room and the vigour of my hand withdrew, I'd feel a thrill of memory: Wendy sitting on the end of my bed, the smell of the radiator, her voice catching because she had a cold. She was talking intently, using her hands to explain something, smiling at the end of a sentence.

And then I'd see myself in the mirror, my face and

neck red like a sunburn, running my hand under the tap instinctively. Sometimes I'd look round into the hall to make sure she hadn't seen me.

By New Year I was going out with Dave almost every night, always hoping to get off with somebody, but usually too drunk to get anywhere. He still insisted on going round the student pubs, trying to drink as much as they did. I went along with it because it ensured that I got to sleep. My only worry was that he tended to get a bit loud once he was pissed.

'In our day, students looked like students: long coats, books, tousled hair. We looked the part. But this rabble, look at them. Reeboks and tracksuits and labels. Designer fucking labels. What happened to the rebellious spirit?'

'This from a man who just got himself a mortgage.'

He'd bought a house on Grange Road and talked me into putting the carpets down with him. It took a couple of nights' frantic stapling, and then another afternoon carrying furniture in. The next evening he rang me from his newly connected phone, his voice thin with agony. He managed to tell me that his back had gone and that he was lying on the floor, his muscles spasming so that he could barely breathe.

'Do you want me to come round?'

He managed to say, 'Rachel's coming.'

She'd dropped everything when he'd rung and was going over to help him, even though they hadn't spoken for weeks. All he wanted was to hear my voice while she drove over there. Although I was concerned for Dave, I felt angry, because he was going to be nurtured and looked after. Although he was suffering, he could relax in the knowledge that somebody he loved was going to look after him. He didn't put the phone down himself but let it go when he heard Rachel coming into the house. I'd expected her to sound efficient, like a nurse, but she said something warm; I couldn't make out the words, but I could picture her face. And I imagined him looking up at her and knew how he'd feel. She must have put the phone down for him.

The flat stank of Wendy. It was as though she'd left little bombs of perfume behind to prevent me forgetting. I'd cleaned the sheets immediately and hoovered to avoid finding hairs and fluff from clothes of hers, but I kept finding smells that reminded me of her. Under the bed I found three aniseed balls screwed up in their paper bag, so old the colour had mottled off them, staining the paper like lipstick. In an old toilet bag there was the soap we'd used on holiday and a moisturiser as familiar as her skin.

These discoveries reminded me that Wendy used to have a habit of sniffing her clothes each night to see if they were clean enough to wear again the next day. I'd feign disgust, saying, 'If you need to sniff, it needs to be washed,' but then she'd look hurt, and I'd have to assure her I didn't think she was dirty. 'I didn't sweat today,' she'd say, insisting it had been too cold. I lectured her about how clothes fill with dead skin, and she'd say something like, 'You think I'm foul.' Seeing her distress, I'd assure her that the habit was endearing, but my words must have had an effect. She'd often put things in the washing basket when I was watching only to retrieve them when I was in the shower the next morning to hang them up again. She'd been the same with food; if it wasn't completely off, she thought there was no point in throwing it out. We'd go away for a day or two and come back to find a bottle of milk in the fridge that had separated into a cheesy residue topped with water the colour of urine. She'd sniff, then even taste it, and eventually, after a couple of gulps, she'd say, 'It's off,' with a look of complete surprise.

My post-New Year plan to tidy her out of my life backfired, because every cupboard or space I cleared out revealed evidence of her presence. At the back of the bathroom cabinet I found a bottle of Mum for Men. It was Wendy's favourite deodorant. She'd bought one by accident but preferred it to the usual women's brands. They'd stopped making it a few years ago so she'd stockpiled a store of them and always left one at my place. I took the cap off, a dandruff of chemical fluffing away from the lid. The smell was something like soft toffee and mint.

For a moment it was like being with her again, the memory clearer than the empty flat I was sitting in. After inhaling a few times, I could no longer smell it, so I'd leave it for a while then go back for another sniff and be shocked by the recognition all over again.

I got as far as putting the deodorant bottle in the bin but couldn't bring myself to throw it out. The most frustrating thing was that it was only teasing me, because it reminded me of the smell that was above hers, not her skin. Her own smell was like that of a baby, or a young child. She called me sick if ever I said that, but there was something milky about her, as though she'd never been fed on solids. It was this smell that I tried to recall, but it was like searching for a word that you can't quite remember; trying made the memory more remote. The only time the memory of her smell came back was on waking, when I'd smell my own skin, heat in the sheets, and think she was beside me.

People say January flies by, but in 1993 it dragged. I find it difficult to remember much of what happened, but I know that each day I woke too early and unless I'd been drinking I couldn't sleep until late. Dave rang me up occasionally but sounded distracted, and the one time we went out to see a film he kept looking at his watch. He denied that he was seeing Rachel later, but we didn't even go to the pub.

It was in February that I determined to do something about my state of mind. When I woke up, the air in my bedroom smelled of cold glass, which could only mean it had snowed. There was a corona of paper-coloured light around the edge of the curtains. The last time I'd seen that, Wendy had been on the bed with me, eyes closed and sleepy.

I went to get my hair cut – always a symbol of renewal – then bought some new clothes. I didn't want a cheap shag but a new girlfriend, and probably somebody my own age this time. As I went from shop to shop I planned to go out every night, to accept all invitations, and even to go to pubs on my own in an attempt to meet somebody new.

I might have stuck to that except that I bumped into Linda and Laurence outside Burtons. Laurence looked so cold he appeared bad-tempered and managed only a brief hello then stood quietly while Linda talked. I can't remember what she said because I was watching him. His hair, I noticed, although thin and wispy, was exactly the same blonde as Wendy's.

I asked if Wendy had a phone in the flat, but Laurence interrupted. 'She's moved on, Nick.' He shrugged then smiled as though embarrassed. 'Eh? I'm sorry, but I think she's moved on.'

It was such a mean thing to say, but I determined to prove him wrong. He obviously wanted the conversation to end there, but I asked a few more questions about her life in Bath. He turned away, to look at calculators in the window of a stationery shop.

'I believed in you two,' Linda said. 'I'll get her to call you.'

That night I spent a while trying my new clothes on but

didn't get to go out. Although the phone rang three times, it was only ever Dave, bored because Rachel was refusing to speak to him. They'd had their first row, this time round.

'Get off the line, would you? Wendy's going to call.'

It was another week before I heard from her.

She rang me because of something that had happened at the hotel. She'd been working in the kitchen, and the chefs had ordered her to kill a tank full of fish for a banquet.

'I had to pull their stomachs out to make them die.'

'Couldn't you have smashed their heads?'

'They wanted the head intact,' she said, 'so I had to twist their lower fin off and drag their stomachs out. It was horrible, Nick. Horrible.'

It was strange talking so freely. I'd planned so many lines and speeches about my regret, and hopes, and details of how things could be worked out, but we were chatting normally. That conversation didn't last long, but after that she rang me every night, usually late. The phone was by her bed so she'd talk until she was ready to drop off.

Once she said, 'I'm so cold tonight,' so that I could respond with, 'I wish I was there to warm you up.'

'I want to come,' she said, and while I struggled to find the correct response, I heard her breath catching, then stuttering in little pained sounds, far more intense than she made during actual sex. It went on for about four minutes, and then she held her breath, her orgasm sounding like she was on the verge of crying.

The next time we spoke she invited me down for a week.

Chapter Four

Somewhere in Wiltshire the train stopped in a landscape of fields, and I spent almost an hour urging it to move. It would creak, take the strain against the couplers, than sag back to stillness. The people in the carriage spontaneously lost their patience as one, moving to a new level of fidgeting and muttered annoyance. There could almost have been a community spirit, except that a baby started hacking out a series of elongated wails. I managed to smile, because I imagined Wendy waiting at the station, cold and expectant. It was strange to be so close – a few miles, a few minutes – both anticipating the other. It was almost as good as being together.

There was something about the twilight that persisted into darkness, so that, even when the sun had long gone, the air remained misty blue rather than clearing to black. And within it, the only movement was the unfocused glow of distant headlights. I thought for a while that it reminded me of another evening, but then realised the moment was so distinctive that if ever I came across these conditions again I would be reminded of now. It's so easy for potent moments to be triggered by the merest smell or colours and recalled exactly, but it's rare to recognise a moment as it happens. I couldn't help but see significance in that.

Arriving in Bath was like driving into a town in the Lake District, the black hillsides veined with lights so small I couldn't make out the buildings around them. The main glow of the town came into view at the last moment, the huge abbey so floodlit its stone looked purple.

Wendy was standing by the steps and rushed forward to hug me. The size and shape of her was more strange than familiar. She let go, then backed off, as though to indicate that she wanted to build up gradually rather than be overly familiar. As we walked, we acquired a formal tone of voice, almost like we were at a job interview, over-sincere and direct. Our progress was hampered by her attempts to guide me by gestures made with her body, so she could carry on talking, with the result that we kept bumping into each other. I would have told her off for that once, but I was glad of the contact.

The pavement had frozen into fern-shaped patterns, glittering like zinc, and it was only when I pointed this out that she warmed and said, 'I'm so glad you came.'

Her flat was at the highest part of Bath, behind the Lansdowne Grove Hotel. Now that Caryn had gone back to London she had the whole top floor of a building that looked like it could have been property of the week in a local paper: yellow Bath stone, Tudor frontage, shuttered windows and tall lampshades. Her bedroom at the back was too small, so she'd converted the main living-room, which overlooked the town, into a large bedroom. She'd put Monet posters on the green-plaster walls, bought a few plants, piled her books up against the wall without a shelf. Her mattress was the centrepiece of the room. I dropped my bags, and we rushed off our coats; it was as though we'd set up a rhythm of undressing and couldn't stop. We were on our knees as the last clothes came off, and then on each other. As soon as I was inside her, the urgency relented.

Afterwards, we lay with the curtains open, a streetlamp so close to the window that we needed no light. Her skin looked luminous, but her nipples were black and her eyes hidden in shadows. It was cold enough for our breath to show in the air, but we lay with the blanket off us, to cool. The traffic outside was a constant rush of noise, but sometimes it would clear, and for a few seconds there would be silence.

A calm came over us. For the first time we began to make plans. Being together, we decided that night, would be better than being apart. We barely even mentioned the intervening months but treated them as though they'd been a forced separation. I don't remember saying good night, but we must have slept, because we woke in the early morning while it was still dark. There was no tiredness, as though we were too excited to sleep next to each other, so rather than fight it we talked as we watched the dawn lighten through the ice-laced window.

I'd been making breakfast for a few minutes before I noticed a birdcage in the corner of the kitchen. Inside, a blue budgie was watching me.

'Is this Caryn's?' I said when Wendy came in.

'No, he's mine.' She looked nervous, as though I'd be cross with her. 'I know it's cruel keeping them in cages, but the boy downstairs was emigrating to Australia, and he was going to set it free.'

'I didn't know you liked birds.'

'My dad hates them,' she said. 'But I used to have one, you know.'

We sat down in the freezing kitchen, and over a cup of tea she told me the story. When she'd been about eleven, she'd longed to have a yellow-grey cockatiel and finally her mum had bought her one.

'Dad was livid, because she did it without consulting him. I think they'd had a row, so the bird was an issue for him. He went on and on about how cruel it was. As though he cared. It was called Mike, but I only had him for a few months. I loved that bird.' She paused as though she wanted to add more, but then said, 'There were magpies in the trees outside, and Dad told this story about one coming down and opening Mike's cage. Because they're spiteful like that.'

'Bollocks.'

'I know, but I was eleven. I believed him. So Mike escaped, and we got everybody out looking for him. It was put out on local radio. And somebody caught him, three days later. I got him back.'

I could picture Laurence, infuriated by this, but hardly wanted to hear the end of the story.

'So what happened?'

'Dad set him free again a few months later. He didn't even pretend he'd escaped, but just took the cage out in the car and let him go. He kept saying it was cruel to keep birds in a cage. He'd have died of hunger within a week.'

'The fucking bastard. Why didn't you tell me this?'

She carried on talking, but I was hardly listening, aware that if she hadn't told me this story, I'd probably have been lecturing her about how cruel it was to keep birds in cages. Even though she'd inherited this budgie out of compassion, I'd probably have been giving her shit about it.

'So what's this one called?'

'Joey. Not very original, but I inherited the name as well.'

She thought the kitchen was too cold for him and wanted to move his cage into the bedroom, but budgies are known to die when their cages are moved. 'They can't stand change. The slightest disturbance and their hearts give up.'

'Imagine that.'

We spent the rest of the morning moving the cage inch by inch, until Joey was safe in the warmest corner of the bedroom. I felt an intense hatred for Laurence and wished he could see the effort we'd gone to, and that there was nothing he could do about it.

'As soon as it gets warm enough, I'll start drawing again,' Wendy promised. She improved on that with a little encouragement by saying she wanted to do something concrete with her art. Maybe a course, but a better one. Perhaps work towards doing it full-time.

Our plans grew more hopeful, and they included each other. For the first time since we'd met, we got up early every day. We ate breakfast at the Blackwell Café; it was a long way from the flat, but they had a brass broiler which pumped coffee-roast air into the street. We'd watch couples stopping to take it in, smiling at each other for a moment.

It was getting colder each day, but we'd walk for as long as we could.

On Sunday it was so cold we were the only ones out. Twilight began just after lunchtime, and the low cloud was so featureless you could mistake it for clear blue sky if it hadn't been so dark. The footpath frosted as we walked, glittering when the streetlights came on.

'I don't feel quite real,' she said, 'being here.'

'Meaning?'

'I still feel like I'm a child half the time. I don't feel like I'm renting a flat, so much as pretending to. You know, it's as though that's something grown-ups do, so it can't be happening to me.'

'I had that feeling when I passed my driving test. I

thought, *Here are all these adults who can drive, and I've tricked them into thinking I can too.'*

She stopped, leaning against the park wall, her arms by her side, seemingly unaware of how freezing it had become. I held one of her hands between mine to warm it, but she didn't seem to notice.

'It's strange being able to make my own mind up. If I go out or spend my money on CDs, I know Dad would be cross, and it's weird not having to get his permission.'

'That's pretty normal when you first leave home. Wait until you buy your first toothbrush. You'll feel like a real adult.'

'You don't think I'm abnormal then?' she asked, looking into my eyes again, more worried than she sounded.

'I'm sure you're not.'

Then she gazed off again, looking up at the sky.

'But it makes me feel like I'm on holiday. I dread it coming to an end.'

When we went out in the evenings I was more eager than Wendy to get home, probably because we'd been having such good sex. But Wendy was keen to go to pubs, to see films, or to eat out. Once, I pretended to be too tired, so we could go back and get into bed, and when we were naked she was surprised to see that I wasn't tired at all.

She made me feel guilty by saying, 'You love my body. You never just rush to get inside me.' I'd never heard such confidence from her. There was some truth in it, because although I was often anxious to get her into bed, I didn't hurry things once we were there. I knew that being a frantic lover was unappealing to women, but I'd often found it difficult to find the correct tempo between passion and desperation. With Wendy, I'd learned to take my time, but this felt more like a gift from her than any skill on my part.

'But fuck me,' she said, catching my attention again, and lying back, closing her eyes, and clasping her arms behind her head. I'd never heard her use the word, except as an insult. That night, she yelled it. It reminded me of porn I'd seen – I must have been about seven – where a tiny blonde woman kept yelling *fuck me* while this black bloke spanked her. Her face had been crimson, and although it was confusing the whole scene had thrilled me. Wendy's cries did the same; she seemed willing to take our sex to a new level, so I went with her. Towards the end, I pushed on her face, pulling her hair as she came.

We hadn't eaten, so the exertion left me gasping with a pleasant headiness almost like flu.

'Are you all right?' I asked. A classic phrase when you've tried something new in sex.

'I loved it.'

The only time I worried about her that week was when she drank too much coffee. She'd been getting excited about plans to move to London, perhaps to live with Caryn, so she could look into college there. I was a bit bad-tempered, because this was the first time she'd considered doing something that didn't necessarily include me. I tried to encourage her, but because we'd stayed in the café for longer than planned she'd had four cups of black coffee. I could tell she was struggling to keep herself in a good mood, and when she snapped at me about something she followed it with, 'Sorry. I'm so sorry, Nick.'

'It doesn't matter. It's probably just the coffee.'

'Why is it the coffee?'

I didn't know what she meant, so looked blank.

'Don't look so stupid. Why is it the coffee?'

'I thought it was making you jumpy, that's all.'

'If it isn't hormones, it has to be drugs? I'm not allowed to have moods in my own right?'

'Of course you are.'

'There's always some chemical to blame,' she continued, as though I hadn't spoken at all.

She paid then walked out ahead of me, making sure I was following but keeping a few steps ahead. I caught up with her when she got stuck behind a group of old people who were shuffling so slowly they were almost standing still. She still looked mad but held out her hands; the fingertips were shaking, and when I held them they were juicy. I couldn't tell whether or not she was blaming me. We caught a cab back up the hill, and I left her in the bath for an hour. When she came out, naked apart from a green towel-as-skirt, she apologised. Normally I'd grin seeing her dressed like that – I knew she did it to please me – but I felt sad for having won the argument. I didn't want to accuse her of having a personality composed of nothing but reactions.

'There's more to you than your moods,' I said, but she ignored me.

'I shouldn't mess with caffeine.' The way she said it, the word sounded as frightening as heroin.

The long nights must have taken their toll, because on Monday morning I felt the first tickles of a cold. By sunrise my throat felt like it was cut, and my head ached with the pressure of mucus. Instead of getting my train home, I rang in sick. Wendy went to work and came back at lunchtime with a paper bag full of medicine: Lemsip, Strepsils and Chloroseptic throat spray. I spent the rest of the week in bed, too tired to even read, smelling nothing but catarrh and menthol. Although unpleasant, I enjoyed the anticipation when Wendy was away; all her returns made me smile.

When you have a cold or pain, or even an itch, you swear you'll be a good person if it will go away. It's like making bargains with a god you don't really believe in. You say to yourself, *if I get better, I won't get mad at her again. I'll be patient. I'll stop being so lazy.* As though it will make a difference. I spent so many hours in that room feeling sorry for myself that I convinced myself to be kind to Wendy. I don't think my cold cleared up all that hastily, but by Friday I felt a renewed sense of responsibility. I'd made a million promises to be good to Wendy, to listen and understand, so that I couldn't imagine being offhand with her again.

It snowed at the weekend just as I started to feel better. The roads and pavements were scattered with ochre salt that melted clear circles around itself. That night it stayed light because of the snow, and we went down to the park which was full of people snowballing. Some rolled huge chunks of the stuff, which never quite became snowmen but left a meandering trail down to the turf. Children sporadically tried to build igloos by packing ice-cream containers with snow to make bricks, but they never got beyond the first layer.

I made a feeble attempt to attack Wendy with snow, but she got one straight back in my face and I called the game off. I felt too weak and frozen to carry on.

That night Wendy trailed the phone into the hall and closed the door to call her parents. I could hear her voice, but no words, so I busied myself with the budgie. We'd let him out for hours at a time, taking it in turns to collect his tiny pieces of crap. I opened his cage, but he was too occupied with the toys she'd bought for him to come out. There was a mirror and a white plastic bird. The mirror did nothing but drive him into a frenzy of head-butting whenever he caught sight of himself. The plastic bird, I maintained, was like a blow-up doll. It reminded him that he wanted company without providing any. It was a model canary for a start, which seemed somehow unnatural, but he was still enthralled by it. We'd find him talking to the bird: 'Budgie, budgie, budgie, boy. Joey, Joey, Joey.' That was about all he could say, but he'd say it as though he was desperate for a response.

Wendy was taking her time on the phone. I could hear long pauses between rushed sentences, so I read through her *Book of the Budgie*. According to the text, Joey was initiating the mating ritual, expecting the female to lower her head in acceptance of his proposal. I put my hand in the cage and held the plastic bird by its tail, nudging it towards him. He tapped her beak, so I tapped back. He turned his head, tapped again, and started singing, puffing up on either side of her. It was sad, but I couldn't resist lowering the bird on her spring, leaning her over in submission. Joey's posture changed; he looked like he'd been offered something wonderful and his chirrups became higher-pitched. Then he vomited up seeds, a wet trail of millet coming out on to the plastic bird. I was terrified that I'd overexcited him and shut the cage.

Wendy was shouting something, and I heard her slam the phone down, three times. It was an old phone, with a metal bell, so that each time she hit the cradle, the bell chimed.

She came back in, her face wet with crying, glanced at the cage, then hugged me.

'Your dad?'

'No, my mum. She's leaving him.'

'Fuck. Does he know?'

She didn't answer but cried into my shoulder.

When she did start talking, I sat back and listened. She

wasn't mad that Linda was leaving Laurence, but that she was going on her own.

'She promised we'd go together. And now she doesn't want me. She says it would cause too much trouble between me and Dad.'

'Does it matter?'

'She won't stay away from him unless I'm there. He'll get her back.'

'Would he want her back?'

'Nick, he won't let her do that to him.'

'When's she leaving?'

'As soon as she can. It could be any day now, or it might be months.'

I didn't understand what she meant, so she explained about joint bank accounts, ownership of the cars, credit cards. Linda had gradually been transferring power into her own hands. That way, she'd be able to get away, start a divorce, and stay one step ahead of Laurence.

'She's done everything he's asked for in the past year. Everything. Never given him any shit, so that he trusts her more. As soon as she can afford to she'll be off.'

'Surely, if she really wants to leave, she'll just go. You don't need money to leave somebody.'

She shrugged. 'You do if it's my dad.'

Sunday wasn't just cloudy but skyless. There was no fog, but a mistiness that obscured the roofs of buildings, and above them the air was a dim, featureless blue. We spent most of our day on the mattress with the lights out. When we stared out at the city, the lit-up rooms in buildings looked so warm it made the rest of the town uninviting.

It went dark prematurely, making us feel like we'd spent too long in bed. We forced ourselves to get up and shower, then went for a walk without drying our hair. It was colder than it looked, and dark, because the streelights had yet to come on.

I can't remember what we talked about on that walk, because we didn't talk much, but I remember feeling as though I'd forgotten something important. It was like the tension you feel when you've insulted somebody without knowing why. Something was nagging at me, and I couldn't place it. I remember wanting to tell Wendy, and her response being, 'You're probably not getting enough light.' The problem was that, even at the time, I couldn't be sure whether I'd imagined her responding that way or if she actually spoke.

Everything was slightly dewy: a thorn hedge, the pavement, a newspaper limp over the kerb. There wasn't enough wet to form droplets, but without touching you knew everything had a film of cold.

When the streetlights came on, we headed back. We bought chips on the way up the hill, both too tired to cook, unwilling to eat out. When we got back inside, we undressed and got into bed.

The room was different that night. It might have been the cold that felt strange, but there was also a smell that felt out of place; I couldn't tell where it came from, but there was a strong smell of rotten wood.

Inexplicably, I started crying. Even if she'd begged to know what was wrong, I couldn't have answered, but Wendy just lay there, holding me tightly until I went to sleep.

In the morning Wendy left the flat before I got out of the bath and returned in ten minutes with a paper bag from the chemist's. She held it out like a present, but inside there was a pregnancy testing kit.

'Are you late?'

'Only about five days.'

'You didn't seem worried.'

'I got this so that we don't have to worry.'

Dressed in nothing but a towel, I wanted to get dressed, but she asked me to stay with her. She squatted over the toilet, and I held the plastic stick between her legs, keeping it in her piss for ten seconds. Then we pushed it into a plastic holder, where the chemical reaction would take place. We had to hope that it would come out white. If it looked slightly blue, we had a problem.

It took two minutes, and we counted down the last seconds out loud. When the stick was withdrawn its tip was the deepest, richest blue, a thick drip of blue water hanging from it, trembling with the shake of Wendy's fingers. I felt like I'd been winded. Wendy put her fingers into her hair, then touched her heart. For a moment she took on the expression of crying, but it was replaced by a blank, pale stare. She touched her stomach, her palm resting there gently.

Chapter Five

We left Bath in such a hurry it was as though she blamed the place rather than me. She went into work to pick up her money and I lay on the bed, unblinking, my eyes filling with dust until they stung. When she returned, she stripped her wall of posters, tearing them so much that she ended up leaving them screwed up in the corner. Everything else we could carry was stuffed into a combination of cases and carrier bags and taken downstairs in shifts. She covered Joey's cage with a silk scarf and carried him down. I was left to lock the flat. It looked like it had been empty for weeks, already feeling cold, the torn paper on the floor making it look like a room in a derelict house. We left pillows, towels and a few old socks, but they looked like they belonged to strangers. The only trace of our presence was the unmade bed, our imprints resting in the sheets.

We caught a taxi to the railway station, and a train to Leicester, talking quietly at first, but later arguing loudly enough for the whole carriage to get the picture. Trying to make it sound like I was advising, it must have been obvious I was doing more than persuading. She concentrated on the birdcage, peeping under the scarf to see if Joey was still alive. We heard nothing from him all the way back.

Wendy wouldn't even let me go home with her, so we

parted at Leicester railway station. It was a bewildering feeling to be walking home again when only a few hours earlier we'd been planning an evening out in Bath. I expected my flat to be stale, but it smelt lived in. I'd left T-shirts to dry on the radiator, and they were still giving off the smell of washing powder. It smelt so much like home, which didn't seem right, because I was the only one there.

I didn't see her again that month, not even on my birthday, but rang every night. Sometimes the conversation was cut short because Laurence wanted to use the phone.

'You haven't told them, have you?'

'Of course not.'

She'd spun her parents a story about being offered a better job in London, which would keep them off her back for a few weeks.

She wanted to talk about the future, the different futures that could exist, but I just pestered her.

'If you have it, your life will mean nothing. You've achieved nothing yet.'

'I want to go away with Mum.'

'Is she leaving him?'

'Soon.'

I hoped Linda would leave it a while, because I could picture the two of them buggering off to start some Gypsy existence, bringing the baby up together then coming back to me when the money ran out. When I said that, she surprised me by laughing. I took the opportunity to strengthen my argument, repeating the key points to her silence down the phone.

It would be good to say that I was panicking, that I couldn't help myself, but I calculated every argument in an attempt to convince her. Worst of all, I tried to make it look like compassion rather than my own desire. I think the ferocity of my argument surprised her.

'Why do you hate babies so much?'

'It's not a baby; it's a blob of cells,' I countered. 'You sound like a fucking Pro-Lifer.'

It was difficult finding the right balance of argument. If I was too kind, she might keep it, thinking I'd be there for her. But if I only put the other argument forward I could be accused of forcing her to get rid of it, and I'd never be forgiven. I even found myself saying, 'I'll support you whatever you do,' to make her feel close to me, then followed it with, 'but it would be so much easier if you got rid of it. For you.'

I dialled myself out of the equation at all points so that I wouldn't sound as selfish as I was being.

When I told Dave about this, he was as incredulous as Wendy.

'So you're going to play at being an artist your whole life.'

'If we had a baby we'd become like everybody else.'

'You are like everybody else. Except you're more of a bastard than most. Don't be so selfish.'

'Selfish against whom? It doesn't even exist. I don't want a baby yet. Does that make me a bad person? Everybody else is allowed their opinion; why the fuck aren't I?'

I must have sounded more desperate than I realised because he calmed down then and tried to rationalise, rather than argue me down.

'You're always harping on about experience and living an extraordinary life – whatever that means – but as soon as something unexpected happens you're petrified. You want to cancel it out.'

It was the first time I'd stopped to think about why it bothered me so much. I'd been so busy, trying to persuade Wendy, telling her she was too young, that I hadn't thought about why I couldn't face her being pregnant. Most people my age were getting to the point where they wanted to get on with it. The thought of staying with Wendy was good, we could afford it, and I liked children, so why was I so desperate to avoid it?

'There's nothing unusual about having a baby. Everybody does it. The thought bores me.'

'And yet you want everything to be predictable.'

'I want things to be like they were in Bath.'

'And you think if she gets rid of it, everything will be fine?'

That was the most depressing thing he'd said all night. I can't remember where we were, whether this was over the phone, or if we went out. The whole of March was like that. I can remember the sounds of the month, tones of voice and words spoken. I'd run speeches through my mind; things that had been said, things that could be said. I knew the best thing to do would be to support her, to stay with her no matter what, but if I ever said anything like that I'd back off again and begin my lecture about her age, her life.

In the end, to shut me up, she said, 'You won't be held responsible whatever I do.'

She began to distance herself even more when she agreed to have an abortion. Even after she'd booked the appointment, I didn't let up with my insistence that she get rid of it. She was too young for a baby; it would ruin her life; it was such a responsibility. She didn't want me at the clinic with her, which is partly why she'd booked it in London. The other reason was to be near to Caryn. She didn't even want me to go halves with her on the cost, preferring to pay for everything herself.

The last thing she said to me before leaving was, 'Don't worry. I'll go through with it.'

She rang me afterwards, in my office, to say that it was done, and asked me to give her space for a few days. I was so relieved that I didn't complain.

'I thought about you,' I said, realising I'd been working so hard that I hadn't thought about her at all since breakfast. She started responding to that, but her money ran out.

A letter arrived a week later saying that she'd stayed in London. She'd joined Caryn in a tower block in Wandsworth. There wasn't much logic to her letter, with thoughts interjected as they occurred to her, ideas tailing off as something else caught her attention. 'I'd better start taking myself seriously at last,' she wrote.

The writing was tender but casual, so it surprised me that she ended so abruptly.

'I made the decision to have an abortion that day we left Bath, but after your reaction on the train I wanted to see how you'd be about it all. If you'd been completely open about our future, I'd still have got rid of it, but I might have kept you.'

In a way, I used that to absolve myself. Who wouldn't react badly, when tested in such a calculated way?

I found myself thinking about Linda more often, even though no news was coming through. If Dave and I ever got on to the subject of Wendy, I'd end up talking about Laurence and Linda, hoping she'd left him.

'It sounds like you miss them more than Wendy,' Dave said.

'It pisses me off that he got his way,' I said. He'd effectively written me off as part of Wendy's life, and I'd been so pleased when we were in Bath to have proved him wrong. 'If there's any justice, she'll leave him.'

'You're obsessed. Your own parents are so happy, you can't cope with it.'

He was wrong about that, because I found out that week that Dad had been ill for months. As usual, he'd kept this to himself, sneaking off to hospital on his own, until Mum had found him crying in the bedroom. It was related to blood pressure, and there was the risk of a stroke. I only spoke to her on the phone, but I could picture her face because she sounded so puzzled. 'He was such a bad-tempered sod for months. I can't tell whether that made him ill, or was because of it.' They'd put him on beta-blockers and told him to take it easy. Which was like telling somebody with depression to cheer up. Mum acquiesced whenever he got uptight, which only made him angrier. 'He's after a reaction,' she said. 'If I go along with him he gets worse, until I end up crying. It's easier if I explode straight back at him.' They'd never argued much in the past, except in traffic jams, and now that she wanted to look after him she found him tiresome. She speculated briefly about a holiday alone, or even just a weekend in Leicester, but I knew this was her way of releasing the tension of a fantasy. Once it was aired, she'd settle back to looking after him.

I didn't get out as much as I should have done during the following months, convincing myself that I was wrapped up in work. Uni slacked off in mid-June, so I busied myself with painting. Normally, that would get me out, looking for ideas, but I started developing an idea that Wendy had been keen on which relied on the past rather than on new sights. I became interested in the coding of emotions, to store memory. The way she'd worked was to reduce an image down to bare colours and shapes. Where she had used abstraction as a personal reminder, I tried to find a way of repeating conditions of light and weather and the time of day to encode a moment. I was fascinated by those moments when light seemed to mean more than it should. If I was trying to get anything across in my paintings, it was times like that, when you see something ordinary, which makes you feel more than you understand. So I painted actual scenes, sometimes from photographs, sometimes made up or from memory, but rather than painting them as they had been I gave them the weather and light of a meaningful moment. There was often a sense of distance in my work; you'd see a house with a light on, rather than the room itself. It was suggestion, rather than revelation. There was always this sense of contrast and dislocation, and overall I thought it was the best stuff I'd done.

I was starting to get quite proud of my work and risked showing it to Dave. I might have kept it from him, except that he found his way into uni on a Saturday, bored and looking for something to do. I explained that my painting was meant to be a sort of heightened realism.

'There are no people.'

'There are traces of people. Memories of them. In the locations. It's about how people perceive the world based on their experience.'

'Is it because you can't paint people?'

'Don't be thick,' I said. 'People would get in the way. You'd focus on the action rather than the feeling.'

'Pretentious twat.'

This was better than him being polite. If ever Dave said, 'No really, it's good, well done,' I knew he thought that I'd done something dreadful.

He dismissed my work and rambled on about his own job

as we walked to the pub. It made me feel a bit stupid for getting so excited about my ideas, but after we'd been in there for a while he brought my painting up again. I loved talking about it usually, even when he was offensive, but this time he sounded worried.

'You're always reminding yourself of things, rather than getting on with life. It's all about the past.'

'So we should just write off our history? Live for the moment?'

We swapped insults for a while, but I must have sounded subdued because we left soon after. Walking home on my own, after he'd dropped me by the fire station, I couldn't help but think about what he'd said. Nothing new happened to me. Wendy had been gone for months, and although I'd pretended to start a new life she was colouring everything I did.

Diverting on to a path that ran between Welford Road Cemetery and the school grounds, I headed for uni. In my office I set up my paintings against the walls to assess them. There's something about being in a building late at night that makes you nervous about putting the main lights on, so I looked at them with the glow from my desk lamp. In a way, that lighting was better; the dark colours faded, bringing out the glowing places: windows, fires, distant traffic. But every painting, no matter what it showed, reminded me of Wendy. Months had passed, I'd been out with other people, but it was difficult to recall anything other than her. My recent past seemed irrelevant. There were impressions of working and seeing Dave, but I couldn't place any day with certainty. The memories that came back could have been from any time since she left. I wasn't even sure what the weather had been like. I felt irrelevant in my own life, as though nothing I did counted, unless she was there.

Still mildly drunk, I wrote a long, disjointed letter to her, full of the apologies and kindness I hadn't offered when she'd needed them. I posted it on the way home.

Two days later Wendy sent me a postcard of the BT Tower. She wrote in note form about her new job at W. H. Smith, the food Caryn cooked for them, a life-drawing class she was thinking of joining. Things were looking up. At the bottom she put her phone number. I didn't wait for the cheap evening rate but called that morning. Our conversation covered the basic pleasantries for less than a minute, and then we established that we were both still single.

'Did you give me your number because things are getting better, or because you're missing me?'

'Both,' she said. 'I missed you the whole time, but I couldn't be with you while it was all so close to the surface.'

'And what do you want now?'

'To see you for a while. That's all.'

I went down that Friday night, the train drawing into London as the sky yellowed. I half-hoped she'd be waiting at the station for me, but headed for the Northern Line, with its distinctive smell of oil and dust. By the time I got out at Tooting Bec the sun had set, so I caught a cab to her flat. She lived on the seventh floor of a white tower block, one of five identical buildings set between Wandsworth Prison and an art college. The lift smelt of bleach, which was marginally worse than the piss it was trying to cover.

Wendy's hair had grown, running over the shoulders of her cardigan. I wanted to touch her, but she didn't even hug me hello. Instead she led me out to the narrow balcony, for a good view of the prison. You could see Battersea Power Station off to the left, its four creamy towers at exactly the same angle as on that Pink Floyd album, only smaller. On the other side, the shining railway line, and a sandstone building that looked like a country mansion, except for the pollution that had soaked into its stone.

'That's the art college. Mostly it's acting, but they run some freelance courses. Life drawing. Painting.'

Her conversation was more nervous than the first time we'd been out, but I couldn't think of a way to relax her.

Back inside the flat, I saw Joey's cage. The budgie was facing his mirror, tapping his bald head against it.

'He made it here without a heart attack?'

'Of course.'

She beamed at the bird, leaning down at him, calling his name. He responded, chirping it back at her. I thought about the time we'd shuffled him across the room, thinking he was so fragile that the slightest movement would break him. Now he'd been up to Leicester and back to London without any sign of dying.

The flat smelt unfamiliar, probably because of Caryn. She wasn't going to be there until the morning, but there were traces of her: silver bangles left on the arm of a chair, body spray instead of deodorant, a hair dryer, striped tops that I'd never seen before. There were ashtrays, emptied out but not cleaned, the glass milky with ash.

'She's smoking too much,' Wendy whispered, as though she might be heard.

I suggested eating out, but Wendy said there was nowhere nearby. She didn't mind cooking, because she'd been practising. I offered to go out for wine, but she said it was too far.

'Let's just stay in tonight. I'll show you round town tomorrow.'

She was serious throughout dinner, and when I tried to make her laugh she'd look off to one side, trying to work out what I meant. She became happier when I grew tired, lighting up enough to say she was glad I was there. I couldn't take my eyes off her hair, wondering whether it made her look older or younger. I'd expected her to look withered and disturbed by her abortion and imagined she'd have cut her hair, trimming down for efficient city life. Although she seemed tense in her speech, long hair made her look relaxed. She'd lean over to pick something up, and it would fan out in front of the lamp before swinging back. I imagined it on her collarbone or falling away from her spine as she bent forward.

'You look well,' I said, then realising it might lead to a discussion of the abortion, I said, 'better than you ever have.'

We went through the motions of pretending we'd sleep separately, even making up the bed-settee in the main room. When I borrowed her toothbrush, I felt unexpectedly pleased to be using it, knowing that it had been in her mouth that morning.

I got into my bed and listened to her brushing her teeth, washing her face. There was a long silence after that, and then she came through.

'I don't think I can sleep yet,' she said, so she sat at the edge of the bed. I let her make the first contact, touching my knee through the covers. Without looking at my face she wrapped her arms around me, pressing her head against my solar plexus. She turned so that her face was closer to my skin, and kissed. The soft spread of her hair excited me, but she seemed desperate to hold me still. No matter how I stroked and kissed her, she just held on to me.

We slept in that position, and in the morning my hand was between her legs before I was fully aware, and wet before she awoke. She was more vigorous during sex than I'd ever known her. That, combined with an exceptionally warm morning, made us slick. When she came, she made a noise so loud and intense it didn't sound enjoyable. Afterwards, her forehead was tight, and she appeared to be irritated with my conversation.

I brought her breakfast in bed, and she smiled; I was amazed at how quickly her mood could change.

'You're so kind to me,' she said, but in contrast her face regained some of its reluctance.

Caryn came home while we were still on the bed-settee. Either she guessed we were in the front room or couldn't be bothered saying hello, because she went straight to the bathroom and turned on the taps. We could hear her breathing, washing, the plastic squeaking as she lowered herself deeper. I felt uncomfortable, because it was forcing me to picture her naked, even though we'd never met.

Wendy was about to speak, but the phone rang. She pulled it over the bed and sounded calm as she talked until she slammed the phone down.

'Two of the part-timers have pissed off again. They shouldn't employ school kids.'

'You sound like your dad,' I said, but the joke went by her, and she went to open the curtains. It was so bright outside I couldn't tell whether the sky was blue or white.

'I have to go in, on a day like this. We were meant to go out.'

She went to speak to Caryn through the bathroom door while I put the bed away and opened the windows. The air already smelt of grass, as though the park had been mown; grass and exhaust, and a hint of tarmac. It wasn't even nine o'clock, but it was the hottest day of the year.

As Wendy dressed in her grey-flecked shirt and skirt, she told me all sorts of obvious things, such as where they kept the bread, what I could have for lunch, how to tune the

radio. She kissed me as she got into the lift, but looked like
she regretted it because it was so brusque.

I listened to the lift unwind all the way down, then went
back in, surprised at how quickly after waking I was alone.
The bathroom door was open, and although there was no
steam its wet air smelt of shampoo. Caryn was in her room,
the door closed. I went into the front room for a while,
unwilling to turn the TV on because the weather was so
good. I was too tired to go for a walk, so went out on to the
balcony to read.

When I went back in, I could see Caryn in the kitchen, a
bitten piece of toast in one hand, a mug of coffee in the
other, a *Guardian* spread out over the cooker. Her hair was
still damp, making the shoulders of her *Time Out* T-shirt
translucent.

'Do you want any breakfast?' she asked, raising her
eyebrows. She looked much younger than I'd expected. In
the only photograph I'd seen of Caryn she'd been drunk, her
pupils red from the flash. She looked so much healthier now.
Her jeans and T-shirt were ordinary, but she was wearing
narrow silver bangles and had put on mascara. It was the
only make-up she wore, and had the effect of making her
skin look pale apart from a flush in her cheeks. Her eyes
could have looked startled, except that the rest of her
appearance was relaxed. She was the sort of person I imagined
having as a younger sister. I could imagine her taking the
piss out of me.

We never did manage a formal introduction, and I could
tell she preferred that. When the conversation lulled she'd
hum, and even break into a line of whispered song, while I
pretended to take an interest in the budgie. Then she'd read
something out of the paper to me, trying to work out what
I'd find interesting.

Once we'd established that we'd both be spending the day in, she became more talkative and came to sit with me in the front room. After a few minutes she said, 'You don't look like I expected.'

'I was thinking the same about you.'

'Wendy makes you sound more . . . I don't know. Taller, I think.'

'I saw photographs of you when your hair was shorter.'

'Yeah, well, I did things the wrong way round. Became a lesbian and then grew my hair. *Became a lesbian*. Freudian slip. I was born a lesbian, according to Louise.'

'Your girlfriend?'

'Sort of. I wish. Nothing much doing there.'

We spent the day making brews for each other. She made a Brie salad for lunch. We opened the balcony door and all the windows, but no breeze came through. I was sitting in the armchair, she on the settee, and we faced each other all afternoon. She smoked for a while, until the heat made it difficult to breathe. It became so hot that her hair never dried, because it became wet again with sweat. All day she looked like somebody who'd just got out of the bath. I can't remember what we talked about, only that she wouldn't hesitate to contradict me. It wasn't done competitively, but if she disagreed she wouldn't say, 'Yes, but . . .'. She'd say, 'No, that's wrong.' Despite her tone, she looked nervous when she did that, so it was impossible to be annoyed.

When she went to the toilet, I realised that I was blushing, as much from talking to her as from the heat. It had been a long time since I'd spent time with somebody new, and I was enjoying it. I'd forgotten how attentive you become to your own speech.

When she came back she suggested we read, and I said I'd been thinking the same thing. It was as though we knew that

Wendy would come back and ask us what we'd been doing, and if we said 'just talking' she'd worry. She wasn't likely to be jealous, but it would underline that we'd been messing about while she'd had a shit day at work.

We took our books out to the balcony, having to sit on the concrete because there were no chairs. It was so bright I could barely make out the words, and after I while I gave up and lay back to watch the sky. Within its white shine clouds began to outline and deepen, blue space appearing between them. The air was so thick with pollution it looked like the sun was setting even while it was high, at five o'clock. Every few minutes one of us would comment on the heat.

'I'm not going to complain, though,' Caryn said. 'The first warm day of summer, and you immediately come across old grannies in big wool coats, moaning about prickly heat.'

'We're talking about the weather. How old are we?'

'Older than we should be.' During the course of the day she'd made a few statements like that, which she'd follow with a look as though she realised she'd said something not quite right but didn't know how to correct it.

I was disappointed in myself for being attracted to her. If Wendy hadn't been around, Caryn was exactly the sort of person I'd have been looking for. She may have sensed that, because for the last half-hour we talked about nothing but Wendy. We made plans for the evening, to play cards, watch a Channel 4 film, cook something together and share a bottle of wine.

When Wendy returned she said she was too tired and went to her room. I went straight in after her and found her curled on the bed, arms folded. I felt the need to apologise, but I didn't know what for.

'Was it shit?' I asked.

'I missed you, that's all.'

Once I'd moved towards her, she didn't let go of me, even as we undressed. I didn't get to open the window. Within minutes we were soaked, the bed so wet I couldn't believe we'd produced that much sweat. We were too hot to sleep, but lay without talking for over an hour.

Caryn cooked for us, forcing us to emerge. We sat on the living-room floor to eat, watching the news. While we ate, the air cooled, and then it began to rain. That high above the ground you can't hear the rain hitting the ground, only the rush of it cutting the air.

'I need a bath,' Wendy said. 'Come and talk to me.'

'I'll just get a drink.'

While I ran the tap, Caryn came into the kitchen and, whispering under the sound of the running water, she said, 'Is she all right?'

'Yeah, fine.'

I felt worse than if we hadn't spoken, even though it had only been a few words. It wasn't just that we'd had a secret moment but that we'd started thinking of Wendy as though she was a problem rather than our friend.

Chapter Six

After that weekend, I went to London every few days, spending so much money on train fares it would have been cheaper to move down there with her. Sometimes I'd travel home on the morning train, only to have Wendy ring me up in the afternoon, asking me to go down again that night. I had enough spare time around lectures to be able to go. My students were more than willing to hand in essays late or put off their appointments with me. It felt like I was living in London and commuting to Leicester. Even so, it was never clear whether or not we were going out with each other. If we talked about the future at all, she would prefix every sentence with, 'If we stay together . . .' At other times she seemed so eager for me I couldn't believe she could accept a future apart. There was one night when I arrived late, keen to talk, but she took me to the bedroom before I could say hello to Caryn and undressed before I'd even put my bag down. She laughed briefly but looked anxious as she lay back, spreading her legs. I was still dressed, tired and hungry from eating nothing but crisps, and she was opening like that. She'd put just one light on in the room, so that as she stretched back I could barely make out her face. Between her legs, the hair looked darker, the only light coming from the shine of wetness.

'Please,' she said, looking up at me, so unhappy it was difficult to become aroused. The only comfort was her warmth as I moved on to her.

When I was getting out of breath I considered faking an orgasm. It isn't too difficult for men, even with condoms on; there's usually enough pre-cum and general foaming of fluids to convince somebody you've come. With some women it was more difficult, because they'd crouch over a pad of tissues after sex, insistent on wiping everything out of themselves. Wendy never did that. She preferred to leave it inside and would sometimes laugh – on the tube, in a bookshop, while cooking – as she indicated that my come was running into her knickers. So I knew she'd lie there, unknowing, if I were to fake it. But it was something I'd only ever done on one-night stands, when I was either too drunk to feel anything or regretting going to bed with a stranger. Even those occasions were pretty hypocritical, because with just about every girlfriend I'd gone on and on about how bad it was to fake orgasms. All this went through my mind, and I was only brought back into the moment by the sound of my own panting, so hoarse I sounded unfit. Wendy was almost rigid beneath me, and then, to my disappointment, she came. I'd been trying to make her, but it disappointed me that just fucking her like that, while worrying and thinking, feeling nothing myself, could make her orgasm. I'd hoped she would sense my distance, almost hear my thoughts, and ask me what was wrong.

'Carry on,' she said, her arms falling away from me.

'Too tired. I just don't think I could.'

She urged me out of her then, which was unusual, but then held on to me. I hoped she wouldn't worry too much.

After a long time, she said, 'You're not one of those people who only wants what he can't have, are you?'

'No, I love it when you want me.' That was true, but her desperation had frightened me.

'I'm really trying, Nick,' she said.

I didn't know what she meant, but it must have helped her into sleep, even though it kept me from mine.

We hardly argued at first, which was a useful habit, but it meant that when we did bicker the insults carried more weight. As a result, I would keep my distance if she appeared angry, because one misplaced comment could make her insecure for days. Weeks after I'd said something insignificant, she'd bring it up again and admit that it had been eating at her.

'If something bothers you, tell me.'

'But then you call me critical.'

We were sitting out on the balcony, too cold, but trying to enjoy the sunset. Facing the wrong way to see the sun, we watched it reflected in the windows of the prison. The other tower blocks, usually as white as paper, looked like orange chalk. It was probably the last time we'd make the effort to go out there. The forecast was for a cold October.

'I can't relax around you,' I said. 'You're so touchy, I have to weigh everything up before I speak.'

'You don't realise how hurtful you can be.'

We were drinking white wine, the glasses made opaque by our fingerprints. We'd been holding them so long that the wine remained chilled only because it was so cold out there.

'We spend too long analysing ourselves, thinking about what we say, what it all means.'

'I thought you liked talking to me,' she said.

'I like talking, but not endlessly about *us*. We just spiral down, criticising each other.' She didn't look convinced, so I said, 'I'm not saying we should never talk, but we're at our best when we talk about what we like, not each other, not our relationship. If you analyse for ever, you'll come to the same conclusion that most philosophers did. Life is pointless and mostly disappointing.' She smiled, her laugh nothing more than a quick breath through her nose, amplified by her wine glass, but it was enough to diffuse the tension.

After that, we got on better. The only recurrent argument we had was when she accused me of being like her dad. She was telling me a story about Caryn and struggling to find a word, so I suggested 'fatalistic', and she looked at me as though she was cross. When she spoke her voice was sad.

'Please don't finish my sentences for me. If there's one thing I can't stand . . .'

'Sorry.' I'd said it without thinking, and that made me angry. 'I was only trying to help.'

'Dad never lets my mum finish what she's saying.'

'I'm not your dad.'

'He takes over stories,' she said, explaining more than accusing now. 'Mum will be telling people a story, and when it gets to the good bit he'll butt in.'

She let it go, but the subject came up again within half an hour when I started whistling. I was washing up and Wendy was carrying toast plates into the kitchen for me. She stopped, looking at me as though I'd called her a cunt.

'What?'

'*I* was whistling that.'

'I didn't realise.'

'You're always stealing my whistles.' I looked blank. 'If I start whistling, you take over.'

She never mentioned her dad, but she'd told me before he was always doing that.

'Sorry for sounding happy,' I said.

Although I remember these incidents clearly, they were minor fragments of anger in an otherwise peaceful time.

I'd avoided going back to Wigan for ages, worried that Dad would go too far in trying to cover his illness. He never admitted to being unwell, and he'd always waited until I was out of the room before taking pills. I'd be able to hear from the next room – bottle open, pills shaken out, glass filled, gulping – and yet he thought he was doing it in private. I dreaded having to spend an afternoon avoiding the subject of his blood pressure. When I got there he was straight out of his chair as soon as he saw my Mazda on the path. I don't know why, but I'd imagined him with a walking-stick, so even though he looked a bit puffed up around the eyes he didn't look as frail as I'd expected.

The afternoon was tense because Mum was tired, and finally voiced her woes in front of me. She'd probably been silent for weeks but was using my presence as a guarantee that Dad wouldn't lash out at her. I kept trying to change the subject, but when I told a story they'd miss the point, focusing on a detail I couldn't have cared about.

'She thinks I'm a burden,' Dad said when Mum was out of the room.

I just wished I could have said, 'You are,' and laughed. I bet he'd have laughed with me. But I couldn't do it and made excuses for him and for her.

A David Attenborough programme was coming on, one about birds, and they wanted to watch it, which gave me a good opportunity to leave.

When I arrived in London one Friday, it took a long time for Caryn to appear. All the doors were closed behind her, and she was whispering.

'We're having a bit of a crisis,' she explained, letting me into the dark hall. Wendy had bought another bird to accompany Joey. It was a cockatiel, like the one she used to own.

'She only decided this morning,' Caryn whispered. 'Once she'd got it in her head that she wanted another bird, she couldn't bear to wait another day. We've been trying to get him in the cage for the past two hours. It was meant to be a surprise for when you arrived. She's trying to tempt him down from the curtains.'

I was pretty angry, because we'd often talked about the bird trade in this country. It was well known that most of the pet shops round here imported them illegally, letting nine die for every one that survived. And I didn't like birds being kept in cages anyway.

'She's having a horrible night,' Caryn said, seeing my face. 'Try to be nice to her.'

We heard a yelp, followed by sounds of the cage being shaken, so we went in. Wendy was kneeling by the cage, her palm bleeding; inside, the cockatiel was backing up against the bars, hissing.

Later, when his cage had been put next to Joey's, she told me she wanted to call him Mike.

'You can't call him Mike if your other one was called that. It's insulting to his memory.'

'Don't be stupid,' she snapped, offering no further argument, so I shut up.

In some tube stations, on certain days, sunlight gets into the stairwells, and the metal casing on the steps looks like gold. The diamond-shaped grooves are blackened with dirt, but the surface is burnished smooth by passing feet. The steps at Tooting Bec were like that sometimes during autumn, but so rarely that I became superstitious about seeing them. If the gold was glowing, I took it as a good sign. Which is probably indicative of how nervous I'd become around Wendy. She wasn't volatile, but sometimes inexplicably sad, and I didn't know how to bring her out of those moods.

She kept creating minor desires, such as the new bird, or a better pair of shoes, which were so easily attained that she was quickly left with ennui. I tried to encourage her to get back to her art, and in principal she agreed. It would give her something to aim for. She wanted to get a better grounding in the history of art before she threw herself into it, which I thought was a good sign, rather than procrastination, so we trawled round the galleries every weekend. After a few weeks we grew so bored that we stopped. The older paintings were too familiar, and I was growing increasingly pissed off by the lack of talent in young artists. I was so used to defending modern art that it had taken me months to realise I'd gone off it.

The reason for my sustained enthusiasm up until then was that my students had grown steadily more narrow-minded during the 1990s, and I'd felt the need to enlighten them. When I'd taken a coachload of first-years to London for the Pop Art Show, I'd been confronted by a girl who, observing a Rauschenberg, insisted, 'That's not art.' I might have let that go, except that a few weeks later she expressed the same attitude to Christo and Goldsworthy, who are so accessible they've made some good coffee-table books. And this complaint was from somebody who wanted to be an artist. Did she want to paint like Constable? I could have understood it if I'd been talking to a banker, but she was an art student.

So I'd become a staunch defender of all non-realism, trying to convey why it could be as valid as more obvious representations. Nothing annoyed me more than hearing people say, 'Anybody could do that.' *Yes, anybody could, but you didn't and Andy Warhol did, thousands of times. Art is not craft.* But because of this repeated rant, I didn't realise for ages how depressing the art scene had become. It was pretending to be clever by being opaque. Which was the height of irony, because the artists in question could barely string a sentence together.

The galleries were like exclusive clubs, the same pale people dressed in black, drinking coffee all day. More of a silence ensued when you walked into the bar of the Photographers Gallery than when you went into a Welsh pub.

None of this was helpful for Wendy.

'I don't want anything to do with them. But I don't want to work in a bookshop my whole life.'

'You could do what I do.'

'I could never teach.'

'I mean book covers, that sort of thing.'

Wendy was in the bath, lying back so that I could only see the top of her scalp. The sun was going down behind the frosted window, casting a blurred, soft-edged circle on the plaster wall.

'Something has to happen to me or I'll go mad.' She sat up and turned round to look at me. 'We should go away again.'

'If we run away everything will be all right.'

'Don't patronise me, Nick.'

'I'm not patronising you. But going on holiday isn't going to help you find out what you want.'

'I haven't a clue what I want. I want to stop feeling like this.'

Her voice didn't sound especially sad, but her words frightened me. I'd been about to make suggestions about doing a degree but could tell the timing would be bad, that she needed reassurance. I said something about feeling certain she'd eventually find what she wanted.

'You really think so?'

'I know you will if you don't panic.'

That night we went to bed early, not for sex but to read. Her eyes were so tired that she asked me to read her book out loud. She was halfway into the first book of *Lord of the Rings*, because I'd gone on at her about reading it. Caryn was out, so I felt able to do the different voices and noises without too much embarrassment. I copied them off the Radio 4 series I'd heard years ago, but Wendy was so pleased with them I had to keep up the pretence that they were my own invention.

We didn't get out much during November because of the cold but managed a brief trip out for Wendy's twenty-first, which failed to turn into anything other than an ordinary night. By December town was so busy that we rarely ventured from the flat. Caryn was always out, but we stayed in, having a bath or reading. It was probably because of this that my visits became less frequent, and I started going down in the car, which made it easier to leave if we were getting on each other's nerves. We talked about driving out to Hampshire and Wiltshire, to see the sacred sites, but either we got up too late or the weather was foul.

At Christmas Wendy came up to Leicester, but I'd already gone to Wigan to spend it with my parents, so we missed each other. She sent me a card saying, 'I'm reading *Lord of the Rings* on my own again. I couldn't wait for you to come back. But I'm using your voices, in my head. They're getting close to Mordor. I miss you.' There was nothing about Merry Christmas or New Year, which made me smile.

It was mid-January when I next saw her. The roads were icy so I took the train, and once I was on my way I couldn't think about anything except getting there.

Wendy looked well, if a bit tired, and her hair was longer. The low sun made the flat warm, and it was good to look out over London, seeing the Battersea towers made yellower by the light. Having been apart, I felt our enthusiasm for each other would probably make this a good visit. I went to the toilet, and as I sat there saw that although the waste bin had been cursorily emptied it was glittering with tiny silver ovals. It looked as if metal confetti had been put in there. I fished one of the ovals out and saw the word *Sol* written on it. After examining a few more I realised they were the pushed-out sections of foil from a blister-pack of Solpadeine. When I asked if they were hers or Caryn's, Wendy just said, 'What's the problem?'

'If you have that bad a headache you should see a doctor.'

She denied having headaches. 'It's to help me relax.'

'What?'

'It evens me out.'

'You sound like a fucking addict.'

'For God's sake, stop lecturing me.'

I would have gone on, except that she was staring, focusing on the space in front of her. It was something I'd seen her do many times, but I'd never realised until then that it was an indication of her proximity to losing it. It was as though she was withdrawing, attempting to be calm, knowing she was about to explode. I stopped talking and waited until she made eye contact with me again. She looked so relieved at my silence that she didn't even continue defending herself.

Our sex life went downhill so gradually that we barely noticed. It wasn't dreadful, but it became a way of trading pleasure rather than something we shared. At first I was certain it was her fault. She was too tired to put everything into it. She said that I wasn't paying as much attention.

'So I'm shit in bed all of a sudden.'

'You're still doing everything right, but I don't feel anything from you.'

'How am I supposed to change that? You're imagining it.'

'I feel like you're working me over, rushing things. You don't seem to be enjoying it.'

'I *never* rush.'

'Well, not rushing, but mechanical.'

We were both so defensive that we didn't discuss it much more and slipped into habits of reassuring each other. Quite often I couldn't come, and when I did Wendy was usually nowhere near. It was because of that and because we were worried about leaving the other out that we got into the habit of finishing each other off. Before long, that had turned into sexual trading. I would usually go first, either being sucked, or fucking her, and then, wanting only to move away, I'd have to lick her. It was even worse if she came first, because I struggled to come, knowing she wasn't enjoying it.

We came to see sex as a favour to each other. I ended up asking for blow jobs, as though I was asking to borrow ten quid. And she'd usually agree, but acted as though it was a minor hassle. She was just as good as ever, but it felt like a performance. That was a shame, because when we'd first started sleeping together she'd delighted in my cock. She wasn't the sort of woman to feed me lines about size, but she genuinely enthused. Until then I'd always thought women hated dicks, but that was probably because I'd been out with so many young women. Wendy had loved taking my cock in her mouth, but her reason had shocked me. 'Most men think the best way to wash your knob is to shove it in somebody's mouth,' she'd said. 'I never knew they could be so lovely.' Remembering that enthusiasm made it difficult to watch her laboriously wanking me off into her mouth.

Even when I went down on her, our position changed. We always used to be in sixty-nine, and even though our difference in torso size made it impossible for her to suck me, she used to bury her face in my balls or against my thigh, her tongue occasionally pressing between her lips, licking and sniffing at me until her face was grimy with spit. Now, she made sure I was lying on my front, between her legs, watching her face for any sign of arousal. Her eyes were tightly closed, the skin folded over the lashes – the only indication that anything intense was happening to her. Her orgasms passed silently, but she said that was because Caryn might be in the house.

That sort of sexual trading wasn't as bad as when we started exchanging sex for non-sexual favours. I offered to do the washing in exchange for being able to fuck her. 'If you're quick', she said, lifting her skirt and pulling her knickers aside.

When she wanted to come, she simply offered to bring me off first, knowing I never refused.

It sounds obvious that something was severely wrong, but we didn't even realise we'd stopped kissing.

I also found myself imagining Caryn while we were at it, and sometimes I made more noise, knowing she might be able to hear us from her bedroom. I felt like shit afterwards, because it was as bad as being unfaithful, but bad habits are usually made stronger by guilt. It was like throwing porn in the bin after a wank; five minutes later I wanted it again. It got to the point where I couldn't come without imagining Caryn. And by repeating that to myself during every sexual act, I started associating her with sex. Putting it down to boredom, and with no intention of following it up, I enjoyed being attracted to Caryn. She was rarely in, though, because she'd been seeing this bloke who, as she put it, confused her. They hadn't even kissed, but it was a possibility. And then her old girlfriend had shown up, jealous and desperate. Caryn had virtually moved in with her after that, so we were left alone in the flat most nights. Her absence made me think about her more than when she'd been there, but my thoughts became less sexual. I missed her presence because she'd had such a calming effect on Wendy.

By late February we were arguing more often, and after my birthday I became impatient. As soon as I felt a row brewing I'd say, 'Do you want me to leave?' but she'd say that I should stop threatening and go if I meant it. I was never sure why I stayed. Was it because going would make me feel worse, or because I didn't want to hurt her? Even when I was trying my best, she could lapse into a mood. There were a few times when I thought back to how much fun she used to be, and almost found myself saying, 'You never used to be like this.' I never voiced this thought, because I didn't want to remind her. If she once started blaming me out loud, it would never stop.

Some nights we didn't talk at all but watched television. I was surprised when, partway through an obscure Swedish film that I'd lost interest in, Wendy's face contorted. I thought she was in pain, but she was crying. When I asked her what was wrong, she couldn't think of an answer.

The next morning we caught a series of buses to Alexandra Palace for the sake of somewhere to aim for as much as for the view. It was a perfect winter day; no snow, no wind, no rain, just watery cloud and icy sunlight. The leafless trees were a shiny grey.

That night she was particularly tense. She went for a bath, and I guessed that it was more to be alone than for its soothing effect. She snapped at me when I went in without knocking. Caryn was still away, so I called Wendy a cunt at the top of my voice. When she was dressed again, she came into the front room with a book, biting her lip in concentration.

'I can't carry on like this,' I said. She didn't answer, so I got straight to the point. 'Should I go?'

'Stop *threatening* me.'

Her eyes were teary, but I couldn't prevent myself from saying, 'Why should I stay? So that you can sulk at me all night and ruin a good day?'

'You don't give me enough room to recover.'

I was shocked by the momentum of the argument and what sounded like a rehearsed line, so I tried to calm her.

'If you have problems, fine, share them, but please don't take them out on me.'

'Then stop threatening to leave.'

'Why should I stay?'

'Because you love me?' It was definitely a question.

Cruelty is more difficult to resist when you know it will really hit home.

'When you're like this,' I said, 'what is there to love about you?'

She started to say something, but I cut her off.

'I'm not interested,' I said, going out and slamming the living-room door. There was nowhere to go unless I left the flat, so I sat on the edge of the bath, wondering why she wasn't coming after me. There was already a tinge of regret, immediately countered with justification; we couldn't get anywhere if she insisted on blaming me.

There was a loud noise, like a door being slammed, and

then Wendy's voice, somewhere between moaning and screaming.

I ran back in and saw her kneeling in the centre of the room; her mouth was a distorted hole, her face redder than I'd ever seen it. She looked terrified more than upset. Behind her, there was a hole in the window.

'What did you do?' I asked, the sadness in my own voice making me want to cry. I had never seen anybody look so despairing. I said, 'Please,' unable to believe I had brought this on. She looked so afraid, so utterly lost, that I immediately knelt to hold her. The relief that flooded off her body in sobs made me feel worse. Even at that point, she'd thought I was going to carry on being mad at her. That, more than anything, made me want to help her.

'I had no idea,' I said.

This time, when she cried, there was no restraint, and it went on for minutes. Over her shoulder I looked at the hole in the window, the trails of fracture spreading a few inches around it. The window itself was largely intact. Cold air blew in through the hole, making my eyes water.

When she went to get tissues I stepped out on to the balcony to see what she had thrown. Among the shards there was a drinking glass, still whole, not even chipped. It felt fragile and light. I couldn't imagine how it had passed through the window and on to the balcony without shattering. Wendy came back, blowing her nose, and I showed her the glass. 'I don't even remember doing it,' she said.

I sat with her for hours, apologising over and over again for being thoughtless and taking her for granted.

'I just couldn't understand what was wrong. I thought today was lovely, that was all.'

'It wasn't today that hurt me,' she said.

Chapter Seven

The day after I got back to Leicester, Wendy rang me up to say it was over. There wasn't much of an explanation at first, so I pressed her for one, hoping she'd say it wasn't me but that she needed space. Instead, she said, 'I can't cope with you.' I was angry and argued it out with her, close to tears, but once the phone went down I felt relieved. She'd shocked me, but I wasn't that bothered.

All the way back on the train the day before, I'd been watching a woman – she could only have been about eighteen – sitting across from me. It was a cool evening, but the train's heating was on full so that her forehead was damp, turning her hair from strands into black quills. We'd glanced at each other a few times, and I'd passed the journey by fantasising about her. That might not have been so bad, but I've always had difficulty separating fantasy from reality. I've often felt that if you picture something, it's because you intend it to happen. After an hour or so of picturing this woman, seeing myself taking her into the train toilet and fucking her, I'd begun to contemplate it. When it went dark, we'd both pretended to stare out at the landscape, using the dusty reflection to look at each other. It was incredibly exciting to think it might actually happen. She'd got off at Northampton, and I'd tried to tell myself that it had just been a way to pass the time, but I knew if I'd had the chance I would have done it. Only after I'd got home and had a wank did I realise how unrealistic it had been. She probably hadn't even been looking at me. But I'd felt the desire, and that was enough to taint the way I felt about Wendy.

When she rang the next day, it seemed as though it was my own fault that she'd ended the relationship. Not that I was being punished for having wanted somebody else, but that by picturing a future without her I was making it happen. In a way her timing was perfect, because I must have wanted to move on. All that bothered me was that we'd invested a lot of time in each other for it to end without explanation.

She rang again at the weekend, furious that I hadn't contacted her.

'I can't believe you were prepared to let it go.'

'You were the one who dumped me.'

'Don't I mean anything to you?'

I made it clear that I wanted some time apart, and she put the phone down on me after calling me a selfish twat. Dave agreed with her.

'Isn't it obvious that she's hurting?'

'What the fuck are you on about?'

We were both a bit aggressive, probably because we'd spent so much time apart and were half-drunk. The jukebox was on in the pub, but our voices rose above it.

'She's scared you'll leave her, so she's testing you. She didn't want you to roll over and accept it. She wants reassurance that you can't live without her.'

'If she wants to be with me, she has a funny way of showing it. Besides, we get on better when we're not going out with each other. We have friendship, and sex, without the other problems.'

'You're saying all this because you're too scared to make a commitment.'

This was ironic coming from him, because Rachel kept hedging about marriage. Yes, she loved him, but it was a big step. She made a bit of a mockery of his talk about commitment.

'Not scared. I choose *not* to make a commitment. I don't want middle-class predictability. If I had your attitude I'd be working in a fucking bank. I'd never be doing what I do.'

'And you're really changing the world with your art.'

He said the word *art* in a posh accent, so I said, 'Don't piss me off. You're a smug fucker.'

'I'm a damned sight happier than you are.'

'If I had a life like yours I'd be miserable. You have the fucking *Hay Wain* on your wall. If I saw that every morning, I'd weep.'

'At least I have somebody in bed with me when I wake up.'

'You're not even married. You just act as though you are.' Before he could respond, I said, 'The ridiculous thing about middle-class security is that it's an illusion. It's just as likely to fall to pieces as what we have. In fact, what we have is stronger.'

'You talk about her as though it's still going on.'

'Perhaps it is.'

In some ways I think I went back down there to prove it to him.

I didn't want to risk delays on the train, so I drove to London as soon as I got out of uni. The sun was in my eyes all the way down the M1, the roads white with dry salt, the sky veiled and glaring. It ended up taking longer than the train because of roadworks, and I parked outside the tower blocks after dark. All the way down, I'd gone over the things I'd say. I wasn't going to make promises, but I would be kind and generous, let her do what she wanted. If she wanted to be friends, fine.

Caryn opened the door, and at first I thought she looked angry with me. I wanted to reassure her that I'd be reasonable with Wendy, then realised she wasn't cross but scared.

'Is she in?'

'Yes, Nick. But her boyfriend's here.'

Her eyes were wide, and she was holding on to both sides of the doorframe, as though to stop me getting in. Did she really expect me to burst in there and hit him? I felt so weak with shock that I couldn't have done anything. I heard Wendy laugh, then some mumbling. Joey was chirping his name over the sound of the television. There were obviously quite a few people round, which was unusual. The flat had always been so empty.

'Who is he?'

'He's from over there,' she whispered, gesturing out of the window.

'The prison?'

'The art college.'

She must have judged that I wasn't about to start a fight, because she invited me in. I hesitated, unwilling to see Wendy with somebody else.

'Come into my room. I'll tell her you're here.'

The flat stank of dope, which disappointed me. Already I could imagine Wendy spouting bullshit about it helping to release her artistic abilities. I resolved to say nothing about it, because if anything was about to show up the age gap between us, that was it.

Caryn closed the door, and her room went quiet around me. I sat on the bed, realising that in all the times I'd been

down I'd never been in Caryn's room. It was strange seeing
things that I associated with her – silver bangles, a navy
cardigan – separate from her. There was a smell which was
hers, and for a moment I entertained the idea that she had
perfumed the room with her presence, even though I
recognised it as Impulse body spray.

Wendy came in with a look of pity on her face.

'Oh, Nick.'

'Well, I hope you're happy now,' I said immediately,
forgetting my resolve and getting up to walk past her. 'Go
back to your cool dope-smoking boyfriend.'

I felt stupid, and when the front door got stuck I
overreacted, pulling it open so hard that it hit the wall. Acting
more angry than I was made me feel worse, so I slammed it
as I left. If she followed me I didn't see her, because the lift
was still on our floor, its door open as though waiting for me.
In minutes I was back in the roadworks, wondering how
things could have gone so wrong.

Waking in the middle of the afternoon I rang Dave and
told him we had to go out driving. He moaned a bit, but I
said, 'At least I didn't turn up at midnight, chucking stones
at your window.' He promised he'd be round after Rachel
had gone to sleep, no later than ten. It was half-eleven
when he turned up, beeping his horn even though I'd told
him not to.

'I should have just gone driving by myself,' I said, getting
in.

'He keeps himself to himself for months, and then expects
instant support the minute he gets a bit depressed.'

'Fuck off, Dave.'

'Don't tell me, you've split up with her again.'

'She's got a boyfriend.'

He said 'I'm so sorry' with such tenderness I was close to crying again.

I'd wanted to talk about it, but Dave realised the best policy was to change the subject, make me laugh and construct plans to meet other women. It was something he used to do at school. 'You've got to have targets,' he would say, expecting us to find that a reasonable approach to meeting women. 'There's nothing sexist about it,' he'd say lamely. 'Women have targets as well.' Every time I'd say he was treating women as commodities to be acquired, he'd get personal, saying, 'Which is why you're on your own.' That night, however, I didn't argue with him, because I wanted targets. I couldn't bear for Wendy to be with somebody while I slept alone. Dave's responsibility was probably to tell me it was advisable to wait, get some breathing space and calm down, but he said, 'I'll pay for you to go to Dolly Birds.'

He'd had this vague prostitute fantasy for years, which he'd always projected on to me. Nearly every time we walked back from town, he'd urge me to go into the massage parlour for a hand job. I think the seediness appealed to him because his life was so clean.

'I want a girlfriend,' I said.

'That's the last thing you need.'

'So speaks the expert on matters of the heart.'

By the time he'd dropped me off, the intensity of his wank-fantasy and the determination of my desire for a new girlfriend had culminated in a feeling close to desperation.

When I'd been going out with Wendy, I must have looked calm, because I'd had more looks, offers and flirtations from women than ever before. That calm must have left me and been replaced with a look of urgent need, because it took me until April to find a girlfriend.

She was a Spanish waitress called Joanne, who worked in the university canteen. She was about the same height as Wendy, a couple of years younger, and although she wasn't fat, her skin had a turgid feeling, making it incredibly smooth. Although she had black hair, you wouldn't have known she was Spanish, because she was so pale, and her accent was so subtle it only made her sound thoughtful rather than foreign. She slept with me on the first night, but not until she'd dragged me down to Mosquito Coast until two in the morning. I saw half my students there and had to get drunk enough that I didn't care if they saw me dancing. Once you're past the age of twenty-five you can feel a certain stiffness to your movements, and you just know you're going to end up dancing like your uncle – vigorously, but looking like a twat. I tried to enjoy myself, not expecting much, and was a bit worried when Joanne acted as though she owed me sex. We went back to hers in a taxi and started undressing as soon as we were through the door. Which was weird, because we hadn't even kissed until then. I was so drunk I don't remember much about it, except that she wouldn't let me go down on her.

'I couldn't do that to you, so please don't do it to me.'

In the morning she showed me her teddy bears, as though I'd never seen a girl do that before, so I acted suitably charmed. Then she shocked me by saying, 'I like you. We can work on the sex.'

It almost turned into an argument, which was strange having known her for such a short time. I managed to stay calm, asking her what she wanted.

'I don't like it too wet,' she said. 'I like it to hurt as it goes in.'

I felt like a bastard because I never called her again, but I couldn't face sex where the main aim was to hurt my girlfriend. Dave said I should have expanded my repertoire, but what if I'd got to like it? Imagine carrying that fetish around with you into a new relationship.

That night hadn't been enough to get Wendy out of my system, but the desperation had gone and I started to relax. Perhaps because of that, I received unexpected attention from one of my students. It sounds like a classic male fantasy, but Chelsea Hay irritated me at first because she flirted as though it was a gift I should be grateful for. She was twenty-three and determined to appear wiser than the other students, talking in conspiratorial tones to me as though it was obvious she was brighter. At the same time, she didn't want to look stuffy, so went through exactly the same patterns of drinking and late nights. After tutorials she would always find an excuse to come back to my room with me – to pick up notes, to check on her studies, to ask me endless questions about my paintings, even though none of them had been worked on for months. She looked younger than her age, except that her hair was the sort of thin, dull blonde that could almost be grey, and she was frequently tired.

I went out for coffee with her when she asked me, which was probably a mistake. I'd discussed this with colleagues before, because it's almost inevitable that it will happen one day. If a student asks you out, the best response is to say yes, but suggest it would be better if a few others came along. Making a public occasion of it discharges the tension without offending anybody. But Chelsea looked so upset when she asked me, before I'd even replied, that I found myself attracted to her. Not because she looked vulnerable or weak, but because all her pretence was dropped and she risked letting her emotions show.

My next mistake was to acknowledge that there was something slightly risqué about our meeting. I wanted to go somewhere other than the canteen, mostly to avoid bumping into Joanne, but Chelsea misinterpreted my suggestion.

'We're not doing anything wrong,' she said.

'No, but I wouldn't want people to talk.'

We went to a dismal café next to the tattoo shop, made too hot by the cloudy sunlight. It smelt of steam rather than coffee. She drank three cups to my one and talked about her work, then her childhood, gradually asking about my life. I told her about Wendy, probably because I needed to talk about it, and she listened. It was peculiar feeling an attraction to somebody I didn't really like. The more she talked the less she smiled, and that wistfulness held my attention. I ended up with a raging hard-on, my left leg so wet with pre-cum I wondered if it was going to show through my jeans. When the conversation lulled I took the opportunity to make an excuse and leave, but while I went to pay she wrote her phone number down for me. On the walk home I thought about nothing except calling her and inviting her to my flat. She could come round that night and stay. Even though the age gap was small, there was something exciting about knowing I was going to fuck one of my students.

Wendy had called, leaving a short message on the machine for me to ring her at her parents'. It felt as though she knew what I'd been planning, and I felt horribly guilty for having even considered sleeping with Chelsea. When I rang Wendy she sounded bright, then bored. She'd been back in Leicester since April. Her boyfriend had been visiting at the weekends for a while but they'd split up now. She didn't even hide the fact that she hadn't bothered to call me until he was off the scene.

She came round that night, and we quickly established

that we were going to be just friends, which made the whole evening all the more erotic. It was unusually warm for May, the sky remaining clear, the air smelling of blossom and grass. Even when it cooled, we left the window open because of that smell.

She told me she'd pretended to sign up for a secretarial course, to keep her dad happy. Before September came, she intended to leave with her mother.

'You think she'll do it?'

'She's almost ready. And we've nothing to lose.'

'To do what, though? Where will you go?'

'It's a secret.'

'For fuck's sake, Wendy, you can tell me.'

'You're one of the first people my dad will go to.'

'And you think he'd get it out of me? What's he going to do, beat me up? Bribe me?'

'Grow up.'

'Well. You make out like he's going to chase you.'

'He won't let her go. You ask her.'

I didn't get to ask Linda because I refused to go round to their house if there was any chance of them being in. I'd always been uneasy around them, but after her dad had effectively written me off, that had been it. I'd be polite if I had to, but if I could avoid him I would.

Staying away from the house wasn't too difficult, because Wendy and I didn't get back together officially, even though we saw each other every few nights. At the time it felt like our relationship was progressing, but it was a backward step, because the only sense of commitment was an assumption that we'd continue to see each other. Wendy wouldn't even stop over but would catch a taxi home after we'd had sex. I wouldn't mind until morning, when it felt daft to be making breakfast on my own.

Our relationship had all the bad things about familiarity – the nagging, criticism and predictability – without the pleasant knowledge that the other person is there for you. But we couldn't give it up. We thought it was largely because of the sex, which had improved vastly. With no real plans to stay together, there was an intensity about us that made sex feel almost desperate. For whatever reason, we managed to find the balance between losing ourselves in pleasure and giving to the other. The payoff was that afterwards we wouldn't even hold each other.

We started going out more. Her other boyfriend had insisted on taking her out, and she'd got into the habit. That in itself pissed me off, that he'd been able to get her to go along with him when she'd always wanted to stay in with me. And when we went out, she got into the habit of putting lots of make-up on. I hassled her about it, because one thing I'd always loved about us was the way we could just be so casual. In the past, when we did go out it was on the spur of the moment. Now, I had to sit around while she made herself up. My bathroom had more make-up in it than my own stuff. I should have been more tactful, but one night I spoke my mind, saying she looked like a corpse with bruised lips.

She said, 'I put this effort in for you.'

Seeing her face I felt stunned that I could be so cruel and tried to make up for it by saying, 'I just mean that you look lovely without it.'

Our bickering might have carried on like that, but perhaps in response to my thoughtlessness Wendy took things to an extreme. We spent Saturday at her parents' house because they were in the Cotswolds, visiting that cottage he'd bought. Lounging in the front room, we were debating whether to go out or play Scrabble when she offered to suck me off. I thought she was kidding, but she said she meant it. When I tried to get up she pushed me back on to the settee and told me she was going to do it there. The living-room window was huge, and although nobody could see in it made me nervous.

'I've got a treat for you,' she said. At that point she looked so young and happy. She went to the kitchen and came back with a jar of honey.

'You're joking.'

With my pants around my ankles, she began to layer my dick with honey. It felt like putting on a melted condom, heavy and numb. I was quite eager for her to get on with it, but she kept grinning, putting more and more on. I held my cock up, away from my stomach, while she went to put the jar away.

'Come on,' I said.

'I can't hear you,' she called through.

'Wendy.'

She didn't come back, and most of the honey was pooling in my pubic hair. I kicked my pants off and went looking for her, cupping my knob to prevent it dripping. I was still hoping it was part of her game, but she was sitting at the kitchen table reading her dad's *Homes and Gardens* magazine.

'Well?'

'I changed my mind.'

I felt like an idiot for having wanted her.

'How could you lead me on like that?'

'Oh, get a grip, Nick. Christ, anybody else would have laughed.'

'So you're just going to leave me like this?'

'I'm not putting that in my mouth.'

Thinking about it now, it's easy to forgive her, to say that there was laughter in her voice, but at the time I was livid. When I told Dave about this, he said I should have laughed, that it was hilarious. Wendy would never back down, insisting it was a joke, but whatever her intention I can remember that when she'd looked up at me there wasn't even the hint of a smile.

I rang Chelsea from a phone box at the bottom of Wendy's road and told her I wanted to see her. She hesitated for so long I thought she was going to say no. Instead, she planned the night out before I could contribute my ideas. I'd been steeling myself to suggest she come straight to my flat, but she opted for the more polite pizza-first route.

While we were sitting in Pizza Hut that night, she suggested going on to a pub called the Marquis, and then perhaps for a dance at Lord Byron's. I thought to myself that she was making it hard work, then I wondered what she'd think of me if she knew I was already condemning her as a difficult shag. I probably laughed too loudly at her next few jokes.

My efforts went astray, though, because she must have sensed my withdrawal. The silences between us grew longer, and I didn't have the energy to fill them, because the whole affair was making me feel unaccountably sad.

'Something's wrong, isn't it?'

'Not at all.'

'Is it that girl?'

'No.'

She copied my silence, forcing me to ask her what was wrong.

'I just had visions of us, tonight, you know.' It sounded as though she'd planned to say something much bolder but had then tried to cover it up.

'You can come home with me,' I said, risking outright rejection because I'd run out of patience.

'All right.'

She held my hand in the taxi and talked about a holiday she'd had in Greece while I nodded in appreciation. Once we were in my room, she stripped quickly then lay on the bed. I felt more self-conscious than usual as I undressed, because I couldn't get a hard-on. I'd expected that doing it with a student would be exciting, but there was a surprising amount of guilt. It wasn't illegal, or uncommon, but the vague naughtiness worked against me. It was also occurring to me that she'd probably have high expectations, and my paranoia was kicking in. I was about to start fumbling with the condom, knowing how difficult it would be to get it on to a lob-on, when she took the rubber from me, popped it into her mouth, and rolled it on by going down on me.

'There,' she said, wiping lubricant from her mouth. 'Easy.'

In the end I couldn't complain. She was communicative and experimental and guided me without being forceful. The only thing that bothered me was that she talked so much it felt like I was listening to a porn script rather than a real experience. But it was very Protestant porn: 'Oh, yes' rather than 'Fuck me'.

When I woke up it was past nine, and she was already out of bed, pulling on her underwear.

'Morning,' she said, coughing. 'The worst thing about unplanned sex is putting on your dirty knickers before breakfast.'

'Are you off then?'

'I don't want to pester you by hanging around, but I'll see you again.'

I always feel a bit dropped on when women bugger off that quickly. Most think they're doing you a favour, but I feel cheap unless there's a bit of larking about in the morning.

I can't remember how it happened, but she ended up on the bed again, fully clothed, but holding my face and kissing me. I think she made a joke about me being her teacher. What I remember clearly is the phone ringing and knowing it was Wendy before I even picked it up.

She was trying to tell me something, but I cut her off.

'Wendy, I'm with somebody.'

'I don't care,' she said, crying openly.

'All right, what's wrong?'

From the hall I could see Chelsea sitting on the bed, reading titles on my bookshelf. She looked round at me without smiling.

'Dad's let my bird go. The cockatiel.'

I winced at the thought that she hadn't called him Mike, because I'd got at her about it.

'He didn't even pretend it was an accident. When they got home last night he just put the cage in the garden while I was asleep. When I got up it was empty.'

'Where are you?'

'At the bottom of your road,' she said, the waver leaving her voice.

'Wendy,' I said slowly. 'I'm with somebody.'

'We're going away.'

'Who?'

'Me and Mum. Dad's out this morning. She's packing now. We'll be gone in an hour.'

When I said 'Wait there' Wendy's money ran out.

The sense of panic made me rush to get Chelsea out of the flat. I wasn't even subtle about it, telling her a friend was in need and that I had to go. She said she hoped that didn't mean it was over. When I told her it was, she cried, and I realised just what a cunt I was being. I put my arm around her, expecting to be shrugged off, but she held me.

'I knew this would happen,' she said.

The worst thing was that no matter how bad I felt, I couldn't stop myself from trying to get rid of her. She was still there when I was fully dressed, and left the flat with me. It would have been too difficult to send her away, so I let her walk down with me, baffled as to why she wanted to put herself through this.

Wendy was sitting on the ground by the phone box, her eyes hidden behind sunglasses. She looked up at us both briefly but didn't even seem concerned by Chelsea's presence, and neither acknowledged the other.

'I'd better go then,' Chelsea said.

'OK, thanks.' I didn't even realise at the time I'd effectively said, *Thanks, I'm glad you're going*.

Wendy watched her leave, and when she was only a few steps away said, 'Did you fuck her?'

'Yes,' I said, sitting by her. She put her arms around her knees and leaned her head on them. 'But I didn't enjoy it, if that matters. I was just so sick of things going wrong between us.'

'Me too.'

She told me they were going to head north but to keep that to myself if her dad came looking. They might be gone for months, depending on his reaction.

'Can I come with you?'

Her eyes were so wide I could see them through her sunglasses.

'Don't you have commitments?'

'Term's over. I can put just about everything else on hold.'

'We've got half an hour. Can you be that quick?'

It shocked me that I could shut down my life so rapidly. You always think there are bills and meetings and things to do, but you can throw clothes into a backpack, lock your house up and abandon the familiar in about seventeen minutes. All it takes is the decision to leave.

Chapter Eight

On the first day we made it as far as Longframlington near the north-east coast. The Golf was laden down with as much essential stuff as Linda could gather. I'd been stuffed in the back with the birdcage and spent half the journey watching Joey keep balance on his perch. I'd expected him to die from the shock of it, but Wendy wouldn't risk leaving him with Laurence.

The journey had taken so long because Linda wanted to cover her tracks, being certain that Laurence would be following us by the next morning. I'd always scoffed at Wendy's claims that he would do that but was polite enough to say that it was better to be safe. I imagined Laurence coming back to an empty house, crying as he realised what had happened and then waiting by the phone. But she said he'd be tracking us down the moment he got home, so her plan involved heading south for an hour to use her credit card at a service station. When he traced that, it would make him think she was heading towards her brother's place in Devon. In an attempt to slow his progress she'd left no letter and hadn't told anybody that she was leaving. She wouldn't even tell me where we were heading, but it was clear that she was pleased I'd come along with them.

The bed and breakfast we found was set away from the

road, so we could keep the car out of sight. It was run by a woman so close to being blind that we wouldn't have any problems with being remembered. Even if Laurence tracked us this far, reports of a group of three would lead him astray, because as far as he knew Linda was travelling alone. Wendy had told him she was visiting Caryn in London in the days leading up to this, so he wouldn't know she was involved. I did wonder, though, what he'd think if he went as far as contacting me or my parents. He'd soon become suspicious if all three of us had vanished.

We were all tired, but there was a certain excitement about what we were doing and we were unwilling to sleep. Linda didn't want us to go to the pub so drove out for wine, bringing back seven bottles of something Australian, a corkscrew, and a box of wine glasses.

'On the credit card,' she said. 'They used one of those old paper things rather than an electronic one, so I thought where's the harm. It won't be processed for weeks from up here.'

We stayed in her room, the three of us sitting on the double bed, drinking more wine than felt comfortable. Considering how quiet we'd been on the journey up I was surprised when they started talking about Laurence. It was as though they both needed to justify what they were doing and were finally telling a third party what they'd always kept to themselves. They didn't spend so much time slagging him off at first as they did speculating about his reaction. Linda worried constantly about the methods he'd employ to get her back. She sat cross-legged, cupping her wine glass in both hands, her hair coming down around her face. Although she was nervous about what she was doing, her posture, her movement and voice were more relaxed than they had ever been around Laurence. She looked more like Wendy's sister than her mother.

'He can't report the car stolen,' she explained, 'because I've made sure it's in my name. It's taken me years to get him to do that.'

'Couldn't you have bought your own?'

'You've no idea, Nick. I've worked for him for years at that bloody factory and I've never seen a wage. He just paid me bits here and there as I needed it. It's taken me a long time to save up for this without him noticing.'

Wendy looked uncomfortable, and I thought she was going to start defending her dad, but she said, 'He controls everything. I told you about him throwing my dresses out. It wasn't just that. He chose what books we could read, what music we listened to. If there was something he didn't like, it would just vanish. He wouldn't even let Caryn in the house.'

They told me about his obsessions, swapping details and finishing stories for each other, eager to give me the full picture. Laurence had kept a cardboard pyramid next to his bed, supposedly to help him sleep better, and around the garden he'd buried ceramic rods to discharge negative energy from nearby power lines. In the morning he'd go into Wendy's room to strip the covers off her and pull open the curtains when he decided it was time to get up. He'd lied constantly, telling stories about himself that he found impressive, such as driving his Jaguar at over two hundred miles per hour, rock climbing in the Lakes and getting his pilot's licence.

'He used to lie in front of me, and after a while he started expecting *me* to believe it all,' Linda said. 'He'd tell Wendy these stories, and she didn't know any different. And he'd tell complete strangers the most astounding bullshit, and they'd believe it because he's so bold. Nobody ever challenges him. I don't think he knows what he's made up and what's true. Now I'm away from him it sounds ridiculous; I should have

just said, *Come on, Laurence, don't be a prick.*' She laughed.
'But you can't do that around him.'

He'd also lied about violence, saying he'd beaten up people
who were rude to him, or slapped restaurant owners when he
wasn't happy with the service. Mostly his peculiarities were
relatively small things like that, not enough to start a divorce
but enough to make you think him weird. Collectively, they
went beyond idiosyncrasies, and painted the picture of a man
obsessed with control. Apparently, he wouldn't have anything
aluminium in the house, not even deodorant. Wendy had
been hiding hers at the bottom of a cupboard for years.

'He's got this thing about metal,' Wendy said. 'He had all
his fillings replaced with white ones, because he's afraid of
the metal getting into his system.' She looked a bit guilty,
and then said, 'That's why all my fillings are white too.'

'You're kidding?' I tried not to act too shocked, because I'd
always been impressed by how unblemished her mouth was.

'Oh, yes, he made sure we got our fillings replaced,' Linda
said. 'But the weird thing is, he has metal pins in his leg from
a car crash. He always says he has a metal shin, but I think
it's only the pins. He tells this story about kicking a bench in
half when he was a foreman on a building site. A park bench.
He did it to frighten the others into working harder.'

'Fuck.'

'He tells our friends he was in the SAS,' she was laughing
loudly now. 'I can just imagine him coming down a wall on
a rope dressed in black.'

'People believe this?'

Wendy laughed, but I could tell it was difficult for her. If
I thought about it, I could imagine going along with his lies,
because when the grin left his face he looked as though he
wanted to twat you.

'He never mentioned any of that stuff to me,' I said.

'He knows you'd have challenged him.'

'I don't know if I would. I wouldn't have accused him of lying.'

'He's weird, Nick. Completely weird.'

'Are you frightened of him?'

Wendy wouldn't answer that, but Linda said, 'Yes, we always have been.'

It was peculiar knowing she was being more honest with me than she could be with her husband. Usually with people's parents I slip into the habit of treating them as much older than me. Sometimes that's because parents will always treat the generation below them as children. My Uncle Steve used to refer to my cousin as *the boy* until he was nineteen. And even when I was in my early twenties I remember borrowing a bandsaw from Dave's dad, and as he'd showed us how to use it he'd said, 'Now, it's not a toy.' On the few occasions I'd gone to stay with Mum and Dad in Wigan, they'd give me a lift into the centre of town, telling me to be careful, and they'd still be awake, listening for me when I got back. Setting off on this trip with Wendy, I'd imagined us stealing away from her mum, perhaps even being left somewhere else for a while, because it would be uncomfortable being around her. But she didn't feel much older than me. After all, the age gap to Linda wasn't that much different from the one between Wendy and myself.

'So what happens now?'

'Once it starts to dawn on him that I'm serious, I'll start proceedings. But it has to happen at a distance or he'll never give up. I need to keep away from him for a few weeks at least. Make the most of his precious bloody money while it lasts. And keep out of his way for as long as we can.'

'But even if he did find you, so what? He can't force you to go back.'

'You don't know what he's like,' Linda said. 'He's obsessed with keeping me there. I've left before, but he's always found a way of getting me back.'

I was worried by that, hoping I hadn't been dragged into a protest display of separation that would end with her going back.

'If you don't love him and want to get away, what could he do?'

'There are always threats,' she said. 'I won't tell you what he says he'll do. But once he's put a threat in place, he comes over all lovely. He goes to Wendy, he goes to our friends and talks them round. He makes everyone think he's the innocent one being abandoned by a heartless woman. Even my brother falls for it. He promises to change, but the minute I'm back he takes over again.'

Not much else is clear from the next few hours, although I know we talked for a long time, drinking so methodically we didn't realise how pissed we were getting. It's strange, though, because my memories up until then are clear, and of the next few weeks they are exact, but from the rest of that night I can remember only two more things. When we first got into bed after we'd gone back to our room, Wendy said, 'Why are you doing this?'

'For you.'

'Really?'

I couldn't say *yes*, but I hugged her, thinking to myself that I was glad to be getting back at Laurence. I wanted the fucker to suffer.

And after that I remember the most intense fuck. We made a noise so loud everybody else in the house must have heard. My eyes were open, but I was almost blind from the booze; at times I could see the lace curtains glowing with streetlight, but I don't remember seeing Wendy at all. I don't know why we were so frantic, but it felt like she was fighting through me and I was having to hold her down, pulling her back on to the bed by her hair, licking the sweat from her chest. I don't remember much else, or how it ended, but afterwards we were both covered in semen; it was on my stomach and her chest. We were so hot we couldn't hold each other and fell asleep apart.

In the morning she said it was a one-off. Not that she didn't love me, but that this wasn't the time for us to be working on our own relationship. I was so happy to be heading north with her that I didn't even argue.

They must have got Laurence out of their systems, because he wasn't mentioned that day. The plan was to get to the Isle of Skye before nightfall, which shouldn't have been too difficult, because it was the longest day of the year. We kept stopping, and by the time we reached Glen Coe it was threatening to go dark. Wendy ran out of words trying to express how beautiful she found it up there, which was little wonder, because the road snaked between mountains that were so impressive it was difficult to believe we were still in Britain. There was low cloud around the tops, mostly grey but lit in patches the colour of sunset. It made the air around us seem pink, the heather and grasses inflamed. I could only imagine the sun was setting in the west and some of its light was leaking into the thin clouds.

On reaching the Kyle of Lochalsh hours later, we were shocked at the masses of industrial machinery, railway tracks, gas holders and factory buildings that cluttered the shore. It felt as though civilisation was making one last attempt to look powerful, before giving way to the wilderness. Across the water, beyond the lowlands of Skye, we could see the sharp ridges of the Cuillin mountains. It looked so extreme you couldn't imagine anybody living out there. The light behind the mountains was blue like midday sky, making the rock black.

'It looks like Mordor,' Wendy said. I hadn't realised until then that she'd even finished *Lord of the Rings*. It made me sad to think that we'd stopped talking about what we were reading and thinking about. All we'd talked about recently was ourselves.

'Mordor? I don't like the sound of that,' Linda said, sounding cross for the first time. I couldn't tell if she thought Wendy was being negative or if she felt left out, so I just said, 'It's beautiful,' to defuse the tension.

Hours had passed since sunset, but there was still a lingering twilight as we drove on to the ferry. On the top deck there were rows of red plastic chairs, each cradling a shivering puddle, so we stood by the rails, the journey taking less than ten minutes. To our right there were three brand-new cranes lit by clusters of halogen lamps at their bases, their shine plating the waves. Huge stone blocks jutted out of the water where the new bridge was being built. It hadn't yet joined in the middle, so we felt like we were going to a real island.

At Broadford we turned inland towards Elgol. Most people shoot north at that point, heading for Portree and fake traces of Bonnie Prince Charlie, but Linda wanted to keep away from the busy areas. She'd found out about this road years ago, and it was hidden so well between the bakery and the hotel it looked like a private drive. She said it led to the best part of Skye, even though nobody went there. The single-track road was patterned with cattle-grids and strewn with shreds of sheep's wool which caught in the beam of the headlights. Without any streetlights to warm the clouds we could see nothing other than tarmac and an impression of barbed-wire fences rushing by. Diamond signs with *Passing Place* written on them flared up as we approached, their paint looking granular.

Wendy read directions from a scrap of paper, and we managed to find the unmarked turning for the cottage Linda had booked. The key had been left in the door, and we had a quick look around, checking beds and cupboards, finding Monopoly, a pack of cards and books on farming. The rooms smelt of stone and old carpet, something between dust and damp, without being unpleasant. Joey was installed in a corner of the room, still alive but silent. When we'd finished unloading I closed the car for the last time and saw that there was some light left behind the mountaintops. We were so close to them now that they obliterated a third of the sky, and until then I'd assumed their darkness was the black of night above a moorland. When I told them about the view, Wendy and Linda came out with another bottle of wine, turning the cottage lights off. We sat on the grass, noticing the smell and the sound of the sea for the first time. Nothing was said, but I got the feeling we were waiting for the last of the light to leave the sky.

Long after we'd stopped talking, it had still refused to die completely, so we gave up, and as we stood to look behind us we saw that the sky in the east was beginning to brighten with morning.

Wendy and I stayed in bed, talking quietly, to let Linda sleep off her hangover. Despite insisting that the last time had been the last time, Wendy pestered me for sex. I don't think she was even half-serious but was just enjoying messing about in bed. She kept grabbing my dick and saying, 'See, it's hard,' and then lying back, she'd say, 'Just lick me.' I laughed so much I couldn't possibly have done anything. She managed to calm down a bit, and while we talked one of us was always hanging on to the other, but it didn't feel claustrophobic. It was the first chance in ages we'd had to talk and be close, just mulling over anything that crossed our minds. She didn't bring up Chelsea again, which was a surprising relief. I found it difficult to accept that the whole drama had happened just two days ago. It felt as though Wendy and I were on equal ground now, and that rather than plunging back into a relationship it would be better to spend time together without worrying. I felt like going for walks, doing crosswords and reading, rather than bothering about painting and light and meaning. We'd always taken ourselves so seriously, making things seem more important than they were, and this was our chance to get away from that. While she was telling me something about the day she moved home from London, I was resolving to myself never to hassle her again. It was up to her what she did, I thought, and even if I didn't approve of her plans I should let her get on with it. So long as she was happy.

'Are you listening?'

'Yes. You said it was the longest you've ever queued on the motorway.'

'Just because you can quote me doesn't mean you were paying attention.'

We heard Linda in the kitchen and went through to find that she was already up, had been out to Broadford for food and was being quiet so as not to wake us.

'I should have left a note,' she said. 'I only realised when I got there, if you'd seen the car gone you'd have thought I'd been kidnapped.'

After we'd eaten, Wendy ran a bath and let me get in with her. It reminded me of the times in London when she'd been relaxed. I could even hear Joey chirping in the next room to add to the effect. The water was so peaty it looked like whisky, the air in the room cool; there was only one window, filthy with age, making the light in there the colour of honey.

'You look beautiful,' I said.

'Fuck off.'

She realised immediately she'd hurt my feelings, and said, 'Thanks. You surprised me.'

There was no plan for the day except to walk down to the sea. Outside, bulls and sheep roamed the fields, which were crossed with high dry-stone walls. In sunshine, the two domed hills behind the cottage were ruddy like granite. The main ridge of peaks looked more imposing in daylight, and their slopes were folds of mould and ash, creased with shadow. The long slope of Blavan, even in full sunshine, was black. The only other building in sight was the farmhouse, where the owners of the cottage lived, almost hidden in the trees at the bottom of the hill. The road we'd driven down was blurred by the grasses, and the overall effect was of being remote.

The sea was further away than we'd thought, and as we walked down the slope we saw that a huge area of land had been hacked out into a jagged white quarry, presumably marble. Everything there was veiled in pale dust; the digging machinery and JCBs, which should have been bright yellow, were dusted with white. The prefabricated huts that were spread through the quarry looked empty and unused, their windows like cataracts. Linda voiced disappointment and kept apologising. It was as though she thought we'd complain, that we'd be mad at her for bringing us to somewhere slightly less than perfect.

'We should pretend it's snow,' I said. 'That way we get summer and winter at the same time.'

My effort worked better than I'd expected, with both of

them laughing, and Linda was quite taken with the idea of imagining something out of existence.

I felt mildly irritated by her complaint about the quarry, because I'm never upset by intrusions of so-called ugliness on the natural world. I'm usually wary about admitting that, because people then assume that I have no pantheistic tendencies, which is far from the truth. But I can get as much pleasure from a rusted tractor as I can from a tree. That's what the world looks like; the sky has aeroplane contrails, the hills are dug over and the space between places is full of power lines and roads. To deny that reeks of guilt about what we've done to the world. Which would be a good thing, except that it's hypocritical, because these are the same people who pay for the environment to be so readily plundered. So I get pissed off by people who think that it's only a beautiful view if you hide the roads and buildings and quarries. It's like those bastards queuing around the Lake District in their BMWs, thinking they're getting back to nature, without ever climbing anything or walking further than the Ambleside car-park. If you manage to get a blinkered view of an untouched landscape, that means the natural world is still out there, surviving. It's as though they're saying, *We'll have our four cars, several TVs, countless ornaments and salad bowls, but we'll pretend there isn't a price to pay. We'll whine on about the environment, and believe that recycling our wine bottles is enough to save the planet.* They'll happily put a hideous figurine on their mantelpiece but will complain when they see the quarry it came from on their Sunday afternoon drive. Linda's distaste made me wonder just how different she was from Laurence, so I tried to explain what I thought.

'The whole thing is so stupid,' I said, 'because it's nostalgia for a world that never existed. Those paintings of idyllic rural life are actually depictions of hard labour and painfully backward industry. Even *The Hay Wain* is a picture of a traffic accident when you think about it, farm machinery gone wrong. It's a shame,' I concluded, 'because people don't paint the beautiful things that *are* out there. There's nothing to match a line of electricity pylons at sunset, but nobody will paint it because they think it's *meant* to be ugly.'

We'd reached the beach, which was mostly grass, like tended turf, with a short stretch of pebbles and rocks down to the water. The ocean was still and white, interrupted by islands on the horizon, hazy with distance.

When I thought the subject had been dropped, Wendy said, 'But without the sunset your power lines would be nothing, and that's a natural phenomenon.'

'Sunsets are caused by pollution in the air, usually. Dust and skin, everything we shed.'

'Those things contribute, yes, but natural dust can create a sunset.'

I started to say, 'Look, nobody loves nature more than me . . .' but Wendy cut me off.

'Some of my best friends are black,' she said flatly. It wasn't entirely fair, because I was being honest, but her wit surprised me, and I was left trying to come up with a response.

I think most of this was lost on Linda, because she said, 'I just thought it was a shame, spoiling the view. This place feels like heaven, except for that.'

'It feels like heaven anyway,' Wendy said.

Although I remember everything clearly from that week, the order of events sometimes gets muddled. I'm fairly sure it was the next day that we went for a long drive, because that was the first time we'd seen the single-track road in daylight. What had been a narrow, enclosed lane in darkness opened up across the base of a valley and past a reed-fringed lake. Where the land sloped away from us, the grassy ground was broken through with rock and trees. On the longest stretch of road it felt like we were driving through the crown of a volcano, a plain of grassland ringed with mountains. The size of the place felt greater than if the mountains had been absent, as though by enclosing it we were more able to appreciate the space. In the middle of all this there was a tiny derelict church on a mound of grass, a rubble of gravestones around it. It felt a bit disappointing to be driving away from the place we'd discovered, but Linda wanted to go around to the other side of the Cuillins to see a view of them from the west-coast sands.

It was a good drive over, but when we arrived an hour later the weather had dulled. From the beach we could see only the base of the mountains, because low clouds obscured them. It was windy, the grey waves breaking into spray.

'It's a shame,' Linda said. 'I really wanted you to see that view. It's such a shame.'

'Mum.'

'Well, it's disappointing.'

'It doesn't matter.'

The lowlands and the mountains were the same muted grey as the sky and water, so there was almost no colour. We sat away from the car, arms around our legs for warmth, and watched a group of people further up the beach who were going into the water, despite the rough weather. At the edge of the sea there was an enormous naked woman, absolutely pale apart from her saucer-sized nipples that were the colour of lipstick. She was thudding in and out of the waves, her children dashing around her. She'd never go in more than knee-deep, so her body was always on show. It was impossible not to stare, and I said, 'Now that's the view we came to see.

Just because it isn't the mountain we expected doesn't mean it isn't a good view.'

I'd been trying to raise a laugh, but they nodded seriously. At first I felt angry for having said something unfunny, but I realised that more than anything I was concerned by the way they'd both responded. They were more than willing to listen to me, whereas if one of them had said it to the other they'd probably have bickered.

'I'd rather see it like this,' I said, settling into my role, 'with those people and this light, than if it looked like something from a tourist brochure. And remember where we are; it's a damn sight better than being in Leicester.'

'You're so right,' Linda said, putting her head on an angle to nod at me.

Wendy glanced at her mum, raised her eyebrows at me, then smiled, as though to say that even though she'd heard it all before she was glad I was telling her mum. It was the first time I felt as though they needed me with them.

We stayed around our cottage most of the time after that day. On wet days we stayed in and read, making more food than we needed and playing with Joey. We'd let him out of his cage, and he'd take it in turns to land on our shoulders. He'd bite at Wendy's hair, as though stripping it of seeds, and she'd tell him off. 'Naughty boy. Yes, you.' Other times you'd see her holding him, having spent half an hour moving her hand gently over his back so as not to scare him. She loved that bird so much I could barely watch, waiting for it to drop dead from shock at any moment.

When the weather was better we walked along the coast or into the valley. Just outside our cottage, towards the edge of the trees, we found a standing stone, encased in a sheath of lichen like colourless scabs. It was a couple of feet taller than me, even though it had looked small from the path. We put our hands on it, and the rock felt warm to the touch.

The rest of the time we wandered along our beach. There was nothing to do there, as such, but we passed our time just messing about. Somebody else had gathered rocks and made a massive clockface out of them on the grass, so Wendy said we should do something similar. With larger rocks we made a stone circle, and with pebbles we made patterns like snowflakes. On a sunny afternoon we could see the colours of the stones better, so we made piles of stones in a line of gradually changing hue. Linda would sit on the grass saying she was too old to be joining in, and it felt a lot like she was our mother watching over us. Wendy played up to this, saying, 'Come and look,' as soon as we'd finished making something new. 'Come and look, Mummy.'

Linda and I laughed so much that Wendy kept doing that, talking like a little girl, acting overexcited.

At other times she was calmer than I'd known her. When we were collecting driftwood for a fire, she went quiet and I knew not to push her. After a while she said, 'I could do this for ever.' She'd tried to sound casual, but her voice had wavered.

'Perhaps you should be a sculptor then.'

'When I'm this happy I don't want to be anything,' she said. 'And I didn't mean that. I meant being with you.'

I ignored her last comment, thinking it was the place, the holiday feeling, that was bringing out the best in her.

We passed a phone box on the Elgol road a few times, but I didn't even want to ring my mum and dad. Not because I was worried his illness had got any worse, but I imagined everything at home would be exactly the same and I didn't want to be in touch with such familiarity. And talking to

Dave would be another reminder that everything in Leicester was constant. Having seen the change in Wendy, I didn't like the thought of things going back to how they had been, and the longer we stayed away from normality the better.

When other cars came down our valley we viewed them as intrusions, only relaxing once they'd left. In one case the brief presence of tourists helped to make us feel more remote from ordinary life. A Volvo rolled on to the beach nearby, and you could tell from the occupants' pause that they were trying to decide whether or not they were on private land. When they got out, the parents looked innocuous enough, but the father was the sort of man who liked to say, 'Darren, walk slowly,' loud enough for us all to hear. Their mother got back in the car and looked at the map. The father paced for a while, then stopped to look at the view, frowning as though trying to work out what all the fuss was about. 'Keep away from the rocks, Darren.' In among their whining, one of the boys said, 'It's *boring*.' There was water to be splashed in, mountains to be gaped at, a beach to run on, stones to throw, dead seagulls to dissect, but he was probably longing for his Gameboy or a Happy Meal. Within two minutes of arriving they were driving away.

It wasn't that we felt superior, but lucky to appreciate what we had. The less we did, and the less we strived to find attractions, the more we enjoyed ourselves.

Occasionally we'd go into the village for provisions, which was the closest we came to civilisation. You don't really notice the sea at Broadford while you're on the shop front, but a few yards away from the car-park the buildings become distant and the water unfolds. The mainland opposite is mountainous and in the water between there is an island called Pabay, so flat and featureless that it looks like a lawn in the sea. If ever there is sunshine in Broadford bay, they say it falls there, and that seemed to be the case. Even when the sea around it was dull, the grass of Pabay was flaring, the seagulls there made whiter than the clouds behind them. Although it was beautiful, I was grateful when we got in the car and headed back to our valley.

There was an afternoon where we ended up in the graveyard. We'd talked about going there every time we'd driven past but had never got around to it until then. Getting out of the car I felt exposed, because there was nothing in sight except flat land to the mountains.

It was cool and cloudy, the matt light silvering the grassy mound. There was no sound of sea and no cars on the road, so the air felt padded and silent. The church was the size of a front room, its roof missing and the walls half-tumbled. The graves themselves were so old most of their names had been weathered away. We walked around separately, touching the stones, gazing off at the mountains, watching the sheep on the marshy ground nearby.

Nothing changed while we were there. I'd like to say that something physical happened: a shift in temperature or the quality of light. But nothing happened, except that we ended up standing together on the grass, and Wendy said, 'Can you feel that?'

I didn't know what she meant, but said yes.

Linda nodded, and we all looked at each other. There were tears in my eyes, but I couldn't tell whether it was from the breeze or from feeling so close to them.

It was the sort of incident I'd rather not have talked about. If it had been up to me, I'd have kept quiet to preserve the mystery, but once Linda had started going on about it, saying how strange she'd felt, and what a weird place this was, I couldn't resist joining in. We started drinking early that night, which can't have helped.

Before it went dark, we'd got all the maps out and had worked out that the graveyard lay on a line that joined two other churches, the old monastery at Pabay, and our standing stone. The line went right through the cottage, which got us all the more excited. If we hadn't been drunk we'd never have taken it seriously; I'd be the first to point out how easy it is to find ley lines. You can line up all the Woolworths in England as meaningfully as you can line up the stone circles. But given the mood we wanted to be in, it was enjoyable pursuing this theory. Wendy broke up coat hangers to make divining rods, but she cut herself, leaving Linda to stagger around the cottage, the rods crossing every few feet. She pretended to be finding hundreds of ley lines. 'We're living on a power centre,' she said.

'Mum, I'm *bleeding*.'

I knew I should have helped Wendy, but I was enjoying her mum's performance. Once she'd put a plaster on her finger, she came through to watch.

I have a vivid memory of Wendy trying to get the rods off her mum at the same time as claiming it was a load of rubbish. Once she'd got the rods, she took it far more seriously and got mad at herself the few times she did laugh. After Linda and I had lost interest Wendy called through to us. There was definitely one spot, she said, where the rods always crossed, in the hallway. Every time.

Maybe she was feeling left out, because she joined us in the front room and started switching her moods so quickly we couldn't keep up. She would be serious, then mess about, pulling my hair, saying she wanted to play a game. I was too drunk to come up with anything witty, so I sat back telling her to leave me alone. She sat on the floor between Linda and myself.

'I am a mole and I live in a hole,' she chanted, tossing her head so that her hair flew around. 'I am a mole and I live in a hole.' Then she stopped, wobbling her eyes as though dizzy, smiling.

'Fucking hell, Wendy,' I laughed. 'You really shouldn't drink.'

'I am a mole and I live in a hole.'

The more we laughed, the more she said it, and I was a bit worried about her mood, surprised that she was so intense. Joey was squawking and flying from one side of the room to the other, and Linda's laughter was turning into a cackle. It felt like one of those times when the level of excitement is going to keep rising until somebody starts to cry. I imagined this is what it would have been like to have a younger sister. Except that a younger sister probably wouldn't be that drunk.

'I've never *seen* her like this.'

'I am a cat and I sit on a mat,' she said. 'I am a deer and I live in fear.'

She said that so meekly that I almost cried laughing.

I'd known other girlfriends to be like this in private, acting childlike, but there was a desperation about her that concerned me. If she switched to a bad mood that was this intense, we'd be in trouble.

Over her noise I'd heard a lamb calling on the wind, and it was sounding so distressed that I tried to shut Wendy up. When she realised I was serious, she regained her composure in an instant.

'What are we listening for?'

'There. Hear it?'

We couldn't decide how close it might be, and even when

we went outside to listen, it seemed yards away, and then perhaps miles. We went back inside, but just sat there listening to it call, becoming more and more desperate, a long bleat followed by weaker ones. I became convinced that it was trapped. We'd gone over and over the possibilities and what we should do, but I said I couldn't sleep with it out there. We considered telling the farmer but thought that somebody whose job it is to turn his animals into meat might not care about a lamb suffering for a night. I decided it had to be rescued, and they followed me out. The wind was loud, pitted with damp from the sea.

We didn't have a torch, but Linda said she was fit to drive, so we got in the car and headed up the stone path, stopping and switching off the engine every few yards to listen, making sure we were getting closer. It was so dark that the headlights seemed to soak into the blackness, and we could barely see anything except the direction of the road. Where the path became steeper, heading up the rising cliff, it was also rougher, rocks jutting through, scraping the bottom of the car.

'I'll get out,' I said, 'and clear the way.'

I bent down in the beam of the headlights to throw stones off the path. Most were embedded deeply, and by the time I'd rolled them out I'd made potholes in the path, and my hands were stinging from the rain and gravel. Over the sound of the wind and sea I could hear the lamb but was disappointed to find that my energy was gone in minutes. I'd expected its bleating to urge me on for hours, if need be. Enough rocks had been shifted for Linda to edge up a couple of yards, but we might have another mile to go. I stood facing away from the car, wondering how I could possibly back down now. Having made such a show about saving the lamb, turning back would be ridiculous.

I went to Linda's window and over the wind said, 'I'm going to look for it on foot.'

'Why don't we just tell the farmer?' Wendy said. 'He'll probably have a Land Rover.'

'Do you think he'd do anything about it?'

Linda said, 'Yes. I'll go straight down. I'll tell him we can't sleep.'

'Will you do that?'

She dropped us back at the cottage, and it felt hot in there because I'd been exerting myself. There was no water for a bath, so I went to bed sweating, my back already sore. Although we could still hear the lamb's cries, it felt like we'd achieved something, and soon after I heard Linda come back in I was asleep.

I woke to the sound of the bath running, but it wasn't the noise that had disturbed me. Wendy had woken up first and nudged at my ribs, her face right next to mine until my eyes were open. She kissed me and grinned, then got out of bed saying it was time for breakfast. I was annoyed at being woken only to be abandoned, so I tried to get up quickly to go after her, and my back went. I made an involuntary noise, then a louder moan because she hadn't come back. I called for her as I lay down, but all I could hear was the kettle being filled. My back was so tightly spasmed I couldn't move, and the tension crept around my lungs. It was so difficult to breathe I could barely call for Wendy, and my neck was tensing into my shoulders, every muscle hard with pain. She came back after a while, a cup of tea in each hand.

'What are you doing?'

'My back's gone,' I said.

'Just relax.'

'I can't.'

'Well, try,' she said, putting the cups down then standing with her hands on her hips, weighing me up.

'It's not like that, it's completely gone. I can't move.'

There was the sound of a car door closing, and I remembered the lamb from the night before, wondering if the farmer had managed to find it. The wind had stopped now, and although I could hear sheep they were making calmer sounds. Over that there was a knock at the door.

Wendy shook her head. 'You go. I'm hardly dressed. And Mum's in the bath.'

'I can't fucking move.'

'Jesus.'

I closed my eyes, and when I opened them she'd gone. I heard the front door open, and a voice said, 'There's a surprise for you.' I was shocked by how bright he sounded as much as by the fact that he'd found us.

There's a surprise for you.

I could hear him walk up to the bathroom, saying Linda's name with the tone of voice of somebody turning up with good news. Her voice was too much like a moan for me to hear what she was saying, but I could tell she was panicking, and heard the water sloshing around her as she struggled to get up. At first Laurence told her to calm down, sounding gentle, but then Wendy said something quietly to him and I heard her say my name. It was at that point that he started kicking down the bathroom door.

Chapter Nine

Covering my face with the sheet, I wondered if it would be possible to hide for any length of time. I was in no fit state to move, so there was no chance of running away or facing up to him. He knew I was there, from what I could gather, and that more than anything had upset him. He must have thought that once he'd found them, he'd got his victory, but hadn't expected me to spoil his plans.

I couldn't hear what was going on any more, except Linda's crying. The sheet was pulled away from my face and Laurence was looking down at me. He brought his mouth so close I could feel his breath.

'Nothing personal, Nick,' he said, 'but this is a family thing.'

All I could do was nod weakly, and he moved away.

I lay there for a long time, wondering why Wendy was so quiet, what Linda was doing. I couldn't bear the thought of him bursting in on her while she was naked. It bothered me that I felt so powerless. Even if my back hadn't gone, there was something about his presence that made me unable to challenge him. We should have been able to tell him to go away, insist that he leave us alone, and that should have been it. But I'd heard so many stories about his persistence and threats that I was terrified of him without even speculating about what he might do.

When I finally emerged into the front room, Wendy was sitting cross-legged on a settee with her head down. Linda was leaning on one arm, looking tired as much as upset. Her make-up had been applied rapidly and her hair was wet. Laurence was talking continually in a low voice.

'So, we'll just keep calm and sort things out. No need for all these disagreements. All we need to do is find a way to make everybody happy.'

None of them appeared to notice me, even though my posture was so spastic I must have been conspicuous.

'This is a family thing, Nick. It might be better if you went for a walk.'

'Yes,' I said, glad for an excuse to get out.

'You don't have to go,' Linda said.

'Now, Linda, don't go making things difficult.'

Wendy was motionless, refusing to look at anybody. I could imagine the argument flaring up again, almost wishing it would, because his pretence of normality was excruciating. The bastard had invaded our privacy, tracked us down when he wasn't welcome, and was pretending everything could be sorted out rationally.

'I think I need to walk, for my back.'

Outside, Laurence's purple Jaguar XJS was parked at an angle across the gap in the fence where our path came through, effectively blocking our escape. I'd never really noticed his car before, but there, in front of those mountains, it looked like one of those ridiculous Sunday supplement advertisements.

It was a relief to get out, but even from there I could hear the endless murmur of his words, reassuring and convincing. I wished Wendy had come out with me, because I didn't know what to do next.

* * *

About an hour later Wendy came looking for me, with Laurence standing by the cottage, watching. Before she could get near, he shouted, 'You can come back, Nick. It's all sorted out now.'

I didn't like the sound of that but headed back up the slope towards them, wishing I was getting a bit more attention for my back and neck. I was in absolute agony, and normally I'd have been begging for massages and painkillers. I wished he'd leave us alone for that reason if nothing else.

Wendy stood with her arms folded and waited for me. She'd put on a jumper, the sleeves rolled up, and her hair was blowing. I'd never enjoyed the look on her face when she was miserable, but there was something so intense about her concentration that she looked beautiful. She must have been nervous, but she didn't look stressed so much as determined. That thought was with me so briefly that I was barely aware of it. Laurence went back into the cottage and I got my first chance to speak to her.

'What's going on?'

'Mum's agreed to talk to him. Not yet, but soon. He's staying on Skye while we're here.'

'Where?'

'He hasn't found anywhere yet. He only arrived this morning, so Mum's trying to get him to go to that little hotel in Broadford.'

'How the fuck did he find us?'

'He wouldn't say. He just laughed whenever we asked. He kept going on about what a lovely journey it was, as though everything's completely normal.'

'I noticed that.'

'I think he's trying to convince Mum that leaving him's just impossible.'

'So what happens now?'

'We'd better go in. I don't want him to be on his own with her for long.'

Inside, Laurence was leaning in at the birdcage, grinning at Joey, waggling his finger at him. Linda appeared to be sitting in the same place, an undrunk cup of tea on the coffee table in front of her.

'Right then,' Laurence said. 'Hey, Nick, it's a grand place this, isn't it?'

'Yes, it is.' I couldn't believe he was acting so casually, and prayed he wasn't angling to stay with us.

'Right then, Linda, I'll see you later. Bye, Wendy, bye, Nick, heh.'

None of us moved even after he'd closed the door. We waited for the sound of his engine, and then gravel being moved by tyres. We gathered by the window, watching him drive out of view.

'I'm so sorry, Nick,' Linda said, sitting down again. She wiped at her face, as though splashing it with cold water, and made a shocked sound.

'Not at all. I chose to be here, so it doesn't matter.'

'We wouldn't have got through that if you hadn't been with us.'

Wendy said, 'He'd have got his way by now.'

'But he seemed calm until he knew I was here.'

'Don't you believe it,' Linda said. 'That's his version of calm. It means he's happy because he's getting what he wants. We wouldn't have been able to do a thing if you hadn't been here.'

I wasn't keen on assuming that responsibility, but at the same time I quite enjoyed the thought that I'd made a difference.

'Well, my back had gone anyway. I couldn't have done much.'

'Laurence cares what you think, which makes a big difference.'

'How could he have found us?' I asked. 'We did everything right. It doesn't make sense.'

'I don't think he's slept since we left,' Wendy said. 'He looked drawn. He's probably been driving up and down every road in Britain since we left.'

We laughed at that, and Linda said. 'If only he'd put this much effort into being a better person.'

He'd promised to leave her alone for a while but would wait on Skye until she was ready to talk. Linda had no intention of talking to him. If he once got her on her own, he'd start with the threats.

'We have to stay together now, all the time. And we have to get away as soon as we can.'

'This is the one place I've ever felt at home,' Wendy said. 'I don't want to leave.' Linda started to counter that, but Wendy backed down immediately. 'I don't want to stay now anyway.'

We realised that our remoteness was working against us. If we tried to drive to the ferry, we'd probably be seen; even the earliest and latest ferries sailed in full daylight. Linda said he'd be watching, and although I didn't believe he'd be hiding in the bushes I couldn't imagine him having come this far to let us go. I wouldn't like to see his reaction if he caught us trying to escape him. The ferry was a problem, because even if we got that far, we'd have to wait at the docking point for some time, in all likelihood. For once, I wished they'd completed the bridge; it would have made driving away so much easier.

'But what could he do?' I said, trying to rationalise my way around our fear. 'He couldn't physically stop us going.'

'He could get nasty. And I doubt the police here are much use.'

'Oh, come on, I'm not falling for the Laurence-with-the-metal-leg stories,' I said, but didn't sound convinced. Wendy said that if he once got an impression of just how opposed Linda was to going back, there would be much larger problems.

'So we have to escape? I can't believe this. Why don't we find where he's staying, slash his tyres and scarper?'

'He'd have every right to call the police then, and we'd be the ones in trouble. We'd probably be hand-delivered to him.'

We talked over the possibilities until we were starving, and being too tired to cook we decided to go out for a pub lunch, finally abandoning our cottage. The place where we'd felt safest was now the most vulnerable; he knew he could find us there, and we were all eager to get out.

We didn't get further than the end of our path, where it joined the road, before we saw the purple XJS. It was flickering behind trees on the high road to our left.

'See,' Linda said, laughing. 'He's watching.'

'For God's sake.'

He was driving fast as he emerged from the trees, curving down towards us. She stopped, allowing him to pull up alongside her, both winding their windows down.

'Hi. Where are you going?' he said, his voice sounding as bright as ever but his face in an unwilling scowl. He made a slight chewing movement, as though teasing the end of his tongue.

'For lunch, just for a ride.'

He was getting a good look in the back of the car. He probably couldn't imagine us leaving any possessions behind and knew we wouldn't go anywhere without Joey. When he'd reassured himself that we weren't going far, he said, 'All right, have a good time. We should do something like this together, go out.'

'Laurence, you said you'd give me some space.'

'I thought it would be nice,' he said.

'Where are *you* going?' she asked, sounding more confident now she was protected by her car.

'I'm still looking for somewhere to stay. Everywhere's booked up.'

'Laurence, there are plenty of places to stay.'

'I'm not going to sit in the middle of the road and argue with you, Linda.'

My stomach felt hot, not just from lack of food, but as though adrenaline was pooling there. I wanted her to shut up and agree with him, just to make him go away. After a long silence he said, 'Well, I'll see you later,' and drove off before she could reply.

We drove up as far as Portree, talking about our plans, trying to enjoy the scenery as best we could. After we'd eaten, we went to the chemist and I was served by one of those Scottish men with such a strong accent I had to ask him to repeat everything. He sold me a huge plaster the size of my back, saying it was impregnated with medicine that would be better than any painkillers. I kept pressing to buy codeine, but he wouldn't have it and I left the shop with this big plaster. Wendy came into the public toilets with me to help put it on. It made me feel like I'd got numb skin, except where it tugged at the hairs. I was disappointed because it didn't even touch my neck, where most of the pain was. I wanted to ring Dave to ask him what he used when his back went, but I couldn't remember his work number.

Once we'd wandered around the town, we got in the car and headed home. We didn't want to go back but couldn't get into the mood to enjoy anything. As we drove I felt a terrible dread at the thought of being there, knowing every moment we'd be waiting for him to appear again.

'We could just leave now,' I said. 'Pack the car and go.'

'Don't be stupid,' Wendy said, sounding cross.

'We could say I have to get back. He couldn't argue with that.'

Linda tried to calm things by saying, 'I've had a think, and I think the best thing to do, if you two agree, is to go along with him. Pretend I'll reconcile, pretend things could be OK. Take it slowly, make it look as though he's winning me round to going back to him. And then work on getting him to leave me alone, just for a while.'

'God, Mum, he's not stupid.'

'I know he's not. He's a bloody madman, but he's not stupid.'

From the back bedroom I could see Laurence's Jaguar parked in the trees by the farmhouse, the windscreen facing our cottage. I imagined that he'd be sitting there watching for us. If he'd arranged to come round at certain times or made a specific plan, it would have been better than knowing he could appear at any time.

I tried to be logical, thinking that there wasn't much that could happen. He couldn't shoot us, and if he went berserk there were three of us to hold him down. What could he do? But I was thinking about all this while I was on the toilet, the nerves having given me such severe diarrhoea that my arse was beginning to bleed. I felt agitated, as though I'd had too much coffee; anxious to do something, unable to get into anything. I couldn't even read, let alone draw. Which is why we spent most of our time talking about the problem. We went over and over his appearance, how we'd felt, what we'd been thinking. We'd all gone through the same rush of thoughts and panic, combined with an inability to move. It was difficult to remember the things that had happened before, as though our whole lives were focusing down to this.

Linda started making a vegetable curry, using a recipe an Indian friend had given her when they lived in Birmingham. It involved roasting the spices, and took far too long, but it gave her time to tell us more about Laurence. They were stories that had occurred before Wendy was born, and I think she was hearing them for the first time.

She told us about a time when she'd been working at the factory and Laurence was interviewing school-leavers. A black lad had come in, overqualified and polite to the point of embarrassment. Laurence had averted his eyes and left the room.

'I'm not joking,' she said. 'He couldn't even look at the poor sod. *Imagine* how he felt. I was left to tell him we'd already got everybody we needed. He looked at me like I was a piece of shit, and I can't blame him.'

It was partly because of Laurence's racism that Linda had become good friends with Sereta, the woman who'd given her the curry recipe. When she first met Sereta, Linda found her standoffish, but Laurence had kept so well out of the way when Sereta was around that Linda began to cherish her company.

'Sereta was the last real friend I had. Laurence hated her. He called her *that Paki*.'

'To her face?'

'He wouldn't speak to her.'

'I can't believe you put up with it,' I said.

'I didn't say much because if I'd complained he'd have done more about it. In the end he did. We moved to Leicester because Sereta was too much like support for me. He didn't want me to be anywhere near her.'

Laurence must have heard this, because he came in as she

was finishing the sentence. He hadn't knocked, and because the front door opened into the kitchen area we'd had no warning.

'God, Laurence, don't pop up like that.'

'Hey, I thought you'd be glad to see me. I've missed you.'

This was a new approach. Sensitive Laurence, the kind man who missed his wife. I wanted to help with the cooking but just sat there with Wendy, wishing we could think of something to talk about.

'I'm staying at the farmhouse,' Laurence said. 'Can you believe it? It was the only place I could find.'

'Come off it, Laurence. It's not even a bed and breakfast.'

'They seem happy enough to have me,' he said, making it quite clear he'd paid them off and didn't care what Linda thought. 'It's a good location this. They could do a lot more with it.'

Every second he was there, I was dreading that Linda would say something direct and risk goading him. I wanted her to be pleasant, to keep him off track, but at the same time I wanted him to leave. He stayed for dinner, simply by hanging around while we cooked, until it got to the point that Wendy said he may as well have some. I was pissed off with her for that, but she might have had the right idea because it seemed to make him think he was getting somewhere.

I had to go through the motions of pretending to eat, so nervous, so utterly unhappy that I felt I was going to vomit. There was nothing to talk about, so he spent the time telling us what he thought about Skye, what could be done to improve the industry and tourism, and every few sentences he'd drop in something about their marriage. His original intention to keep this a family affair had been replaced by a desire to talk about it in front of me. I was dreading him asking my opinion, because I disagreed with everything he said but was too scared to say what I thought. I had visions of him blaming me, seeing the same support coming from me that Wendy and Linda claimed was there. If he once thought I was pivotal, he'd do everything to get rid of me. The closest he came to broaching this was saying, 'I'm sure Nick doesn't like having his holiday spoilt by all this.' I wondered if he was suggesting that I leave.

'We were all having a good time until you turned up,' Linda said.

Laurence was looking at me as she said that and held my gaze.

'I don't really know what's going on,' I said.

He nodded once, then glared at Linda before resuming his monologue.

Only when he knew the last ferry must have gone did he get up and leave. He barely spoke, as though he was already planning his next move, and having kept us here another night he wasn't going to bother with the formalities of being pleasant.

When we were getting ready for bed, Linda asked Wendy to share the back room with her. She was too afraid to sleep alone.

'What, so he's going to storm in during the night and kill us all?'

Linda laughed, and I realised that she liked it when I personified Laurence as comically violent rather than as I actually saw him.

'I think he'll keep away, but I won't sleep if I'm on my own. Sorry to steal her away from you.'

Wendy made some miffed sounds, saying we weren't even

going out with each other and that it made no difference where she slept.

'Oh, great, so I get left in there on my own all night. What if he comes and gets me?'

'Shhh, he might be listening.' Linda made out that she was joking, but whenever she spoke about him it was in whispers.

'You can sleep on the floor, by all means. I'm not modest,' she said.

Wendy raised her eyebrows to say it was up to me. It didn't take long for me to drag a mattress in, and I slept by the bed out of Linda's sight but within reaching distance of Wendy. I put my hand into the bed to touch her while we talked, but rather than letting me do that secretly she told me to get off. I lay back, feeling nonplussed, hoping we could talk about something else to take my mind off her reaction. Nothing more was said, not even good night, but we gradually went quiet and slept.

I woke early, and crept out of the bedroom. Looking down to the trees there was no sign of the Jaguar. I began to wonder whether Laurence was even staying at the farmhouse or just using its bathroom and sleeping in his car. Whether he was checking on the ferry road, or up to something else, I didn't like to think.

I took cups of tea through to the bedroom, and Wendy said I could get in next to her. I struggled to get in, because my back was still tight, and said something about being an old man because of the big plaster on my back.

'This is the sort of threesome I've always dreamed of,' I said in an old pervert's voice. Although they laughed, I realised I was acting more and more out of character. I was constantly joking and trying to keep them up, rather than saying what was on my mind. It was as though being me was too unpleasant, because I was stuck on an island with a maniac on the loose outside. It made more sense to dick about.

I suggested we take a picture of the three of us in bed and leave it on the front door for Laurence just as we escaped from the island.

'For the best effect you two would have to look worn out and satisfied.'

'*Nick.*'

'I must look shocking,' Linda said, pulling at the clogged mascara on her eyelashes. 'I don't normally go to bed made up, but I couldn't let you see me without it.'

'One of my life's goals is to see you without make-up.'

'Wendy can get away with that, but not me.'

Wendy closed her eyes, knowing I was looking at her skin. The slightest wrinkles were edging up around her eyes, but her skin was so smooth it looked powdered. Watching her quietly, I felt almost as good as I had done before Laurence arrived.

It would have been good to walk down to the grass beach on my own, but I stayed in the cottage because we couldn't risk splitting up. We weren't getting sick of each other – in fact we relied on banter to keep ourselves going – but half an hour alone would have done me good. Wendy showed signs of feeling the same way, an edge of irritation creeping into her voice. For a couple of hours in the morning she contradicted just about everything I said. We were still in the cottage, wondering why Laurence hadn't turned up yet, and I put her mood down to that. The expectation of his arrival was worse than his actual presence.

'That's probably why he's doing it,' I said.

'Stop assuming you know how my dad's mind works,' she said.

Considering what we were going through, I didn't want to
hear her defend him, so I went to the bedroom and sat on
the bed.

Sitting there was the first chance I'd had to get some
perspective on our situation. Months can pass with just one
or two remembered details, but when something like this
happens you're sunk into every moment. My memories of
the past few days were all close-ups of people's faces and
speech. Certain scenes were playing over in my mind so
frequently it was as though they had happened only moments
ago.

There's a surprise for you.

I must have had my head down most of the time since
Laurence had found us, avoiding eye contact. It was almost
as though the background details had vanished; I'd barely
even seen the mountains or the ocean, because I'd been so
focused on our immediate surroundings.

Simply coping was taking so much effort, there was no
time left to appreciate the place we'd found. Even worse,
Wendy and I had spent no time at all discussing ourselves.
I'd complained before that we spent too much time doing
that, but now I felt we were acting like friends. I was closer to
her mum than I was to her, and that bothered me. At that
moment it would have been good to get away from Linda,
for the two of us to sit on the bed and chat. Better still, to go
down to the cliffs. I imagined kissing her, hugging her in
that jumper, feeling it move over her skin. Instead of pushing
me away or saying we couldn't, she'd rest her head on my
shoulder. Then she'd pull back slightly, her arms around my
waist, but staring into the distance, her hair blowing, looking
calm.

I heard her voice and Linda's. They were outside, and it
sounded like they were arguing. I'd heard no car, but Laurence

was there as well, his hushed tones rambling over their voices the whole time. I moved to the window and listened. It sounded like Linda was pleading with him.

'Wendy's not going to start taking sides,' he said. 'You're not, are you, Wendy?'

'Laurence, *don't*.'

'I'm only taking my daughter out for lunch. What gives you the right to keep her to yourself?'

'Mum, it's only lunch.'

His car was so quiet I didn't even hear the doors close or the engine start. When I went outside they'd gone. There was still dust in the air, hanging over the path; it made the mountains behind soft focus, yet brighter. Linda was moving towards the grass at the side of the path, staggering as though drunk. She lowered herself down, looked at me briefly, then put her head in her hands.

Chapter Ten

What seemed like a disaster worked in our favour, because with Wendy out of the way Linda had a chance to talk to me directly. I went to sit next to her and we stayed on the grass by the path, talking.

'Do you think Wendy will be all right?'

'He'll be working on her now, telling her all sorts of nonsense about me. He'll make it perfectly clear that her life will be a misery if she doesn't stop helping me. She won't get a word in.'

Apparently she'd held back half the stories she could have told me, because Laurence was still Wendy's dad. There was a danger in criticising him too openly, she said, because Wendy would go on the defensive. It was better for Linda to keep quiet and to let Wendy voice her complaints about Laurence. If Linda said too much, there was a slight danger that Wendy would take sides against her. I doubted this but wanted to know what she'd been keeping to herself. I was expecting her tell me that Laurence had been violent, but she said that wouldn't have been so bad. The threat of violence for twenty-odd years was worse than if he'd lashed out occasionally.

'I feel like I've been beaten up at the end of every day. If he'd just wallop me I could hit him back or scream at him. At least there would be something I could put my finger on. But his control is so subtle, if I complain he makes me feel like I'm being an unreasonable bitch.'

'That's a classic bullying tactic.'

'Just before we left I had a dream that he was attacking me with a sword, and I only had spoons to defend myself with. That's what it feels like. And I'm always made to feel that if I ever push him too far, he wouldn't stop at giving me a black eye.'

'Has he ever said he'd kill you?'

'No, but he sometimes gives me that look. His eyes go tiny, and you can just see his teeth through his lips.' She paused and said, 'I hate him. He disgusts me.'

'I don't know if I can stand it much more,' I said. 'It's making me sick. I feel like puking the whole time. And I'm so exhausted. It's worse than an all-out battle.'

'I'm so sorry.'

'No, don't be. The one pleasure I get from this is knowing we're pissing him off. It doesn't matter how much shit he gives us if you don't go back to him. The last thing I want is for you to give up.'

'It just won't happen,' she said. 'But I don't know what we'd have done without you. He's so annoyed that you're here, but he daren't get mad in front of you.'

'I just hope he doesn't offer to take *me* out for lunch tomorrow.'

We talked for hours, eventually going in to eat, but we felt so tense we could only manage pesto from a jar. We sat on the floor, our backs to the settee, and I encouraged her to talk. She told me the small details of their marriage, which were somehow worse than the overall bullying. She said she'd made thousands of meals for him, and every single time there had always been some complaint, no matter how small:

too many chips, too few chips, the wrong sort of lettuce. If it didn't suit he'd poke at it with his fork like it was shit. In all those years he'd never said thank you, but if their part-time friends were round, he'd go on about what a great cook she was. If she ever complained to those friends in private, they thought she was being unfair, because they knew how generous Laurence was with his praise.

'I know it doesn't sound like much, but you're meant to get married to be loved.'

'Yes.'

'And I don't want to begin on the sex.'

'That bad?'

I already had an erection, but I wasn't sure why. I wasn't at all attracted to her, but the thought of her confessing how crap he'd been in bed was highly erotic. Laurence was on the other side of the island, thinking he was winning the battle, but she was telling me what a shit lover he was. I didn't fancy her, but it crossed my mind that fucking her now would be a gorgeous victory.

'Let's just say I'm very good at masturbating.' She followed that with a whooping laugh that made it easier for me to do the same. This wasn't the sort of comment a girlfriend's mother would usually make, and I found it difficult to believe this was the same woman I'd seen scurrying around that house to meet Laurence's demands. It was good being this friendly with her, but it felt like a minor betrayal of Wendy. It was an intimacy carried out behind her back.

We were still getting over Linda's comment when we heard the Jaguar on the drive. I went weak again but stood up to watch through the window. Laurence didn't even stop to say hello but waited for Wendy to get out then drove away. There was something so ominous about his smugness that I knew I'd get mad if Wendy spoke in his favour.

She came in, looked from Linda to me and said, 'I *don't* want to talk about it.'

She went to the bedroom and slammed the door. I got up as quickly as I could, my back slowing me. Walking through I imagined her being mad, but thought the best thing was to sound sympathetic. She was curled up on the bed, eyes closed. I sat by her side and put my hand on her shoulder. Linda stood in the doorway, watching.

I thought it would do her good if she had a cry, but I knew why she was holding back. I felt like crying myself at times, but when there was no prospect of the ordeal ending it would feel wrong. If we once cracked up like that, he'd be on to us. I tried to give her room to talk.

'Was it that bad?'

'I'm not talking about it. I've just spent three hours listening to him, and I've had enough. Now leave me *alone*.'

'What the fuck has he said?'

'Nothing,' she snapped, then, 'He's not safe. He's a lunatic.' That gave me hope, because he hadn't turned her against us, but then she looked at Linda and said, 'You're making everybody so unhappy.'

'God, Wendy,' I said, 'don't be so thick. Isn't it obvious he's using emotional blackmail?'

'If she hadn't done this we wouldn't be here. I'm scared of my own dad because of her.'

'You always *were* scared of him.'

Linda interrupted us, sounding furious. 'Right. I'll go back. Is that what you want? Cancel everything. Back to normal.'

'For God's sake, this is exactly what he wants. He wants us to argue among ourselves. That's why he dragged you off, to split us up. You're letting him get his way.'

'He's my dad.'

'Well, he should act like it then.'

It could have turned into a worse argument, except that she calmed down, sat back against the wall and said she was sorry. 'But I don't want to say anything else. I feel like my head's going to burst.'

Linda left us to it, and Wendy said she'd been having headaches since Laurence arrived. She wouldn't go into any more detail about Laurence, saying she wanted to move on.

'There's so much other stuff I want to talk about,' she said. 'Books and ideas. All the stuff we used to go on about. This isn't normal. I miss talking about us.'

'I've been feeling the same way,' I said.

She shook her head and said, 'I don't think you have.'

Soon after that we drove further west than we had been before. Her mood continued to switch from those odd moments of tenderness to frowning temper. I didn't bother talking to her on that journey. The road to Elgol was narrow, often coming so close to the cliffs that the lip of tarmac was cracked where the earth beneath gave way. The road ran out, leading into an empty gravel car-park. Elgol consisted of two white buildings of indeterminate purpose, and from there we walked down to a stone beach. The sea-loch was white with glare from the clouds, only grey at the edge before lapsing back into the breakers. Beyond that was the best view we'd seen yet of the Cuillins. The closest mountain rose from the water with no foothills, like a giant black slag heap. The other mountains arced away behind it, jagged and pale.

We wandered around separately, but I trailed Wendy, hoping we'd get to talk. Whenever I got close, she'd speed up, perhaps knowing my back was so sore I couldn't go any faster.

I'd taken my pencils and pad so I sat down and forced myself to draw. I've never taken less pleasure in drawing, because I kept thinking to myself how unfair it all was. Your life can be relatively normal, and then in a matter of days you end up in a situation as extreme as this. Dave would say the universe was telling me to stick to the straight and narrow, but just because you leave middle-class normality for a while shouldn't mean you're terrorised. And the so-called normality he was such a fan of was really the nightmare that Wendy and Linda had been living out for twenty years. I couldn't imagine how they'd coped; being around Laurence for a few days was making me ill. I tried to imagine it being over but couldn't picture further than a day or two ahead.

My drawing was fairly good. It's difficult to portray the size of mountains; you always forget how imposing they are when you're away from them, but my picture managed to get that across.

We were there for hours, just looking across the water. A lens of milky cloud grew over the closest peak, eventually obscuring the top. I joined Linda, and soon after that Wendy came to be with us. It was so windy we could barely hear each other, but it remained warm.

Our attempts at talking about something else failed. We were no nearer to finding a way off the island, and I was dreading seeing Laurence again.

'Did he say when he was coming back?'

'No.'

I knew I should leave Wendy alone, but I kept saying things like, *Are you all right? Are you sure, because you look upset.* I should have laid off but wanted reassurance that she was still on our side.

She said she was fine, sounding increasingly dismissive every time. I wanted her to be more positive, so kept asking, and in the end she said, 'What do you think, Nick? My life is shit.'

'Then we should leave,' Linda said. 'I'm not having this happen to you. You're becoming so sad.'

'I'm fine.'

'Well, Nick isn't, and I'm not, and I don't believe for a minute that you are. I've had enough of this. We didn't come away to be miserable.'

The cottage wasn't very welcoming, because we'd left the washing-up from lunch and all the rooms smelt of pesto. Wendy said it was like a squat and set to doing the washing-up. I stood nearby, feeling that it would have been rude to go, but I said my back was so sore I couldn't help.

'Can't you dry?'

'I would if I could, but . . .' I gestured behind myself and winced. The muscle was getting so hard I didn't even want to reach out to take plates from her.

'Just relax.'

'It's not like that. I can't relax when it's spasmed.'

Wendy said, 'Spasmed?' as though I'd made the word up.

Linda said she'd help but remained sitting at the table, rubbing her eyes.

'Spasmed?'

'Look, I'd help if I could, but I can't.'

She had a way of looking at me sometimes, a stare that could turn into a smile but often came just before anger. I said, 'Calm down,' intending to sound soothing, but saying it like an impatient parent. She picked up the bowl from the sink and flung it at me. I remember seeing water and crockery coming from it, the image frozen as I closed my eyes. I felt the water hit me. The sound of knives and forks on the floor was louder than the pots smashing. By the time I opened my eyes she was pulling my hair, dragging me on to the ground. I opened my eyes briefly, and she looked terrified, even though she still had my hair in her fist. It was as though she was carrying on to prevent me getting her back.

And then Laurence was in the room. I hadn't even seen him come in, but he was looking from one to the other of us. It was like waiting to be told off. Wendy backed off, leaning against the cupboards, her mouth open with crying but no sound coming out. We were all breathing fast, except Laurence, who waited a while longer before speaking. 'What's going on?'

He directed that at me, but Linda answered.

'Laurence, please leave us alone. This is private.'

'It's hardly private,' he said, angling his head towards Wendy. It was a shock to see her become calm, wiping her face, almost managing a smile.

'It's all right,' she said. 'We just got mad over an accident.'

We were both soaked, the water around us appearing frozen where glass and white china rose from the surface.

He wasn't responding so Linda said, 'Come for lunch tomorrow, but give us some space now.'

Perhaps feeling he'd made another gain, he immediately lost interest in us. 'All right,' he said, leaving the door open as he left.

As soon as his engine fired, Linda said, 'I've had enough. We're leaving.'

It wasn't much of a plan, but we'd got to the point where we were prepared to risk being caught. There had been no apologies between us, because if anything Wendy's reaction created a new feeling of solidarity. After we'd changed our clothes, we went for long walks up the road in both directions to judge where the cottage and the car could be seen from. The main point was to determine where the Elgol road went out of sight for the last time. If we managed to send him that

way, we could leave the instant he went past that point.
Unless he turned back straight away, it should give us enough
time to make it to the ferry. The main thing was to leave
during the middle of the day, when he least expected us to
bother. He was always turning up at either end of the day,
presuming we'd try to leave on the first or last ferry. Our
hope was that, having been around us for a few days, he'd
assume we were staying put and would become less vigilant.
Linda's plan was to stop pressing him to leave but to ask for
more time on the island. That should make him pay less
attention to us.

Once it went reasonably dark we packed as much into the
car as we could. I stood outside and they passed stuff through
to me from the toilet window. By packing it all into the boot,
the car still looked empty. We left a few things out – clothes,
books, tapes and Joey's cage – to make it look like we were
still occupying the cottage. We could pack those within a
minute of him disappearing.

We all slept in the same room, and this time Wendy said
I could get in next to her. Only for the sake of my back,
she said, seeing as I'd put the effort into packing the car.
She slept closer to her mum than she did to me, though,
and I spent a lot of the night awake, listening to their
breathing.

When we woke up, we talked for so long that Wendy
eventually grew bored and went for the first shower. I think
she'd been holding back, because she didn't want to leave
me in bed with her mum. But sharing the bed with Linda
seemed less strange than it would have done under normal
circumstances, because we'd spent so much time together in
recent days. Most of that time had been spent within a few
feet of each other, so being in bed with her barely felt any
different. Nothing much was said, apart from a few comments

about my back. I was facing away from her in an attempt to get comfortable, and when Wendy turned off the water I shouted through to her. I was hassling her into giving me a massage, saying that if she didn't her mum would. It was just a few moments before she came back in that Linda ran her finger down my back. Then she said, 'I want a photo of you two before we leave.'

In the shower I masturbated frantically. The guilt came before my ejaculation was over, and although I felt relieved at having come again, I was disgusted with myself. Being so close to the two of them was beginning to confuse me.

Linda took a photo of us standing outside the cottage; Wendy was still a bit sulky, but I held her with such joy and pushed my face into her hair until I could feel her smile.

Laurence stayed for lunch and tried to give his usual lecture, but we kept talking over him. I'm not sure if it was confidence or an attempt to put him at ease, but we were quite bright. When we'd finished we went through to the front room, and I told him about Elgol and the view from there. I showed him my drawing and casually urged him to go there, managing to get him to say, 'Yes, right, Nick, I'll do that.'

I wanted him to go immediately. 'I'm not sure what the weather will be like today,' I said, hoping he'd contradict me.

'Oh, it'll be fine.'

'Are you going to go over this afternoon then?'

'Do you want to come, Linda?'

'I've already been. We just want to stay here.'

'Heh,' he said, with a sound that was almost a laugh. 'You love it here, don't you?'

'That's what I keep trying to tell you, Laurence. We just want some time here.'

I could see him wondering what was going on, how best to respond to this.

'You can't stay here for ever, Linda.'

'I don't want to, but we came here for a break, and we're not really getting it.'

He went quiet again, then said, 'I'm not planning on leaving.'

'That's all right, Laurence, but think about it; if I need some space to sort myself out, you're not helping by hounding me like this.'

'I'm not hounding you. Can you hear what your mum's saying, Wendy? Eh, Nick?'

I wished she would stop talking and just let him go for his afternoon drive to Elgol. I don't know if it was her sense of confidence or our imminent escape, but rather than being compliant she started to be more contradictory. Throughout all this she sat with her arms around her knees, while Laurence moved closer. It was like watching oversized teenagers. I'd never seen him sit on the floor before, and there he was, trying to look natural. As he spoke he toyed with her hair, putting one finger on her leg and smiling. He worked his way closer, so that she backed away and ended up lying back in the centre of the room. I wanted to leave, but it had got to the point where I would have been drawing attention to myself, and was probably the last thing she wanted. He was craning towards her face, talking softly, then put one arm across so he was leaning right over her. Wendy had pursed her lips, not quite believing what she was seeing. He moved to sit over Linda and put his hands by her head, leaving her arms free, as though he wanted her to hug him.

He kept saying that he loved her, and that things could be worked out. The one thing he kept repeating was that he didn't mind if she had a holiday.

'That's not what I'm doing.'

'It's a holiday.'

'No, Laurence. I'm leaving you.'

'You just need a break. There's no need for all these problems. You're on holiday. Be reasonable.'

'Laurence.'

'Holiday.'

I counted, and he said the word 'holiday' forty times. It was like he was trying to hypnotise her.

He stayed on top of her until, without any conviction, she said, 'All right. A holiday.'

He got up, looked around the room grinning, and said, 'Right, I'll go and see this view then. And when you're ready, you come to me. You know where I am.' He looked towards the cottage. 'Have your holiday, but don't ignore me for too long.'

As soon as the door was closed, Linda got up. We gathered our stuff by the door, and then I watched the road from the spare bedroom, telling them when it was safe to transfer stuff to the car. I could hear Joey's cage being manoeuvred into the back seat, the door closing, the engine starting. When the Jaguar curved out of sight for the last time, I ran back round and got in.

Linda drove faster than felt safe, and I kept looking back, making sure there was no sign of him driving back over the ridge. There was just a chance he'd parked up there to watch the cottage. I was fairly sure he'd watched us from there previously, but there was no sign of him. I pictured him driving to Elgol, making his plans, thinking he was getting somewhere. Linda was leaving her braking until the last moment, flying over cattle-grids at full speed, cutting corners to keep her momentum. From Broadford, the road was quite straight, allowing her to get up more speed.

The worst part was getting close to the ferry and seeing the road busy with cars going in the opposite direction. I imagined being too late, getting there only to see it leaving again, knowing there was a half-hour wait ahead. Even if that happened, I reassured myself, he might not get to us in time; the journey to Elgol, then back to the port, would take too long. But I needn't have worried, because the ferry was taking on cars as we drove up. We were the last to drive on.

We got out and stood at the back, looking down at the water. There was a foaming gap between us and the shore.

'That's it,' Linda said. 'Even if he gets the next ferry, we have half an hour's start. He can't catch us, but we'll have to drive all night.'

'Where are we driving to?' I asked.

Having spent so much time trying to get off the island, we had no idea where to head next.

Chapter Eleven

The smell of my flat was familiar yet soured by the stillness of the air. The curtains were closed, so that the only light in there came from the gaps around them, making the whole room slightly yellow. It felt like I'd been away for years, but also that I'd been gone only a few hours, because although so much had happened, nothing had changed. The same scattering of papers and clothes were there from the week before, making the intervening time seem irrelevant. What had seemed like months while Laurence was chasing us now felt like a few moments. I was reluctant to open the curtains, because I knew that as soon as I did normality would be restored. I'd wipe down the surfaces, open the windows, put on some music and it would be my flat again, as though nothing had happened. Twenty minutes earlier, they'd asked me if I was sure I'd had enough, and at the time I'd thought I was.

The journey down had been almost nonstop, going without pause until we were out of Scotland. From then on toilet and food stops were kept to five minutes. The whole time we'd debated where to go next, and as they'd gone through the list of potential places I began to lose my enthusiasm. The thought of Laurence popping up again was too much. By the time they'd settled on Wales, I said I'd had enough and asked them to drop me at a station. Linda had insisted on running me home. Leicester was the last place he'd expect us to go, and she could use the opportunity to draw more money out.

Sitting there, with my bag still packed, I considered calling the bank and asking them to make her wait. There was nothing to stop me joining them again. Instead, I set the answering machine to playback. The first voice was Laurence, asking for Wendy to call him. That was followed by the same message repeated almost word for word, this time from his mobile phone; both must have been from the day we left. A couple of messages followed from Dave, in which he obligingly stated the day, saying, 'Where the fuck are you?' His most recent call was from that morning, saying to phone him at work. That was followed by a series of beeps, where somebody had rung and hung up again at least five times. I didn't like the thought that Laurence might have been the one ringing me so consistently in the past few hours. He was meant to think we were elsewhere, but it was as though he'd guessed I'd be coming home. I wished I'd gone with Wendy and Linda, because hiding in the countryside suddenly seemed more plausible than hiding in my flat.

I rang Dave, told him what had happened, and he had that tone of voice that meant he was typing while talking to me. 'Sounds dreadful,' was about the best he could manage. He said he'd be round later. I rang Mum and tried to explain, but she just kept going on about how beautiful it was up on Skye and told me not to get involved with family arguments. When she put Dad on, I told him, and he responded as though he thought I was exaggerating.

With the phone down, I felt nervous again. While I was there, he could just keep turning up. I left the machine on to screen my calls, but it didn't ring again. I tidied the flat, unpacked, washed my clothes, ate, and then soaked in the bath to get the medicine plaster off my back. I tried to busy myself until Dave arrived but couldn't bring myself to read or watch TV, so when he arrived I was jittery with tension.

We went to the usual pubs, and whenever I tried to talk to him he kept running through the same old banter of insults.

'So anyway, it was absolutely fucked,' I said, trying to keep him on the subject.

'Did you fuck Linda?'

'Piss off, Dave. We shared a bed because of him. It was terrifying, so don't make it sound so trivial.'

'Hey, you brought it on yourself. You weren't obliged to stay up there.'

'So I should just have abandoned them?'

'It was your choice.'

He moved on to his own life and how he and Rachel were bickering more often. She kept getting jealous if he talked to other women. They didn't get out enough. I wanted to tell him what a middle-class twat he was, that his problems were tiny compared with what I'd been through, but it was pointless. It was going to be difficult getting it across to anybody without it sounding ridiculous. *Why didn't you just leave?* people would say. *What would he do? Kill you?*

So I let Dave get me drunk. If nothing else he was generous with his drinks.

When I got home there were no more messages on the machine, but unwilling to go to sleep I looked through my address book for people to ring up. It's a bad habit, but when I'm drunk I tend to call up old girlfriends. Relationships that might have ended with great dignity years ago could be reduced to sordid embarrassment when I found myself suggesting casual sex.

I considered phoning Chelsea, but given the way we'd

parted it probably wasn't fair. Instead I phoned Caryn, because she wasn't likely to be bothered by a late call.

'Oh, hi, Nick, I was just thinking about you.' She had a way of saying my name that made it sound like the most important word in any sentence. Before I could respond, she said, 'What have you been up to?'

I managed to get the story across in a few minutes, and Caryn asked how Wendy was and where she would be now.

'I just don't know.'

'Shit. I wish she'd come here. I wanted to spend the summer with her.'

'Oh.'

'And you, if you liked. I've got two months off.'

'Yeah, well, perhaps you'll be able to catch up with them. Or are you planning on coming back to Leicester?'

'I dunno. I'd like to see you again.'

The drink was really getting to me now, but it was so pleasant to be talking to Caryn that I couldn't help but feel loved. We said we'd keep in touch, but as soon as I put the phone down I wished I'd invited her up. I was angry with Wendy now. I'd been through all that for nothing, in effect, because she'd made it clear we were no more than friends. That in turn made me angry about the feelings I was having for Caryn, because that could only ever be friendship as well. I found myself hoping that she'd be one of those lesbians who went back to being bisexual after a while. I'd been out with a girl called Melanie Jones who'd been a lesbian for years before going back to men. I think I'd have remained completely shit in bed if it wasn't for her. 'Forget your dick,' was her mantra, which at first I'd thought was some sort of lesbian throwback, but she'd insisted it was the best way to please a woman. *Make love with everything but your dick*, she'd explained, *and your dick will look after itself.* I'd never told anybody about that, because I didn't want it to sound like a technique, but I had a lot to thank Melanie for. I pictured myself sleeping with Caryn, feeling terribly guilty as I did so, because I knew what people would say; typical man trying to cure a woman of lesbianism. You can't argue with accusations like that, because you'll just be told it's a socialised response or an unconscious reaction. Whatever the truth, I wanted to sleep with her not because she was a lesbian but because I adored her.

It was one of those nights where exhaustion and booze combined to ensure that I barely slept but crept through the night in something resembling fever.

I could hear Wendy's voice, distant, and realised it was coming from the answering machine. I must have slept through the ringing, but I caught more of her words as I ran to the phone.

'Nick? If you're there please pick up the phone. Mum's been caught. Dad got her at the bank. I need to speak to you.'

'What's happened?' I asked.

'Has he been to see you?'

'No, why, what's going on?'

She told me that after they'd dropped me off, they'd gone to the bank to draw money out with a cheque. When they tried to clear it something had come up on the screen. The bank had said the guarantee card was registered as stolen, and took Linda to the vault and locked her in there.

'So your dad reported the card as stolen?'

'It's worse than that. I waited outside, thinking the police were coming, but they hadn't even been called. The bank manager is Dad's friend. He kept her there until Dad arrived.'

'That's illegal. That's kidnap. Call the fucking police and tell them.'

'It's too late. She gave up. He spoke to her for half an hour.'

'In the bank vault?'

'Yes. And she gave in.'

'So that's it. All that for nothing?'

'Don't get at me. At least it's over now.'

She said that Laurence had taken Linda to the cottage in the Cotswolds, for them to have some time alone.

'Nick, it's probably better this way. She wasn't happy.'

'How can you say that? How can you possibly believe she's better off with him?'

'Just let it drop.'

The sad thing is that I did. I was furious with him for having won, but from a purely selfish point of view I was relieved. It meant I could spend time with Wendy again without worrying. Laurence and Linda were over an hour's drive away, leaving Wendy in charge of the house for the rest of summer.

I imagined a sense of normality returning to us, but Caryn's arrival made that impossible. For a start it confused me. I still wanted to be with Wendy, but she was being so distant that I kept picturing myself with Caryn. It occurred to me a few times that I wasn't acting completely normally, and that my obsession might be a result of having had such an intense summer. It was also a bit annoying that I was being so predictable, and I knew if Wendy got a whiff of it that's the first thing she'd say. But mostly I gave in to the feelings, enjoying the fact that I could casually long for Caryn without really doing anything about it, because she'd be there until autumn.

Caryn turned the place into an open house, which I would have found stressful, but it was such a contrast to what

Laurence must have envisioned for his obscene little palace that I enjoyed her minor debauchery. She'd never been one for excess company in London, but she was keen to give Wendy a good time. Wendy went along with it because it kept her occupied. There were never parties as such, but every night they'd go out and bring back more friends; there were usually five or six people sleeping over, so drunk they slumped on chairs and in corners. I didn't go on most of the pub-crawls but often ended up at the house later on. It wasn't that I was particularly into getting pissed and talking until the early hours, but I'd have felt left out if I hadn't been there. But I was always the first to leave in the morning. Unable to stand the reek of stale breath, I'd tiptoe out between the snoring bodies. Wendy and Caryn would spend the morning getting rid of people, watch TV in the afternoon, then start again after dinner. A few weeks previously I'd have been critical of that, but I was tired of telling Wendy what to do and didn't want to give her an excuse to get mad at me.

I don't know how much of a part she played in choosing their house guests or controlling the numbers, but by July there was a small group of fairly regular hangers-on. There was a German traveller called Martin they'd met at the club who'd virtually moved in. Like all Germans he was training to be a doctor, but other than that he was all right. There were other students, somebody from the uni café and one or two of the people Caryn had been to college with. Their conversations were endlessly dull; fierce debates about pornography (the men nodding sagely about the exploitation of women), political rants that made me embarrassed to be a socialist, out-of-date arguments about the use of the word 'cunt', and the usual crap about the size of the universe. The topics weren't so bad as the earnest belief that they were discussing them for the first time. If I'd had anywhere else to go I would have done, but Dave and Rachel had become such dreadful company I avoided going round there. And despite her attitude to me, I wanted to be near Wendy.

'We should go away,' I said to her.

'Caryn was talking about that. We're thinking of going to Cornwall.'

'Without me?'

'Won't your term be starting soon?'

She knew it wasn't, which made it clear they were planning to go alone, and I'd be left with nothing. Although I didn't want many more parties, I couldn't bear to be parted from Wendy and Caryn for any length of time. I wouldn't know what to do with myself.

Linda rang every few days. She was taking advantage of Laurence's promises to change and using the phone as much as she wanted. He even let her go out on her own, because she insisted they had to have trust. She never said whether she was happy or not, and I only got to hear this second-hand because Wendy wouldn't let me talk to her.

There was a rainy week in August when we barely went out, and nobody came round, so I spent the evenings at home, knowing they were doing the same at Wendy's. It was probably this let-up in the activity that made the next night out more frantic. There were more of us than usual, with general talk of a party at Wendy's. It didn't happen, because she and Caryn urged everybody into Mosquito Coast. It was dark in there, and too loud; most people were too drunk to dance. At one point Caryn sat by me, and it was one of those situations where everything feels like it's going perfectly without the need for a plan. She was managing to talk softly over the music and said she was bored. I asked what she wanted to do, and she said we should go for a walk. But we kept talking, and Wendy came over wanting a chat with Caryn. When I finally got her attention again and asked about our walk, she said we were all about to leave. I was pissed off at that, but hopeful. Back at Wendy's, people went their separate ways to sleep, Caryn being the first to disappear, walking virtually with her eyes closed, she was so pissed.

There was no lock on that bedroom door, so I went in without knocking, not really considering that she could have been getting undressed. She was still fully clothed, with one sheet over herself, foetal. I don't remember how, but I ended up sitting by the bed, leaning on to it. I could smell her perfume in the sheets. She was leaning up on one arm, watching me; there was almost nothing to see of each other, because we had only the glow of distant streetlight. I asked her what was happening and she said, 'Do you mean about us?'

The door opened and Wendy was standing there. She was wearing a white nightie, back-lit from a lampshade in the hall. I could see her body through the cotton, and her hair glowed. At any other time I'd have loved to see her like that, but I was furious at her intrusion.

'What's going on?' she asked.

'Nothing.'

'Nick, come here.'

Caryn urged me to go out to her. I said I wouldn't be long, desperate for the moment to remain.

Wendy had moved towards her mum and dad's room, which was where she was sleeping these days. She urged me to follow her, but I wouldn't go further than the door.

'What the fuck is wrong with you?' I asked.

'She's my friend.'

'So am I.'

'You can't do this. In my own house, with my friend.'

Caryn came out and said, 'You sleep in here; I'll stay with Wendy,' and they both disappeared so quickly I was left standing on the landing wondering what had happened.

By the time I got up Caryn had left and Wendy was sitting on the wide windowsill, looking out. She was pleased to see me, as though there had been no argument, and for a second it felt like this was our room. I sat on the edge of the bed and we talked. I was honest about being attracted to Caryn, and Wendy seemed unfazed by that.

'So what did she say?' I asked.

'She said she was drunk.'

'And?'

'That she's still a lesbian, but that sometimes there's nothing quite like a good hard cock up you.'

'She said that?'

'Yes.'

'It's nice to know I'm nothing more than a cock. What enlightened times we live in.'

'Stop sounding like such a woman-hater. You were the one who wanted to shag her.'

We kept trying to get mad but found ourselves laughing. I wasn't entirely comfortable with this. It was as though we were becoming so familiar we could treat each other like shit and it didn't have any effect. If that was the case, then our kindness was a waste as well.

We spent the day apart, but the night that followed was difficult for two reasons. Caryn came back and was more distant than she'd ever been. And one of my students from a couple of years back turned up at the house. Stephen Bidden didn't appear to know anybody who was there that night, and I never got to find out who he was with, but he acted like he owned the place. He said hi to me, and that was the last time he spoke to me directly. Stephen was about three feet taller than Wendy, so he moved slowly, as though it was impossible for him to be anything other than cool. Wendy had always said she liked people who enjoyed life, so I was pissed off at her obvious attraction to somebody so dull. He had this brilliant act of looking completely uninterested in her, moving around the room as he talked so she'd follow him. I'd never liked him; he was one of those people who refused to wash his hair, insisting that it cleaned itself, even though we could smell the truth. He smoked roll-ups, making a big show of his finger technique, pinching tobacco off his tongue. When he loped off to the toilet, I went over to Wendy and said, 'Well, seeing as you're so in love I'll be off.'

The morning after, she came round to my flat, denying that her flirtations with Stephen Bidden had been anything other than genuine. There was no way, she swore, it was to get back at me for Caryn.

'So what happened? Did he fuck you?'

'Yes.'

'That bothers me less than I thought it would. Was it any good?'

'It was awful. He was huge.'

'His dick?'

'Don't be pathetic. His body. It was like being with a giant.'

She looked so disgusted at the thought of him that I was happy to let her tell the story.

'We started kissing after everybody had gone to bed, and after about five minutes he said, "Go into the kitchen and sit on a chair," and I said, "What for?" And he said, "Because I want to lick your genitals." ' She did a good impression of spewing, but there was a nervousness in her face, hoping I'd laugh with her.

'Lick your genitals? It makes you sound like a horse.'

I'm not one to hold back when it comes to sexual patois, but there's still the matter of style. I must admit I prefer some crudity. A woman who hints that you *kiss me down there* is being too euphemistic. Something more direct is required, but talk of genitals strikes me as clinical.

'Did you let him?'

'I thought I may as well.'

I wasn't too upset by this, because I got the feeling she'd come to spend the day with me. It was only when she had to go because she was meeting Caryn in town that I felt a bit nonplussed.

I rang Linda at the cottage, thinking that if Laurence answered all I had to do was put the phone down. He wasn't in, thankfully, and it was good to hear her voice. I told Linda exactly what had happened.

'I thought things were going well for you two.'

'Not for ages.'

She told me how her life was going, and I asked about her plans. She kept alluding to the impossibility of escape, until I asked her directly what she was on about.

'Didn't Wendy tell you?'

'What?'

'About Laurence. He said he'd get you if I didn't go back to him.'

'Get me?'

I was terrified at the thought but astonished that Wendy had hidden this from me. If it had been up to me, Linda should have buggered off and let him make his threats. I immediately made a speech about not giving in to violence, and within a matter of minutes I'd talked her into leaving him.

'I'm prepared to take the risk,' I said. 'Otherwise I went through all that for nothing. If you want to leave him, leave.'

When the phone went down I felt dissatisfied, because I hadn't really talked out my feelings for Wendy, and once again we'd focused on Linda's problems.

It was less than an hour later that Wendy rang.

'Dad's on his way to Leicester. Mum's left him.'

Her mum had rung to warn her, and her dad had rung a few minutes later, telling her not to leave the house. 'He thinks Mum's coming to pick me up. I've had to evacuate the place. Even Caryn's gone.'

'And Stephen?'

'I sent everybody home when Mum rang.'

'Do you want to come here?'

There was long pause, and she said, 'Thanks, but there's no point. He might even go to yours first. But I don't want to be here when he gets back. I can't face the endless questioning. I want to be with Mum.'

We compromised by heading up to my parents' house. I hadn't been to see them for ages, and it might do them good to see Wendy and me together again. I picked Wendy up twenty minutes later, loading Joey's cage first, then throwing her bags in around him. There was no way Laurence could arrive for at least another half-hour, but we rushed as though he was a couple of streets away.

We never found out whether Laurence had gone to Leicester first or second-guessed us by heading straight to Wigan, but he arrived at my parents' house five minutes after we did. We'd barely had time to get the basic story across to Mum and Dad when we saw the Jaguar outside.

I suggested pretending we were out, locking the doors, keeping back, but Wendy said something about being sick of it all and went to the door. Laurence asked where Linda was, and as he talked I could hear him work his way into the hall. Wendy was telling him that she'd had nothing to do with any of it, that she just wanted to be left alone. He kept saying that if she wanted some peace, she should help him. Things would only calm down once Linda was back. For the first time she started answering him back, saying that if Linda wanted to leave, that was up to her.

We were all listening from the front room. Mum stood nearby, one hand over her mouth. Dad walked around with his head down. He kept moving as though about to get something, or to go to the phone, but would then stop and stand for a while longer. Laurence started getting more angry.

'If you don't help me, Wendy, there'll be problems. I'll sort you out.'

I found myself in the hall, yelling, 'Get the fuck out of here, you arsehole.'

His expression was almost comical. I'd shocked the bastard. I'd given him a moment of fear. It passed quickly and he came towards me. Wendy had backed up against the wall but put her hands out, a palm towards each of us. She was crying, pleading with us to stop.

I felt weak but managed to put my hands up and say, 'Come on,' looking as angry as I could. It was going through my mind that if he attacked me, at least I'd have grounds for getting him arrested. He motioned towards me but thought better of it.

'You're trespassing. If you don't go, I'll call the police.'

'Go on then, Nick.'

'Right. I will.'

'You can't stop me talking to my own daughter.'

'You were *threatening* her.'

'Now that's just not true,' he said, but I left them there

and went to call the police. He'd obviously been relying on the fact that we wouldn't do that.

When I got off the phone, Wendy was in the front room, her head buried in Mum's neck. Laurence was outside talking to Dad. He was saying, 'I respect Nick for that. Nobody ever stands up to me.' I was livid with him for sounding so rational. He was making out that this was a small family debate and that he could just chat and leave at his leisure. His timing, as ever, was perfect, because he drove away as the police arrived. I explained the situation to them, and they sounded so disappointed they considered going after him, but let it drop.

Linda rang later that afternoon, and without asking me along Wendy arranged to meet her. She asked me to take her to the station.

'So I'm not invited?'

'This is nothing to do with you,' she said. 'Imagine what I'm going through, seeing you do that to my dad.'

I felt so relieved at having finally stood up to him that I couldn't bear for her to criticise me for it.

'He was threatening you.'

'But he's still my dad,' she said.

Chapter Twelve

My usual policy of avoiding uni during freshers' week was reversed in favour of the company. I felt more like a first-year than I had ten years ago, because I was desperate to distract myself with people. I even bought a kettle for my office, so I could invite students in for coffee when they had queries. The first-years were as nauseating as ever, but it was better than being stuck in my flat wondering what to do. I'd been left with Joey, to prevent him being dragged further round the country, but having him there served only to make me feel more alone. I'd find myself talking to him, thinking *this is what it must be like to be an old person.* Talking to a fucking budgie and being delighted to see him every day. It gave me an insight into how Wendy must have been feeling in Bath before I arrived.

Dave kept cancelling on me, sometimes talking for so long on the phone I'd get mad, saying he should just have come round to talk. He invited me round a few times, but the plans to play Pictionary or Jenga (which hadn't exactly enthused me in the first place) always collapsed. Rachel would go to bed early and we'd be left watching *Star Trek*, getting pissed because we'd nothing much left to talk about. He'd got into this habit of mixing whisky with bitter, and although he insisted that I drink the same I'd catch him pouring the cheap whisky for me while he had the Bushmills. I was too embarrassed to point it out.

I tried to throw myself into teaching as a way of taking the focus away from the events of the summer. That worked reasonably well at first, but by the second week the standard depression was descending on many of the students. They couldn't understand why everybody else felt so at home. Even during tutorials you could see them close to tears, wondering how they would cope or how they'd tell their parents that they couldn't cope. And I found it difficult to sympathise with half of them, because the GCSE had brought standards down so low I was effectively having to run remedial classes.

I didn't let them go through the usual motions of posing to each other and tried to be one of those inspiring *Dead Poets' Society* teachers who gets to the point, rather than dicking about with books. I'm not sure what good it did them, but they started inviting me to their parties, which was something. I only went to one, because most of the people there were dumbed out on Ecstasy, talking about nothing other than the drugs they'd had last week, the drugs they were taking tonight, and the drugs they were going to buy next time. I'd have preferred predictable conversations about existentialism or David Lynch to that obsession with chemical entertainment.

It was a relief to find a drunk girl, because she wanted to talk about herself rather than substances. She looked only about sixteen but claimed to be at the uni, and as we talked she backed me into a corner by the fridge. She kept tapping her fingers on my chest each time she laughed. Her nose and eyebrows were strung through with piercings. I coped with her predictability until she started saying *I'm completely mad*.

After that I couldn't even bring myself to fuck her and

walked home through the frost, finishing off a can of Boddingtons as I went.

I rang Dave in the morning and he said, 'What do you expect if you try to shag children?'

That pissed me off, because although I was sick of kids I couldn't face a night out discussing mortgages and tax with the uni staff. Give them a chance and they'd all go on about the inevitable trauma of forcing their parents into homes. My few other friends were either set in relationships or had moved to London. It was only natural that I should start thinking about Wendy again. I had difficulty remembering what our relationship had been like before that summer and didn't know if I wanted to be with her again. But I wanted to see her.

When the post arrived I'd check through it for Wendy's handwriting, and when I'd been out I'd listen for her voice on the answering machine. Nothing came through until October, when Linda sent me an envelope of photographs, all taken in the Lakes on the same day. It must have been a week or so earlier, because although the background looked slightly autumnal, the weather was clear and she and Wendy were shielding their eyes from the sun. Most of the photos were of Wendy standing in front of a view, pointing at a sheep or just smiling. In some they'd put the camera on timer, and both were together, holding on to each other. They looked happy, with none of the fear that had plagued us on Skye. It made me angry that we'd been through that misery together and they were having a good time without me.

There was no letter from Wendy, but Linda had included a note telling me about their travels. They were constantly running out of money, and although she'd started divorce proceedings cash flow was a problem. When she'd applied for

Legal Aid, they'd effectively said she couldn't have any because she was married to a rich man. When she stressed that she didn't have access to that money, they'd said it was irrelevant. As far as they were concerned she was loaded. She'd had to borrow from her brother to get things going.

She concluded by changing the subject again, saying, 'You know, away from him Wendy's fine. But she does miss you.' I didn't quite follow her logic but was relieved to hear that I still mattered.

As soon as they'd found somewhere to live Linda invited me down. She would only give me directions once I'd agreed to travel by an elaborate route, taking precautions to make sure Laurence couldn't track me. Wendy spoke occasionally in the background, offering bits of advice about finding the place and reminding me to bring Joey, but when her mum offered her the phone she feigned being busy with something.

'Should I bother?' I asked.

'I think it'll do her good. She doesn't know what to do with herself now we've stopped moving.'

I drove into uni in the morning, taking Joey into the office with me so I could leave straight from the car-park without going home. That way there was less chance of Laurence being able to follow me. I wanted to leave before it went dark, but the weather meant twilight began shortly after lunch, and it was pitch-black by the time I set off. The journey was an awkward one, taking hours longer than I thought it would. I avoided major junctions and took back roads, pausing frequently to read the map. Whenever I came to roundabouts, I had to drive around them until all the cars visible in the rear-view mirror had gone past. It was Linda's idea; something they'd developed on their travels, to make sure they weren't being followed. It felt ridiculous, but I couldn't put anything past Laurence, so I went through the process all the way there. The roads were quiet and there were few streetlights, so it was always easy to see the few vehicles that came up behind me. Each time I circled, it would be nerve-racking waiting for the headlights to approach and resolve into the shape of a car. I kept picturing the Jaguar, wondering what I'd do if it turned up.

She'd said they lived in Ludlow, just this side of the Welsh border, but the house was ten minutes away from town, in the hills. It took me several attempts to find the driveway, because it was an unmarked gravel path that looked like a farm track. At the base of the hill, completely hidden from the road, was a row of four identical houses, brand-new and looking like they'd come out of a box. It was the sort of place Linda and Wendy would normally have sneered at, but it served its purpose. And given their lack of money, it was quite an achievement to have found somewhere so large and well hidden.

Linda checked through the window, waved, then let me in. Once I was inside I put Joey's cage on the floor in the hall and she bolted the door. Wendy was waiting there and hugged me. Her hair smelt as though it had just been dried, but she pulled away and bent down to talk to the budgie, nodding at him as she carried the cage through.

I went to the kitchen with Linda to help make tea, and we talked through the journey and what they'd been up to. The units were lined with bottles of home-made wine and jars of pickles, a hobby they'd started.

'It's not much,' she said, 'but Laurence would never have allowed this sort of stuff in the house.'

'And the divorce?'

'Getting there. Money's a problem, and he's absolutely refusing to cooperate, but I have grounds.' She lowered her voice. 'Getting Wendy to sign an affidavit wasn't easy. But I needed it, not just for the divorce but to get a restraining order if he comes after us again.'

'She did sign, though?'

I could still hear Wendy talking to the budgie, and we spoke quietly, letting the sound of the warming kettle mask our voices.

'She did, but it was a struggle. I put in that stuff about *holiday, holiday, holiday*, and she was livid because he'd get to read it. *He's still my dad*, she'd say.'

'It's difficult.'

'She was never on his side when we lived there,' Linda said, 'and she is staying with me, so she should be helpful.' We heard Wendy coming through, so her mum changed the subject slightly, saying, 'The car's in the garage; the curtains are closed. Even if he turns up on the doorstep he won't know we're in here.'

'Nick's car's visible.'

'I don't think he'll even get near,' Linda said, and I assured them I'd been careful all the way down. Wendy took her brew and gave me a look that meant I should follow her.

She sat in the armchair, lacing her fingers around the cup on her lap. She looked down at my bag, which I was still carrying round with me from room to room.

'You can sleep with me,' she said quietly.

'Oh.'

'Do you mind?' she asked, and although I tried to reassure her that was fine she talked over me, saying, 'Only we haven't set up another bed. We thought you wouldn't mind.'

'It's fine.'

'God,' she said, sounding angry, 'it's not as though you have to fuck me.'

'Wendy.'

She was all right after that, talking more than her mum through dinner, telling me about their trip. She'd shown her mum round the Lakes, taking her up mountains she'd never even seen before. They'd stayed in caravans and tents, and then when it turned cold they'd headed down here for something more permanent. Wendy had given her the wrong directions when they were looking for somewhere to stay, and they'd come down this drive to turn round.

'It was fate,' she said. 'Just what we needed.'

Their wine was nowhere near ready, but they'd bought some cheap stuff in, and we drank until late. The evening was nothing like as desperate as those when we'd been away, but it was pleasant for the three of us to be together again. I could have talked for longer, but Wendy was tired and urged me to follow her up.

She hadn't been able to buy a bed but had a mattress that took up most of the small room. I stripped off without hesitation, to avoid the brief show of false modesty that could make things more exciting. She went to the bathroom and came back wearing a new nightshirt. She got in next to me without touching.

'Why do you and Mum always get so drunk?'

'To spite you,' I said. 'What do you think?'

'Well, I wonder. You make me feel left out.'

'You drink as well.'

'Not half as much as you two. It doesn't agree with me.'

'I can think of loads of times when you drank as much as we did.'

'You're wrong, Nick. I was hardly ever drunk.'

I didn't know what she wanted me to do and didn't want to start denying being drunk, because it would make me sound worse than I was feeling.

'Why does it bother you?'

'I don't have anybody else except you two. And the minute you're together I feel irrelevant.'

'Don't you understand? I'm here for you.'

'Really?'

I nodded, and she went quiet. After a while she said, 'But what am I meant to do now?'

It turned out she'd been planning a foundation course at the local college, but now she was worried about starting there in case she found herself leaving the course again. She didn't want her life to be a process of running away and giving up.

'I thought you enjoyed this summer.'

'But I'm not getting anywhere. I don't want to start anything else unless it's going to last.' She sounded like she needed a good cry, but her voice kept that tension without breaking. 'I don't know what I'm doing here. I always seem to be in places by accident.'

'Then leave. Your mum wouldn't mind.'

She was worried that she had nowhere to go, and then said, 'And I don't know how I feel about you. I miss you all the time; you're all I think about. And then when you're here I get annoyed with you.'

I told her it was the same for me, which made her laugh. I said that it was better to be confused than to know you're going to be an accountant for the next forty years. And if she didn't want to draw any more, so what?

'You mean that?'

'Yes. There's no point in being unhappy. Do something else.'

'I wouldn't know what,' she said, but the thought must have calmed her, because while I waited for her to speak again I heard her breath deepen into sleep.

* * *

In the morning her mum went out before we got up. Wendy said that was more usual these days. Linda was always busy sorting out money and the divorce and couldn't stay locked up in the house.

I wanted to have sex, but I couldn't tell whether it was just the habitual need to come or because I wanted to sleep with Wendy. She considered going along with this, getting as far as holding my cock, and I got to kiss her cheek, but then she said it wasn't a good idea.

'So we are just friends then?'

'I don't know. But I don't have to service you every time you feel the need. Go and have a wank.'

We spent the morning wandering on the land around the houses. Behind the back fence and across a muddy stream there was a derelict mansion set amongst a mass of silver poplar trees. Their leaves were so white they looked like they'd been dipped in icing sugar, and they'd set in the grass that led to the house. Wendy had come this far before but hadn't been inside the mansion because she hadn't wanted to go alone. I'd been in abandoned buildings down by the canal in Leicester, but they were usually full of piss and the smell of burning. This mansion looked undisturbed, being so far from town that it hadn't even been boarded up. Breaking in wasn't necessary, because the front door was unlocked.

The rooms and corridors were much as we'd expected, with no furniture or fittings. The only traces of habitation were the fireplaces, a mixture of wrought iron and painted tiles. The floorboards were smeared with dust, and staples betrayed where carpet had been.

'Imagine what you could do with this place. It's beautiful.'

Looking out, it felt as though we were in a remote part of Scotland, because you couldn't see anything beyond the trees except for glimpses of hillside.

'Did I ever tell you I used to have this fantasy about finding somewhere like this and turning it into a sort of hostel? A place for writers and artists to stay. I think it was just a way to meet girls, really, but I always used to picture this empty building being filled with people.'

Wendy ran her fingers over the fireplace tiles.

'A place like this must be worth a lot.'

'You're sounding like your dad.'

'I don't mean worth money. I mean the space could be used. It could be worth a lot to people. You *could* paint here, there's so much light. Imagine turning it into studios.'

'There must be a reason it's left like this. The roof didn't look all that stable from the outside.'

We couldn't get into all the upstairs rooms, as some had been locked. In other places the floor had fallen through, with only one beam across to the other side, and I wasn't willing to balance my way over. Wendy said that nobody would want to buy a house in this state of disrepair. We could move in and live there unnoticed.

'I'd love a fire,' she said, and I suggested we have one in the house instead.

In the afternoon we went back into the grounds, collecting wood for the fire. It was the sort of day where nothing much happened, but we enjoyed being together, and the thought of eating and lighting a fire was bliss. Linda must have sensed our closeness because she went to bed straight after dinner to read, and we stayed downstairs talking about what we could do with the mansion. I think we were only playing, because we knew there was no water or electricity. But we played the game as though we meant it, planning ways of keeping it to ourselves and expanding it into a massive home.

In the morning I woke Wendy just to say goodbye. She

didn't get up, but waved me back for a hug. She felt so warm
I wished I was staying.

When I next went down Laurence had found them. Wendy
was out, having started an evening life-drawing class, so Linda
got to tell me the details. He'd sworn he wasn't tracking them
but that he simply wanted to buy the house next door,
claiming he'd always wanted to live in this area.

'Can you believe that?'

'I can't believe he tries to convince you. Does he really
think you'll believe him?'

'Half the reason we came to Ludlow is that he hates it
around here. I've been trying to move to this side of
Birmingham for years, but he wouldn't have it.'

'Perhaps that's how he knew to look for you here.'

'He was paying cab drivers, from what I can tell, not just
in Ludlow, but in towns all over the west. They've been
keeping their eye out for my car.'

'Just tell him to fuck off,' I said, and she laughed. 'But
seriously, if you tell him that you don't love him, won't he
give up?'

'It'll take more than that.'

She told me there was a policeman living next door who'd
given her his old wooden cosh and his phone number. He'd
said to bang on the wall if she ever needed help, whether
Laurence was breaking the law or not. When Laurence had
first turned up he'd come straight in, acting as though he was
welcome, putting the kettle on. Since he'd been told about
the policeman he'd kept his visits to the doorstep. But he'd
worn Linda down, refusing to leave until she'd given him her
phone number. 'He said he wouldn't have to come round so
much if he could phone. I jump every time the bloody thing
rings.'

She'd managed to get his address, which made it easier to have an injunction served on him. Technically, he wasn't allowed within a few hundred yards of her.

'He still phones, relentlessly, but he hasn't been round since. One thing I've learnt, he's scared of the police. I thought he'd just ignore them, but he cares what they think. You pissed him off so badly when you called the police to your mum and dad's. I was so proud of you, standing up to him like that.'

'I don't think Wendy would agree.'

'She does, but she doesn't like admitting it.'

We heard the bus on the hill and then saw Wendy coming down the path with a torch. I'd expected her to look drawn and miserable now that Laurence was in the area, but she came into the front room grinning.

'I had a breakthrough,' she said, unfurling her drawings on the floor. She'd changed her technique, focusing on specific areas in detail, but at the same time expanding her peripheral vision within a picture. At first I thought the result was a bit too schizophrenic, but in the last few drawings I could see a definite improvement.

'We're going away for the weekend,' she said abruptly. 'Just in case Dad turns up while you're here. Is that all right?'

I couldn't tell if it was that or the improvement in her drawing that had put her in such a good mood.

We had a choice between Hay-on-Wye and Newtown. I would have preferred to go book-hunting in Hay, but Linda wanted us to meet her friend Tessa. By the time we'd finished breakfast she'd talked us into going to Wales. Wendy was pissed off. She had a blinding headache, probably from getting so little sleep, and she'd rather have stayed at home.

I never got the full story of how Linda knew Tessa, but

they'd been friends since childhood. Linda kept referring to a commune that she ran, and I had this image of a bunch of arty, hippie types hanging around and drinking wine. She said nobody was turned away and nobody paid any rent. How she managed to own the place was a mystery.

'Just about everybody in Newtown has ended up there for a while at some point. It's like therapy.'

She was probably keen on going there because we'd get free accommodation, and none of us wanted to fork out for bed and breakfast. The sky was dull, but all that white light made the trees and roads shiny. The yellowed leaves looked brighter than if it had been sunny, and we drove with the windows down because it was unusually warm.

Arriving in Newtown was the most disappointing part of the journey, because it was a dismal town that looked like it belonged in East Lancs, nestled in a valley of treeless hills. On the brief drive through I got an impression of the sort of place we were dealing with, because half the population looked like travellers, defined by the extreme clichés of dogs on string, fluffy jumpers, dreadlocks, piercings and torn jeans, the sort of people news broadcasters focus on when filming a protest. Newtown was a place where people came when they couldn't get over the Glastonbury festival.

'It's like a uniform,' I said. 'They're fashion victims.'

'Stop sounding so old,' Wendy said, which made me feel stupid.

I've never had anything against alternative lifestyles, except that the few hippies and travellers I'd met seemed to have exactly the same concerns as the miserable middle classes: money, booze and a place to live. They were just as obsessed with belonging to a peer group, obtaining soft drugs and avoiding tax. It didn't strike me as much of an alternative, because they had to work full-time to get their dole, food and

shelter. The few I'd been friendly with when I was younger
had an air of self-importance, because they were nothing to
do with vile capitalist society, even though they'd happily set
up their roadside stall selling cheap oil-lamps and bandannas.
They'd assumed that because I had a flat and a job I did
nothing other than watch TV or fight for a managerial
position. At the time I hadn't even owned a car, and there
they were burning up diesel every day and lighting fires. But
so long as you shit in the woods, you're at peace with the
planet.

'You're so defensive,' Wendy said when I tried to explain
this. 'Dave probably thinks of you in the same way.'

'I don't doubt it,' I said, managing to laugh at myself. 'I've
nothing against them, and I'd let them stay on my land if I
had any. But I just don't think it's the big earth-changing
deal they make it out to be. It looks like a shit life.'

'So we should all have a house and kids and two point five
dogs, should we?'

'I've never been one to advocate normality, have I? I'm
always telling you to do what you want rather than look for
job security. All I'm saying is that this—' I gestured at the
town '—is no different from being middle class. The same
tiny concerns and distractions.'

'Tessa's not like that,' Linda said. 'You'll like her.'

The commune was a set of old farm buildings, vans, caravans,
and even tepees. It was at the end of a track where the hills
lulled, so there was no view. People with bad posture were
ambling around, carrying buckets and wood. Not quite the
wine-sipping artists I'd imagined, and I felt ridiculously dull
for having pictured it that way. Despite what I'd said earlier,
I tried to go into the commune with an open mind. It was
disappointing to see there was no vegetable garden, because

I'd have been excited by the prospect of self-sufficiency, but the bins were overflowing with Safeway bags and food packaging.

Linda asked one of the lads where Tessa was, and he pointed to the main building. It was dark in there and felt so much like a barn I struggled to work out whether it was originally part of the house or the farm. All the walls were stone, and the floor was made of compacted mud.

Tessa shocked me with her matter-of-fact recognition. 'Oh, hello, Linda. Come in.' Linda introduced Wendy and myself, but Tessa just said hello and turned back to her friends. She was bundled up in blankets rather than clothes, the lines in her face made darker by creases of dirt. Her hair was white but matted. The couple she was talking to were both skinny, with shaved heads, looking startled, sitting on the edge of the bench as she gave them counselling.

Linda whispered to us about the place, pointing out that the wooden circle in the floor was the cover for a well, and that was where they got all their water. There was no electricity or gas, so they used wood fires for cooking.

'How many people are here?' I asked.

'Everybody's welcome,' Tessa said, turning to us. The thin couple stared at us as though we were lawyers. 'We've got about thirty people here at the moment. People come and go.'

'It's good to see you,' Linda said.

Tessa led us out, struggling to walk, and took us to her caravan. Inside it smelt of wet sheets, and she sat in her armchair while the three of us crushed up on the edge of her bed. I didn't really know where to look or what to talk about. She made us a cup of tea, and when I said thank you she said, 'Don't thank me. No, no, no,' which annoyed me. Was I really just meant to grab it from her? I knew what Wendy would say, though: it was better to be friendly than polite. I could tell we were going to argue about this place later.

Tessa complained about the stink of Linda's perfume.

'I can barely smell it,' I said.

'It's meant to be there to carry your scent, not to mask it,' Tessa said, as though she was an authority. Linda laughed but said she was sorry, which surprised me. It was like seeing her with a parent.

'I know I wear too much, it's just habit.'

When Tessa asked Wendy what she was doing with her life, she struggled to explain, because she wasn't even sure what she was going to do next. She mentioned the art college.

'Don't waste your time with teachers,' Tessa said. 'They can't teach you anything.'

'But they can guide and advise,' I mumbled.

'Huh?'

'Isn't that what you do for people here as well?'

'Everybody's welcome. We don't force any ideas down people's throats here.'

I wondered about that. I could have let them get on with it all quite happily, without anything other than humorous criticism, but I felt like she was attacking me for being a teacher. Which was a shame, because I liked to think I could contribute something original to people's lives through my work. Just because I was a white middle-class male didn't mean I was irrelevant. But it did mean that whatever my opinion, it would sound like the defence of somebody in a position of extreme privilege. And I didn't want to defend the rat race anyway, because it *was* stressful and dissatisfying, so I just went quiet.

To my relief Tessa complained about being tired and started rolling a joint to help her have an afternoon nap. She said we could stay on the land but she wanted to be on her own.

Once we'd left her, Linda said we'd go to a B&B and that she'd pay. She'd feel guilty making us stay there.

'I don't mind,' Wendy said. 'And I think we'd be welcome.'

'We can stay for the afternoon.'

We spent the rest of the day with most of the others, down by the rope-swing. Where the track turned away from the house, it ran between two deep bankings. A precarious tree with most of its roots on show was the anchor for a long rope-swing. On warm days, this was how they passed their time, taking it in turns to swing off the bank and over the path, sitting around smoking and drinking. They were wary of us at first, probably because of how we were dressed, but encouraged us to have a go. Once we'd all swung out once, they were more relaxed. I got talking to a lad called Ian. It was difficult to tell how old he was, because he had the skin of a teenager but he looked worn out. He asked what we were doing here, where we were going next. While we talked I watched the smooth arc of the rope, then the judder as it snagged. I enjoyed talking to him, although when he got up for his go on the swing I realised that nothing much had been said.

I could see the appeal of this place, just letting time pass and arsing about. If the system fucks you over so rigorously, why not drop out and spend your time having fun?

By the time it went dark I was ready for home. Linda had now opted to drive back to Ludlow rather than stay in the area. On the way back Wendy went on about the commune so much I was worried she wanted to move in.

'And what if I did?'

'Fine. Give up on everything you've ever worked for.'

'Why should I do what you order me to do?'

Linda interjected. 'I think you agree with each other, deep down,' she said.

'But what would you do with yourself?' I asked, trying to sound calm, but it probably came out as patronising. 'Nothing? Or go on the rope-swing all your life?'

'Piss off. What a great socialist you turned out to be.'

'You do realise these aren't poor people? They aren't homeless. Poor people stay in their home town and work until they die.'

'Well, I'd rather live like this than die of hard work.'

'Great,' I said, 'but socialism would never work if everybody went on these extended holidays. One of the most insidious things about capitalism is that it makes people believe the only alternative is to drop out completely.'

'I didn't realise you were such a fan of the Protestant work ethic.'

'Sod off, Wendy. I'm not saying that. I'm just saying that what they're doing is a luxury. I'm not criticising it. If they want to live like this, good for them. But it isn't a pattern for the future. If everybody signed on and sat around, nothing much would get done.'

'It's none of your business what I do,' she said.

'I'm not saying what you should do, just that you'll be unhappy years from now if you haven't found something you enjoy doing.'

'You're just like my dad.'

I knew I must have sounded like him, even though that wasn't what I'd intended. I was trying to encourage her to do what she wanted rather than give up. But I felt bad for pushing her and knew anything else I suggested would make matters worse, so I said, 'I'd just miss you, that's all.'

Chapter Thirteen

It probably wasn't a good idea to go back to Ludlow in November, given the weather, but I was anxious for Wendy to ask me back. Snow had been threatening for days, and the sky had become fat with low grey cloud. The roads were icy, a few stretches of salt-melt giving drivers a false sense of security. Every day I'd see the aftermath of at least two accidents; confused people standing calmly by their cars, the windscreens shattered in the gutter with the broken ice. If the roads had been safe I'd have driven the few hundred yards to uni to avoid the cold. Instead, I'd walk in early, because if I left it until later the streetlights would be out, making it as dark as evening. The university was garish during that month, all the fluorescent lights left on, making it feel like a hospital. I couldn't bring myself to get drunk, because suffering a hangover in that light would have been unbearable. So I was keen to get away, and despite the threat of the weather thought I'd risk the journey across country if she wanted me to go.

Wendy had spent the last two weekends in Newtown, but she'd rung me a couple of times during the week, being upfront about the fact that she'd been seeing a lot of Ian. She'd stayed with Tessa in the caravan but had spent the days with him. The next time she rang, she talked about Ian again.

Nothing had happened, she said, almost inviting me to ask if it would. I let her fill the silence on the phone, and she said that her mum had been complaining about paying the rent on a large house only to have Wendy disappear all the time, so she felt obliged to stay in Ludlow for a while. And it was snowing so much in Wales now she'd have had difficulty getting to the commune anyway, so I could go down if I wanted. I wished she'd been a bit more subtle about showing me how much of an afterthought I was but promised to get there as soon as I could.

The car heater wasn't working well, and I was looking forward to getting inside, sitting in front of the fire and catching up with them, but there were no lights on when I arrived. The snow on the roof and ledges made the windows look black. The house was locked up, but they'd left a note on the door saying they were in Ludlow and that I could either wait or go looking for them. It was incredible they could risk leaving evidence of their whereabouts, trusting that the injunction would keep Laurence away. It was mid-afternoon, but it hadn't got light all day, and I didn't want to sit in my car as it got darker. Besides, the Christmas lights might be on, and it would be good to have a proper look around the town in the snow.

The council had picked the build-up to Christmas as the best time to put in new pipelines, so there were roadworks on every corner, each hole surrounded by orange plastic fencing. That stuff could have been designed to make you feel colder, because it holds drips of water and makes a hissing sound as the air passes through it. A few shops had Christmas lights, but the tree was still being erected in the main square, the wind making the bulbs tinkle as they tapped into each other. There wasn't much snow left, only slush and brown water. It was no wonder Wendy didn't like spending much time there.

I hated the place, because the streets were narrow and crowded, making everybody seem a bit bad-tempered. Even the bookshops were contaminated by stationery departments and magazine racks, so you felt guilty if you went in to browse. The cafés were a place to imbibe quickly, rather than somewhere to read for half an hour. I decided to go back to the house and wait in the car, but met Linda outside the post office. She was heading back to the car and told me I could find Wendy at the DSS, two doors down.

'Run her back if you like.'

'All's well?'

'As far as it could be,' she said. 'But I'm glad you're here.'

Inside the DSS there was the predictable sound of coughing and stray children being told off loudly. It smelt of smoke, just from people's clothes. Wendy was hunched over in a chair and didn't see me, but I was close enough to hear the bloke giving her an interview. He had this way of looking through her forms and pausing as though there was a problem. He'd scratch at his moustache and wince. Dealing with unemployed people was clearly distasteful to him.

'Perhaps you could try another job until the sort of thing you're after comes along,' he said, making eye contact with her. He passed her a box of cards, each with a job that might be of interest.

Everybody should be made unemployed at some time, to know what it's like having those smug fuckers make you flick through that box of cards, which describe jobs that range from toilet-cleaner to box-lifter.

At the next desk there was an old man who looked like he should have been retired, explaining that he'd done a few hours' work this week. He looked proud, as though he might even be rewarded, but the woman asked him a few questions and pointed out that he'd lost his entitlement to benefit that week. She went through the figures with him, but he was confused.

'So I'm no better off?'

'I'm sorry.'

'I might as well have stayed at home,' he said, sounding like he was about to cry.

Instead of responding to this, she again explained the rule about how many hours he was allowed to work. I couldn't bear to watch, so it was a relief when Wendy came over. She was so wrapped up in anger she didn't seem to realise this was the first time she'd seen me in weeks and talked as though we'd already spent the morning together. It was only when I said I'd drive her home that it seemed to dawn on her, and she asked about the journey down.

It was darker, and I tried to work out what time it was. As we walked past the school the kids were outside on their break. Most of the snow around them remained untouched, and they stood in groups, talking. One lad, on his own, was playing with a Gameboy, his eyes unblinking and his mouth slightly open. I wanted to chuck a snowball at him, to give him the idea, but Wendy put me off by telling me about her plans.

'I've just been stagnating, waiting for something to happen. Signing on frees me up in a way. I'll have more time to paint, and I can build things up on my own.'

'So you definitely want to do it?'

'I have to do something. And the truth is I was always happiest when we went away, just drawing and messing about. I know it's what I want to do. I just don't want to go to college or anything.'

'What brought this on?' I said, trying to sound proud of her but worrying what the isolation might do to her.

'Being at Mum's is driving me mad. I need something to happen.'

* * *

I was forced to stay beyond the weekend, because the snow fell so deeply on that first night. I couldn't get my car up the hill, and even if I'd managed to we were still two miles from the cleared roads.

The days were dull, but the sky would clear at night, moonlight making the snow bright. It was beautiful, and at first I quite enjoyed the excitement of being trapped; it reminded me of the feeling when school was cancelled because of floods.

Laurence rang on the second night, when we were beginning to grow tired of each other. We hadn't been outside, even for a snowball fight, and the house was too hot because Linda kept a fire burning at all times. Having so few possessions with them, we had no new books to read and no games to play. They'd deliberately not bought a TV, but in that situation we began to regret it. Sometimes we'd split into separate rooms, but the house was so small we all wanted to be in the living-room. We were sitting in there silently when the phone rang. We both looked at Linda.

'Tell him I'm out,' she said to Wendy.

'I'm not answering.'

Linda got up and answered, rolled her eyes, then sat under the stairs leaning against the wall. She didn't get to speak much during the conversation, and occasionally held the receiver out for us to listen to him rambling on.

'Whatever,' she said, then, 'I'm not being rude. Yes, yes, I know that's what you think. No. No, he hasn't. It's none of your business anyway. Look, Laurence, I want to get off the phone. Will you listen to me, please? Laurence.' She put the phone down and came back to sit with us.

'What did he want?'

'The usual. Forgiveness.'

About five minutes later – it can only have been that long, though it felt like ten – I asked to borrow the phone. I wanted to ring Mum and Dad, for something to do as much as anything. There was a sound on the line, like breathing, and then I heard Laurence speaking.

'You see, it's no good having all these opinions about me if you're not willing to give me a chance.' It took me a few seconds to realise he was unaware that Linda had put the phone down on him. He'd clearly never questioned her or sought a response but had kept talking. I put the phone down, and I must have slammed it because they both looked over.

'He's still there,' I said.

'What?'

'He doesn't realise you've gone. He's still talking.'

Wendy was twisting her mouth, thinking, and I could tell she didn't really believe me. Linda went back to the phone and listened.

'I don't believe this,' she said, then to him. 'Laurence, I want to use the phone to call somebody else.'

I had visions of him keeping the line open, unafraid of the cost, to prevent her phone from working. He'd know we couldn't get to a phone box.

'Let me have a word,' I said, feeling relatively safe letting him know I was there, given the snow and the restraining order, but Linda just put the phone down.

It barely came light, which would have been bearable, except that on the next night there was a power cut. Presumably the snow had weighed down the lines somewhere nearby, because the phone was dead as well. With no candles, we had to rely on the light from the fire. Joey was almost silent, rarely moving, and I wondered if it was the dark or the quiet that was making him so still. We went to bed early, not bothering to brush our teeth, feeling our way upstairs and settling in quickly. In the morning we woke while it was dark and the electric was still off. We moved food out of the fridge and into the snowdrift under the front window. With the fire relit we managed to keep warm, and boiled pans of water for tea and fried eggs for lunch.

When the wood and coal ran low that afternoon we had to go out in the grounds of the mansion, digging through the snow for wet branches. They'd provide more smoke than heat, but at least we felt we were doing something.

I wanted a bath, but there was no hot water so I went up to our room and lay on the mattress. It occurred to me for the first time that I was feeling worse than I should, and things were upsetting me more than usual. I'd been obsessing about that bloke at the DSS, worrying what *he* was going through this week. And there had been a few times when Wendy made me feel so sad; not because she was upset, but because she was trying to hope. She'd talk about some plan or other, but that was worse than if she'd just curled up and cried. I desperately wanted to talk to Dave, because if ever I'd shown signs of depression he'd usually joke me out of the mood. This was starting to feel less like a passing mood and more like a way of being.

That evening, with the lights still out, Wendy called us through to the bathroom window. From there we could see a room in the mansion that appeared to be lit up. Until then we hadn't realised you could even see the mansion from the house, because the trees hid it so well. But the moonlight on the snow made its ledges and roofs clear, the windows showing up as black space – apart from one. There was no movement inside, but a steady glow.

We entertained the idea that Laurence had trekked through the snow and set up a squat there in order to keep watch, but none of us believed it. I thought it was probably just a reflection on the glass. We wanted to look, but Linda was complaining about a headache so we went without her.

It felt lighter outside than it had indoors because of the snow, but once we got inside the mansion we couldn't see anything. I edged my way up to the first door and opened it, reflected moonlight coming through the window and into the hall. By doing that we were able gradually to work our way to the stairs, lighting the place as we went.

From the upstairs corridor we managed to work out that the illuminated room was one of those beyond the hole in the floor. If one of us fell trying to cross the gap, getting to a hospital might be impossible in this weather, but we couldn't face going back yet. Wendy went first, tiptoeing across the beam, trusting it to hold her. I followed, glad that the drop beneath was difficult to see.

Wendy pointed to the end of the corridor, where light was coming from under the door. We made our way there carefully, and she said, 'Should we knock?'

She tapped once, then opened the door and freezing air came through. The roof had caved in, its remnants piled on the floor covered in snow. One half of the room was deep with snow, drifted against the far walls. Icicles had formed an inverted crown around the hole, and ice had welded to the window. The room was so bright because the moon was directly overhead.

Wendy said she was cold and put her arms around me.

'I wish it was just us,' she said. 'In the house.'

She put her head into my neck. I knew I should have been feeling more, but although I was pleased by the contact I felt weary. I hardly dared let my feelings for Wendy surface, fearing that she'd disappear again.

'We could light a fire in here,' I said. 'Not this room, but we could stay in the mansion, make some space for ourselves.'

'I would. But Mum wouldn't be very happy if we left her there.'

We were running out of fresh food, so we ate pitta bread, pickled onions and chestnuts cooked in the fire. I had no clean clothes left, and we'd been unable to wash much, each using a pan full of warm water in the morning. Without a radio, we had no way of knowing when the weather was likely to change. Linda trudged round to the other houses, but next door had apparently been trapped elsewhere, unable to make it home. The other house was still for sale, and at the end were an old couple who didn't even have a spare torch to lend us. We started talking about the prospect of wading through the snow into Ludlow. The roads would be clear there. We could stay in a B&B, buy food, go to the pub.

In the night we were woken by the power coming back on, the lights in most rooms having being left on. We got up to make sure the cooker was off, closed the fridge, and put the water heater on. I checked the phone and heard a dial tone. It was raining, and we struggled to sleep, excited at the prospect of getting out in the morning.

When I got up all of the snow had gone. There were huge puddles but no floods, and it was surprising how green everywhere looked considering it was winter; every patch of moss, pine and grass was vivid. Once I'd rung the staff room answering machine to explain my absence, I was able to have a bath. For the first time in ages I thought about inviting Wendy back with me. If Linda didn't mind, it would be good for her to see the flat again and for us to spend time together on familiar ground.

Wendy asked me to run her to the station because she wanted to go back to Newtown.

'It'll be foul out there.'

'I'm going whether you run me or not, so please help.'

'Can't your mum run you?'

'She doesn't like me spending so much time there. She's jealous because she has such a tiny life.'

I asked her what the rush was, why she couldn't spend a day or two going out with her mum, but she said she was sick of being trapped here.

When Linda came through, having made us all a cup of tea, she didn't sound as angry as Wendy had implied. But she made sure I found out that Ian had rung while I'd been in the bath.

'So lover boy clicks his fingers and you go running.'

'Don't be so pathetic.'

The strange thing is that once I knew she was that keen to go, I wanted to get it over with. I said I was going in five minutes, hoping that would be too quick for her, but she'd already packed her bags.

I remember waving over my shoulder as I drove around the station, trying to see her on the platform, but she had her back to me and she was running her finger down the timetable. By the time I made it on to the M54, it seemed like only a few minutes had passed since I'd been lying in the bath, imagining her coming home with me.

The time I spent with Dave wasn't helpful. He came round to my flat, where I'd been festering with my thoughts and indulging my angst, and encouraged me to discuss Wendy.

'So what does she do over there?' he asked.

'Makes tea, collects wood, smokes dope. And probably fucks that bastard Ian.'

The trouble with Dave is that he was persistent about relationships. Even when they were clearly on their last legs, he'd never suggest leaving somebody but would work out a plan for reconciliation. So he developed this ridiculous idea about me driving over there and doing something about it. He thought I should take balloons and presents and woo her that way. I called him a prick, but the more I disagreed the more outrageous his details became. In a way I wanted to be told to forget it, to move on. I'd been through enough and wasn't getting anything in return.

'Summer made sense,' I said. 'Because of what was happening, there was no question about us looking after each other. Since then we haven't known what to do. She's close to me one minute then buggering off the next.'

'Do you still love her?'

'I must do, even if I don't feel it much any more.'

Wendy never rang directly, because she was short of money, but Linda passed on her messages. She was going back to Ludlow in a week's time, to sign on, arriving Friday morning, so I could go for the weekend. It seemed like such a familiar situation that the idea bored me. She would be distant, nothing much would happen and I couldn't really see the point. I was sick of being friends with her because it wasn't much of a friendship.

'Take her to yours if you want,' Linda said, 'or just go somewhere together.'

'Are you worried about her?'

'Only that she doesn't seem happy. She's relying on that place, but God knows what for.'

'Ian, probably.'

'I don't think so. She's just using him as a way of belonging there.'

She was proved wrong that Friday. All the way there I was dreading the weekend, and when I arrived Linda had obviously been crying. Wendy had stayed in Newtown and was signing on there. With no reason to come back she was going to avoid Ludlow from now on.

'She's not coming back at all?'

'She's getting a van with Ian.'

'A van? She couldn't cope in this place. How will she cope in a van?'

'I'm so worried about her, Nick. She says it's to do with her dad. She can't stand the fact that he could turn up here at any minute. But it doesn't make sense. He hasn't been here for weeks. And she always sounded like she was on his side anyway.'

I was shaking, heat passing over my skin as though I was going to be sick.

'And you've come all this way. I'm so sorry. She didn't ring until an hour ago. I shouted at her.'

'Did she know I was coming?'

'I think she's upset. She put the phone down on me when I told her you were on your way.'

I rang my answering machine in the hope that Wendy had left a message that would help me decide what to do. There were a few messages from Linda, hoping I hadn't set off yet, but nothing else.

Linda said I could stay if I didn't want to drive back. She'd already cooked, so there was no problem. I didn't really want to stay, knowing we'd talk about nothing other than Wendy, but I couldn't face being on my own. She opened the wine they'd made and poured me a glass. They'd been planning to open the first bottle together, but she said Wendy had nobody to blame but herself.

I sat in the big armchair while Linda sat on the floor. She'd managed to get a huge bundle of red roses from the market, dirt cheap, and was cutting and crushing the stems. The newspaper she worked on grew wet with sap, and the room began to smell green.

Talking to Linda was the first real chance I had to get everything out of my system. As usual, we went over all the events of the summer and we talked about the past. A few times I mentioned the occasions when I'd first been round to their house, saying it was hard to believe what had gone on since. When I'd first met her, she was just another girlfriend's mum, and it was incredible that we should have gone through all this together. And as I became drunk I started talking about myself. I told her my hopes, how I'd always believed there would be one person, how I thought it had been Wendy but now knew I had to keep looking. Linda went quiet as I talked, giving me long stares as she put the roses into the water. She told me more about Laurence, and how he'd always told her that they were meant to be together. He'd said it so often in the early days she'd almost believed it.

I don't remember ever thinking that I wanted to fuck her, only knowing that I intended to. It wasn't that I particularly wanted her, but I loved the thought of Laurence being a few miles away, still hoping and wishing to get her back. Somewhere in the middle of that conversation I began to drop hints that I wanted to get her into bed. When she went to the toilet I felt my face: it was hot.

And then when we were talking about the summer again, I said I wanted to go away. I hadn't felt the same since we'd been travelling.

'I don't think Wendy wants to move anywhere now,' Linda said.

'We could go without her.'

'Be careful,' she said, and as she lifted her wine glass I could see she was shaking. Part of me hated her for that, for being so obviously excited by me. I considered going to bed on my own, but instead we kept talking.

It was after three in the morning when I finally said I was going to bed. I was drunk enough to say, 'I'll go on my own, but it wouldn't seem honest after everything that's happened.'

'I want to,' she said, 'but I just can't.'

'Well, you know where I am.'

She came into Wendy's room about ten minutes later and sat next to me on the mattress. I was in a state of half-sleep but unable to drop off because of a raging hard-on. She got under the sheets with her clothes on and, without saying anything, undressed, trying to keep out of sight. I said something about her being shy.

'My stomach's horrible,' she said. 'Never get pregnant.' She laughed for the first time in hours, and as her top came off I caught a glimpse of her breasts. I was amazed at how wrinkled they were, with massive brown nipples the size of fruit pastels. She smelt strange, a mixture of rose sap and perfume, and a faint odour like piss and talcum powder.

While we were kissing, I felt bad for finding her so disgusting. I've always believed that people can age beautifully and am thrilled by the phrase *pensioner sex*, but there was something cloying and desperate about her. It wasn't her body, but the fact that she was so amazed by mine. She kept me going by grabbing my dick and pulling at it vigorously. When she wrapped her thighs around my legs I could feel how wet she was.

It was one of the only times I've pictured a man while

having sex. I was saying *fuck you* over and over, imagining his face, wishing he could see me.

Linda came in about a minute, her eyes and mouth tight. Then she hugged me into her, telling me not to go.

'Did you come?' she asked, gasping.

I said no, but that it didn't matter, finding it hard to believe anybody would come in a minute.

'Do you want me to finish you off?'

'No, really,' I said, pulling away and leaving the room.

Sitting on the toilet, sweating, my groin itching and stinking of cunt, I thought of Wendy for the first time. I felt like I should have been crying and kept whispering, 'How could you do that?' – but I didn't know whether I was referring to Linda or myself.

Chapter Fourteen

Linda didn't want to stay in the house and talked me into going south with her. She'd been planning a weekend in Devon for a while, so by the time I got out of the shower she'd booked a place for us to stay. Cottages were almost free at this time of year, she said. I told her I'd have to be back at work on Monday afternoon, and she said, 'I'd better enjoy you while I can.'

On the journey down, sunlight came through tall hedges and dazzled on the grimy windscreen coating we'd picked up on the M5. The roads in Devon were sunk into the ground, so it was like driving down a winding soil tube. When we arrived at the coast it was going dark, the sea black and a wire of sunset on the horizon. I remember those details and the shape of the cliff road down to our cottage, but I can't remember what we talked about. I felt like I was playing a part, pretending to be me-with-an-older-woman rather than actually experiencing it.

The cottage smelt like a launderette, only colder, and over the echo of our breathing we could hear the sea. Our upstairs bedroom was square, with no furniture except the bed. We didn't get much sleep until the morning, because she wanted to have sex all night. She left the dim light on, and when I tried to sleep she sucked me until I was erect again. When she finally turned out the light, morning was brightening the curtains. It took another hour for me to get to sleep.

When I woke up, Linda was staring at me. She kissed my forehead and reached for me, but I got up to open the curtains, wishing she couldn't see me naked. It was pouring down, and she used that as an excuse to keep me inside, telling me to get back in bed so she could bring me a late breakfast. Once we'd eaten she started feeling me again. During the next shag I managed to come at the same time as her. She said *well done* as though sex was meant to be so brief.

After that we spent forty minutes trying to get the bath hot, using boiled kettles to top up cool water from the tank. It was never warm enough to be comfortable, but we both managed to get clean. She wouldn't let me go in to brush my teeth until she'd done her make-up, even though I said I didn't mind. We had a discussion that could have turned into an argument.

'I've never let anyone see me without make-up, not even Laurence.'

'Then do it for me.'

She looked younger without it, in some ways, but greasy and pale.

'There,' I said, 'much better.'

She stayed like that only for ten minutes, saying she felt naked, and then went to put it on again.

We drove out that afternoon, intending to do the tourist things, but it was going dark by the time we arrived at the abbey. I think we talked about Wendy a lot, as though by referring to her emotional state we were proving that we cared. It didn't matter that we were fucking behind her back, so long as we showed that we were worried about her. I could cope when Linda was there, but the few times I was alone –

in the toilet or the bath – I felt a sadness so intense I had to distract myself by whistling or singing at a whisper.

Being with Linda brought out a strange personality trait in me, in that I joked more than usual, making weak puns, going for laughs at every opportunity. At one point, when she asked me to do something, I said 'Yes, Mum,' and that became a constant game, me calling her Mum and pretending to be a boy. I found it difficult to break out of character, except when I was screwing her. In the past, grabbing and hair-pulling was usually done with trust and had never felt violent. With Linda I was having to stop myself from slapping her, and it was the knowledge that I wanted to that made me able to come as quickly as she did. It was on the next afternoon, when we came back from the shops, that it possibly went too far. I was pushing my mouth so hard on hers that her lip stuck to mine, leaving a red pin of blood across her mouth. It spread over her teeth as she came.

Later, she confessed that she'd wanted me since we'd left for Skye.

'In that graveyard I couldn't take my eyes of you.'

'Really?'

'I masturbated like mad, picturing you taking me against the church wall.'

'I never heard a thing.'

'After all that time with Laurence I've learnt to come quietly.'

'Fuck.'

'Don't you remember me touching your back?'

'Yes. But it just didn't sink in at the time. I thought that was because we were all so close.'

'My other hand was between my legs.'

I tried to remind myself that she'd just been fantasising,

which was probably common enough amongst parents. If I had sons I knew I'd imagine what it was like sleeping with their girlfriends. Which was harmless enough. I just hoped she hadn't been intending to do anything about it until recently. If she'd been hoping for that all these months, I'd feel as though I'd been tricked.

We went out for food, making do with a Chinese from Dartington. The last five miles back to our cottage were filled with the stiffest fog I'd known. It felt like the banked roads had collected the mist, thickening it. Most of the time I had to look down to the left, judging how far we were from the road edge, speaking urgent instructions to Linda. At times there was only the muted beam of headlights suffused through the air, and with no sense of speed or direction it felt as though we were motionless.

Not daring to drive down the stone-lined path to the cottage, we parked under the lamp and chose to walk.

'I'll phone Dave before we go back,' I said.

The phone box, an old red one with more metal than glass, was lit by a bulb as dim as a worn-out torch. Linda folded her arms and paced up and down outside.

'Dave, it's me.'

'Are you all right?'

After a brief hesitation I said, 'Sort of.' He must have detected something in my voice, otherwise he'd be asking where I was, what we'd been up to, whether or not I was having a good time.

'What's happened?' he asked.

'Nothing's happened. I'm in Devon.'

As Linda walked backwards and forwards she disappeared into the fog, then fused out of the haze, turning to vanish again.

'Things are getting pretty fucked up. I feel like I'm homesick.'

'You're missing me,' he joked. My breathing came in difficult bursts, because I was almost crying. What he'd said was true, and it felt like the first kind thing he'd said to me in weeks.

My 50p had gone already, and the beeps were punctuated by a whirring sound in the coin box, and fragments of Dave's voice. The last 10p I had was rejected each time it went in.

'I'll be gone in a minute,' I said, but partway through the line clicked and I wished I'd given him the number.

I asked Linda to give me more change, and she headed off to the pub to get some. With the coins she'd given me I rang my answering machine. I had to listen to Linda's messages again, then some from Dave, then Mum, and at the end Wendy spoke. 'I'm at Mum's but she isn't here. I thought you were meant to be with her. Can you call me?' There were three other messages like that, and on the last one she said she'd be going back to Newtown on Monday morning if I didn't call first.

When Linda got back I was panicking, saying that she'd probably seen my car in the garage, but Linda insisted she had the only key. I felt dreadful, knowing she'd come back to see me. I also felt incredibly relieved that we'd left before she arrived, and pictured what could have happened if she'd found us in bed.

I rang her up and she answered after about five rings.

'Hi,' I said. 'How are you?'

'Thank God it's you. I've had Dad ringing up every few hours. Where are you?'

'I'm in Wiltshire with some friends. We've been driving around the stone circles. It's beautiful at this time of year. Are you all right?'

'Mum's not here.'

'Oh, right.'

'She said you were coming for the weekend.'

'I did, but when you weren't there I left. I wish I was there. She said you weren't coming.'

'Are you with Mum?'

'No, I'm with friends.'

'Because I wouldn't mind if you were, if you just told me.'

'No, honestly. I'm here with friends. I don't know where your mum's gone.'

'Which friends?'

'People from uni. Your mum didn't say what she was going to do. I imagine she wanted to get away, seeing as you weren't coming back.'

'Can you hear Joey? He was freezing to death when I arrived. Mum must have gone away for a while because she's left a pile of food for him.'

I told her my money was running out, and she asked for the phone number. As quickly as I could I said, 'I'll come round tomorrow on my way home,' then put down the phone to make it sound like I'd been cut off.

When we walked back to the cottage, the fog had blended with whatever light there was in the area, but it didn't make it much easier to see than walking in the dark, so we felt our way back slowly. By the time we got in I was exhausted, so we went to bed and slept without speaking.

We had to make a plan in order to keep the secret, but I didn't like the way Linda seemed to relish the idea. It was as though we were still playing games with Laurence. The idea was for her to drop me near the house, and I'd hide in the trees across the road. She'd take Wendy out for half an hour, and as soon as I saw the car leave I'd unlock the garage, back my car out and sit there waiting for them to get back. Linda made up a story about where she'd been, but said it was best not to tell me for the sake of realism.

It was more difficult than we'd imagined, because I had to unload all my stuff in a few seconds. It fitted into one bag, but with a coat as well I felt conspicuous as I went into the trees. We had to be close enough to the house for me to see the drive, but that was frightening in case Wendy saw me.

I was beginning to worry that Wendy was refusing to leave, when I saw the car turn out. I could see both of them and knew it was safe to go down. I was still nervous but felt pleased to have seen the outline of Wendy's head.

When they came back later Wendy smiled, and I managed to hold eye contact. She was wearing a dress I'd never seen her in; hundreds of yellow and red flowers, the sort of thing you'd go to a club in.

'I thought you'd be wearing fluffy jumpers by now.'

'Very funny.'

In order to keep her suspicions low I called in sick to work so I could stay a few more days. It wasn't something I really approved of, but close to Christmas nobody was turning up anyway, and I'd never have made it back in time for Monday's tutorial.

Wendy never asked about my trip or what I'd been up to, but in the evening she said she wanted me to go upstairs with her.

'What about your mum?'

'She won't mind. She's cooking.'

I still couldn't tell what she wanted, but when she sat on the mattress and waved me towards her, I said, 'What about Ian?' She shrugged and smiled, so I said, 'Aren't you going out with him?'

'I can't look at you without thinking of sex.'

I lay beside her and pulled up her dress. I hadn't wanked
her off for years, and that seemed like the best compromise.
I didn't get to kiss her mouth, only her cheek, which upset
me a bit. Linda came up the stairs slowly, just as Wendy
reached her orgasm.

'Food's ready,' she said.

'Right,' I called, trying to make it sound as though nothing
was happening.

'I can't believe I did that,' Wendy said, pulling her dress
down and looking disappointed. 'Poor Ian. But it was lovely.'

Linda was so bad-tempered during the meal, slopping food
on to plates and making snide comments, that I began to
think she might let it all slip. When it was time for her to go
to bed, she asked Wendy to go with her. She claimed to be
feeling unwell and wanted the company. Wendy asked if I
minded, but I left a long enough pause before answering that
she said, 'You can come in with us if you want.'

I was annoyed at Linda's engineering of this but excited by
the thought of her wanting me that badly. If I hadn't been
worked up by touching Wendy, I'd probably have kept away.
Linda made sure she slept on the side of the bed next to the
open floor, and Wendy didn't seem to mind going against the
wall, because I think she felt guilty about what we'd done
earlier, possibly because of her thoughts for Ian.

When I told Dave this story, I implied that Linda reached
out for me first, but the truth is that once Wendy's breathing
deepened I was the one who reached under the covers. Her
legs were already open and her cunt spread. I hadn't even
washed my hand since it had been up her daughter. She
turned on her front, trapping my arm but reaching down for
my cock, gripping it like she was arm-wrestling. Her
movements remained silent.

She turned slowly to present her arse, and I risked kneeling up. Wendy was facing away from me. If she turned round I could just get up, or pretend she'd been having a nightmare. I pushed my dick into Linda from behind, but watched Wendy. The guilt hit me at the onset of orgasm, and I pulled out, coming on Linda's backside, lying down quickly. I tried willing myself to sleep, but had to listen for the next few minutes to the wet clicking of Linda bringing herself off.

While Wendy was in the shower I told Linda that that was it, I couldn't do it any more. Over the noise of the water we started arguing, and at the top of her voice she said, 'I *love* you.'

'Don't be so ridiculous.'

That was the wrong thing to say, because she pointed at the bathroom, saying, 'Do you want me to let her know? Do you?'

'If you do I'll kill you. You'll fuck up your own daughter's life for the sake of sex. How dare you? We made a mistake.'

'I can't cope,' she said, 'with you two carrying on like that.' But I could see that she was backing off.

'Don't say anything. What Wendy and I have matters. Think about what you're condemning her to if you spoil that.'

I spoke forcefully out of fear rather than conviction, but somehow we both managed to look normal when Wendy came out.

In the afternoon we went to Shrewsbury. Linda was buying some more things for the house, and Wendy wanted a mirror. I took that as a sign that she might be coming to Ludlow more often. It was shocking that we could carry on so normally, but I was glad.

Laurence walked up to us outside Woolworths and stopped us going any further. He looked smaller than usual, hunched over, and his face was blue with cold. His eyes were so deeply set he didn't seem to have been getting much sleep.

'Still the three of you, eh?'

'Laurence, you're not meant to be here.'

'I've had enough, Linda. I don't care what I'm meant to do. I'm getting sick of this. Now, I want you back. I'm not going to have you insulting me like this.'

'Dad,' Wendy said, but she couldn't look at him.

'And you're being no help,' he said. Then he came towards me, raising a finger and pushing his mouth close to my face. 'I've had enough of you, Nick. Eh?'

I couldn't speak but put a hand up to make him back off. He stepped towards me, and I thought it would be so easy to knock him over if I didn't feel so weak. Wendy moved away from us, and we all looked round to see that she was stopping a policewoman. It was such bliss to see the look on Laurence's face. We could hear Wendy mentioning the injunction.

'See, even your own daughter's scared of you.'

He tried switching to his smiling persona, but it didn't last, because the WPC came straight over.

'Is this correct?' she asked Linda, and we quickly established the facts.

'If you don't leave I'll have to arrest you.'

Laurence shuffled about, a sort of wince making his teeth visible.

'I'll be seeing you, Nick,' he said, taking another step towards me.

'Fuck off.'

'Right, that's enough,' the policewoman said, pointing for Laurence to move on. She watched until he was almost out of sight.

We went through the details with her, and once she'd established that we were all right, she moved on. Which left us realising that Laurence could be watching from anywhere. If we stayed in public it might not be so bad, but I didn't like the idea of him following us to the car-park. We considered splitting up, Wendy and myself waiting on the main road for Linda to bring the car. But then we realised how stupid that was. When you see horror movies, people always split up to find the monster, and you think it's ridiculous. It's incredible how easily you can make decisions like that when you're under pressure.

There was no problem at the car-park, but we locked the doors as soon as we were in the car, and I felt more jumpy than I had since Skye. I kept imagining the Jaguar driving out in front of us, or Laurence standing in front of the car. I spent more time visualising these scenarios than I did looking for him.

It was getting on for four o'clock by the time we made it to Ludlow, which meant that it was dark and Laurence could be hiding nearby. We drove up and down, trying to decide the best course of action. Wendy volunteered for me to run to the front door while they shone the headlights on it. I'd then go in, put the lights on and they could join me. That way, if he turned up we'd have a chance to alert the policeman next door. It went remarkably smoothly, probably because Laurence had been scared off, and we were frightening ourselves for no reason.

Linda thought the best way of dealing with her mood was to have a party, bringing out wine to have with dinner. Wendy and I cooked, and we talked seriously, making it clear that each time Linda came in she was being a distraction.

We went to bed early, and Wendy put her new mirror on the floor, leaning it against the wall so we could watch ourselves making love. She wanted me to take her from behind. She'd never come that way before, but with the mirror there we were able to see each other's face. We made so much noise that just before we finished, Linda slammed her bedroom door.

'I'm coming,' Wendy said. In all the years we'd been having sex, she'd never said that, and the words helped me to finish.

Linda carried on banging around afterwards, and we tried to work out what could be wrong.

'Perhaps we're just keeping her awake,' Wendy said.

'Do you think she's jealous?' I asked, hoping that if I stated the obvious it would seem less likely.

'She's just going barmy.'

Wendy kissed me after that, not for long, but it was the sort of kiss that meant she wanted more from me than sex.

Linda had gone when we got up for breakfast, and when she came back she looked tired. She was carrying a case and two shoulder bags.

'What's going on?' Wendy asked, and I think we were both worried she was bringing Laurence's stuff into the house.

'Don't worry. I'm coming back.'

'We didn't know you'd left.'

She sat down and told us the story.

'I don't know what was wrong with me,' she said, 'but I'd had enough. After what happened, I was just sick of it. So this morning I got up before it was light, packed and went back to him. I drove up to that farmhouse he's got, and thought I'd surprise him for a change. It was about six o'clock when I arrived but he was already up, sitting in the kitchen with the light on. I switched the car off and crept up to the window. He was tapping away at a calculator, this look of obsessive concentration on his face. That was it. I knew I couldn't go back. Not for anything.'

I couldn't tell how much Wendy picked up, but it's possible

she detected something between Linda and myself, because her mood deteriorated. It wasn't particularly noticeable, but there wasn't the same pleasure there had been on other days.

That evening when I thought Wendy was in the bath I went in and found her on the toilet. She'd never been bothered before, even by that, so I was surprised when she screamed at me to get out.

'Don't I have any privacy?' she yelled through the door.

Later, she wanted me to hold her, and we lay on the mattress. I'd got past the point of needing apologies from her and just wanted her to feel better. The strange thing is that as her mood improved, mine became worse. The more hopeful she sounded, the more doubtful I became, because her plans involved us. It could never work now, because I'd always be holding something back. There would always be a lie between us, and a chance of being found out. While she loved me it was fake, because she didn't know who I was.

'We could go away.'

'What for? We're not getting anywhere.'

She didn't have enough enthusiasm for us to argue much, and nothing was resolved by the time I left.

We spoke a few times over the next few weeks and sent Christmas cards, but her plan to come to Leicester was swapped in preference for another visit to Newtown. When we next spoke I said I was losing interest.

'There's always a problem. Something going wrong. Life doesn't have to be that complicated. I love you, but it's too difficult.'

At the time she said she understood.

I spent Christmas afternoon with Caryn. She'd come back to Leicester to see her parents, but they were 'entertaining', as she put it, which made the house unbearable. I wasn't going to Dave's until the evening, so it seemed logical for us to be together. We both felt a bit sorry for ourselves, knowing we were together because we had nobody else. We felt this obligation to go out, so went looking for a pub. I'd never been to a pub on Christmas Day before, so I hadn't realised they only open for meals. At that point in the afternoon most were locked up with no lights on. We eventually found one in Oadby, the door open and people sitting at the bar. When we went in they told us they were closed, that this was a family occasion, but the landlady must have seen how miserable we looked. She set up a table for us and brought champagne and peanuts.

'We must look so lost,' Caryn said.

We left when we'd finished our drinks, but neither of us wanted to go home, so we parked in a lay-by opposite Bradgate Park. There were a few kids trying out new bikes, the odd family going out in their matching Gortex coats.

It was while we were there that the subject of New Year came up.

'Spend it with us,' Caryn said. 'We're having a party in London.'

'I can't be responsible for her, can I?'

It was so quiet in the car, so blue outside. It made me feel hopeful, but I couldn't say why. Although the place and the sensations were familiar – a cold, blue day – being with Caryn felt new. It made me think life could go on. I'd had enough, not because it was too much, but because there was life beyond the events of that year. Moments don't have to poison you for ever. You can let go of them.

I explained this to Wendy over the phone on Boxing Day, but she said, 'That doesn't mean you have to let go of me.'

She begged me to go with her and her mum for New Year. They were going to head for Skye, if the roads were clear enough. She even put Linda on in an attempt to convince me.

I kept thinking of that moment in the car with Caryn, when I'd felt that things could change, and couldn't bring myself to go with them.

'If you don't come, that's it,' Wendy said.

'Don't threaten me.'

'Please, Nick.' She said nothing else for a while, then, 'Please.'

I wanted to end the phone call, and when she eventually put down the phone all I felt was relief.

Part Two

Chapter Fifteen

The drive up to his parents' house took longer than usual, because it was close to Christmas and the roads were busy. They'd planned to get there before dark, but the clouds turned blue earlier than expected. Crossing into Lancashire, where the lighting vanished from the M6, the rain became heavier. To the left of the motorway the ground fell away to the vast black field of West Lancs, patterned with sparse towns. The Mazda's heater wasn't working, so the windscreen was smeared with breath which glared in the oncoming headlights. Sarah was quiet, staring out of the side window. She had turned the radio down so low he couldn't hear it over the weather.

Nick was edgy, because when he'd first brought Sarah here the year before, he'd told her a story that had happened on the M6. He'd realised the story wasn't going well when he'd reached the humorous part and gained no response. Laughing to prompt her, he'd glanced across, but she'd looked at him as though she was disgusted, her eyes watering. It had been the first indication that talking about his past might be a problem. Instead of asserting his right to talk about it, he'd apologised to Sarah for upsetting her. He could have reacted differently, but it was the first time he'd taken her to see his parents, and he'd wanted her to be calm.

Thinking about that journey made him overcautious on

this one. If nothing else, he hoped the visit could pass without them having to talk about Wendy. They'd argued briefly after Wendy's visit in November, even though he hadn't seen her for three years. Since that argument, he'd managed to avoid triggering conversations about her. He hadn't even mentioned her name.

He was hoping to get an indication from Sarah that she was happy. It was a mistake to try, because it wasn't an attempt to cheer her up but a way of angling for a promise that there wouldn't be an argument. Unsurprisingly, that made her withdraw even more, so that she turned her head away. When he asked if she was all right, she said, 'Leave me alone. Stop making me prove I'm happy.'

It was the day before Christmas Eve, and that gave him some hope. There's something calm and moody about the few days before Christmas, which is partly down to the weather. There is always the same thin layer of featureless cloud brightened by sun. It's as though the air could be foggy but stays just this side of clear. By the time it went dark, though, his hands were numb on the wheel and the rain made driving difficult. As they passed the location where they'd argued last time, just beyond Sandbach, he turned off the radio, anxious to do something that might distract her.

The anxiety was annoying him, because the evening before Christmas Eve was traditionally the best night of the year, now that his parents were getting older. At other times they would worry and fuss, but on that night they were usually calm, just happy to get along. The few times Sarah had been in their company, she'd been more pleasant than usual, so she might be the same tonight. It wasn't that she forced herself to look like a tolerable girlfriend, but that she didn't seem as threatened when they were around.

The bungalow was at the end of a cul-de-sac, set back
from the road. The garden was lined with the detritus of his
dad's gardening projects: wheelbarrows, red sand, bricks and
wire. An empty polythene sack held a pool of water, rippled
by the wind. It would have made him feel cold except that it
caught the flashing lights of the Christmas tree, pressed up
against the front window. His dad always insisted on buying
a tree large enough to touch the ceiling, and the top usually
had to be cut away. The house looked so warm and inviting
that he stopped worrying about Sarah's mood and was just
pleased to be home. His mum and dad both came to the
door, a sign that it was a special occasion. Sarah brightened.

'Hello, Michael. Hello, Helen.' The words sounded
uncomfortable, as though Sarah was saying their names to
prove that she was a grown-up.

While they sat talking, Sarah took hold of his hand, placing
it on her lap. It was a test, to see if Nick was willing to show
affection in front of them. That wouldn't have bothered him,
except it was the first contact she'd initiated all day. It seemed
unfair to do this when he was least able to argue. He was
tempted to be upfront, make a joke about how silent she'd
been. She'd have to laugh, and that would ease the tension
for the journey home tomorrow.

'And Wendy got in touch, did she?' his mum asked.
Somehow that must have been related to the present
conversation, but he couldn't see how.

'Sorry?' he said, struggling.

'Wendy rang here, looking for you. I said to try the flat.'

He knew she must be referring to a recent call, but said,
'Yes, she did. I saw her briefly,' hoping Sarah would assume
they were talking about the November visit.

His mum looked puzzled, tilting her head as though about

to add something, but he looked at her sternly until she made a 'hmm' sound. She poured herself more brandy and offered the bottle around. Sarah let go of his hand, and he looked across at her for the first time since Wendy's name had been mentioned.

'I don't feel well,' she whispered, loud enough for everyone to hear.

'What's up, love?' his dad asked.

'Nothing. I'm fine,' Sarah said, following it with forced deep breaths, putting her hand to her forehead. 'I just need to be sick.'

There was a brief debate as to the best course of action.

'I'll go the toilet,' she said. Her face was set, her bottom jaw pushed forward as though she was in real pain. She slammed the door on the way to the bathroom.

'Is something wrong?' his mum asked.

'No, not at all.'

'Has she been unwell?'

'She's fine.'

'You're a hard bugger,' his dad said. 'Shouldn't you go and see her?'

'I'll go,' his mum said, taking her brandy with her. Nick followed her and listened from the kitchen as they talked through the door. When his mum left her alone, he stopped her in the hall, talking quietly enough not to be heard by Sarah or his dad.

'You mentioned Wendy.'

He must have said it as an accusation, because she put her fingers over her mouth.

'Oh, shouldn't I have?' Then she looked cross and said, 'Well, why not?'

'Sarah gets upset. It's easier to keep quiet.' Then, whispering, 'When did she ring last?'

'Friday. Then again yesterday. She'd been calling your flat on and off for days. Is she all right?'

'I don't know. I've been spending a lot of time at Sarah's, and the answering machine's bust. Best not to mention it again.'

When they drove away in the morning it was drizzling, the tops of buildings and trees hazy with white. He wanted to forget the problem, but Sarah's head was turned away from him at such an angle it was impossible to ignore her. He questioned her reaction from the previous night, not even suggesting she was putting it on but asking if she'd taken things a bit too seriously.

'I was ill.'

'So you weren't bothered by anything that was said?'

The speed and ferocity of her reaction surprised him. She cried as she shouted, telling him he was cruel for always going on about his past. At first he told her to fuck off; after all, he was driving and she couldn't exactly get out of the car. It was one of the few places he felt safe answering her back.

'I am sick of hearing that bitch's name. I'm always being compared, *constantly* reminded of how good your relationship with her was.'

'That's not how it is,' he told her, but she turned away, one hand covering her eyes as she cried.

'For fuck's sake,' he said, feeling himself relent, wishing he hadn't upset her.

As they reached the outskirts of the next village, he pulled over by a deserted park. The climbing frame held rows and rows of water droplets; the swings and roundabout were wet. With the engine off, he could hear litter on the tarmac.

'I don't want to upset you, but can't you understand how difficult it is if we all have to pretend I don't have a past?

Imagine if, years from now, somebody said you couldn't see me. If you had to deny that I'd existed.'

'If we broke up?'

'Yes. If we broke up, you'd still want to see me, wouldn't you? If some future girlfriend said I couldn't see you, how would you feel?'

'Future girlfriend?' she sneered. 'I can't believe this. You've written me off already.'

They argued all the way back, and he shifted from reacting to her accusations to feeling bad about upsetting her. Only when he turned up her road did she say there was no need for him to be so final about things.

'It's not final, but I've had enough for now,' he said.

Part of the problem with Sarah was that everything had happened so rapidly. When you like somebody, it's pleasant to be disturbed by wanting them for a few weeks. But when you sleep with somebody on the night you meet, there's nothing much to look back on.

They met at a party just round the corner from the sports department, in a flat that felt like a converted office. The only lighting was fluorescent, making everybody look as though they had a touch of flu. Sarah caught his attention because she was talking so enthusiastically. She smoked constantly, her expressions based around the blowing of smoke. At one point she'd rubbed her eyes, cursing.

'I've been smoking for years, and I still get smoke in my eyes.'

They must have been talking for longer than Nick realised, because she roused him from intoxication when she said, 'God, what is it about you? I hardly ever tell anybody about that.'

Her attention was appealing, and they left before the party

had died down. She talked all night, keeping him awake by giving him blow jobs, mounting him, or just putting her cunt over his face. The age gap was such that if he didn't go along with it he'd feel old, so he enjoyed her persistence.

At one point that night he mentioned something to do with blondes. Blonde is a strange word, because it should create the image of beautiful hair, but it sounds like the second word of a larger phrase: dumb blonde. For this reason people often replace it with *light, fair, golden* when describing hair. Nick preferred *blonde*. In fact, he preferred blondes, and he said something to Sarah along those lines. He risked goading her about it, not thinking about the long-term effect.

When she began to show discomfort, he recalled something Dave had once said. *When people like you, they hang on to every word, and they can use it all against you.* He had no idea what a problem blonde would become for them.

A few weeks later he'd been telling a story involving some mutual friends. He couldn't remember the name of one of the more obscure participants and referred to her as *that blonde*.

'Blonde?'

'Yes, the small girl.'

'Small and blonde, that would suit you.'

The flow of his story was ruined, and he felt nervous. They were taking the short cut across the university field, where the grass was frosty and sunny water melted from the trees. There was the cold sound of traffic.

'She has blonde hair, it's as simple as that.'

'Nobody has blonde hair. They bleach it.'

'Don't be ridiculous, Sarah. What about Swedish people? There is such a thing as a natural blonde.'

'Trust you to defend blondes.'

'I'm not defending anybody. Some people have blonde hair.'

'It's bleach. People with fair hair bleach it.'

'That's rubbish. I've known people with real blonde hair.'

'Then why didn't you stay with her?' she spat, her face bright red.

'I don't know what you're on about. People have blonde hair, that's all. I couldn't remember her name.'

'Whose?'

'That girl. In the story,' he said. 'I was trying to tell you a story.'

'If you're so obsessed with blondes, just fuck off.'

It's no wonder that he became wary of using the word. Even so, in every argument they had, she would bring the subject up.

'Why don't you go back to your blonde bitch?'

The arguments became more ferocious, with Sarah smashing objects, pushing chairs over, screaming at him and pulling his hair, kicking him away, until she broke down with crying. Even then, as he kissed her dark brown hair, he knew what she'd be thinking: he'd rather be kissing blonde.

After three months of this he knew it was a problem that wasn't going to go away. One comment made when he'd barely known her would stay with her for ever: *I prefer blondes*.

If she didn't cry so much, he would have left Sarah within weeks. That she was able to let go of her fury and cry openly meant that he felt sorry for her and tried to be comforting. She was frequently ill, staying away from college because something was making her throw up. Dave had suggested she might be faking it, but she was always so pale that seemed unlikely.

If anything, seeing Wendy again had reminded him of the

damage that can be done when you let things go too easily.
He didn't want the same thing to happen, which is why he
refused to hurt Sarah. The problem was that everything he
did seemed to upset her. Even his work bothered her, because
he was dealing with women her age. If ever there were parties
she'd insist on going along or would wait at his house for
him. *It's not that I don't trust you, I just want to be part of your
life.*

If she was willing to take things so seriously, he had to
respect that. With Wendy, his belief that something better
might come along had contributed to things going wrong.
They hadn't taken it seriously enough, because they didn't
believe it could last, and that had led to their failure. Nick
often thought that if he and Wendy had stopped making life
so complicated, they could have sorted things out years ago.
Doubt in a relationship is a self-fulfilling prophecy, because
while you're hoping for something else in the future you'll
make sure the present relationship can't survive. Sometimes
he'd wonder just what he was meant to be getting out of the
relationship with Sarah, but he reminded himself that she
was young and that things would improve. The worst thing
he could do would be to abandon her as well.

Sarah knew about this but took it a step further, making
Nick feel grateful for knowing her. *Nobody understands you
like I do. You're lucky to have me.* She'd say that she loved him
and found him beautiful, but implied that was generosity on
her part. He would never find another nineteen-year-old
willing to put up with him.

Nick felt there could be truth in this, and reminded himself
that, even if he could find somebody else, newness was a lure.
People you meet seem perfect because they are unknown.
But you can't spend your whole life giving up what you've
achieved for the sake of another attraction. One day you

have to build on something and make it work. That's how it was with Sarah, because it had taken months for them to find any sort of peace. It would be a crime to have gone through all those arguments for nothing.

He told all this to Dave, but he said, 'If that's true, what about you and Wendy?'

'It doesn't apply.'

'So you just forget about her.'

'She's moved on. And I wouldn't want to go back there anyway. You should see her.' That sounded more unkind than he'd intended it to. If anything, he meant he couldn't stand to see her in that state, knowing he'd probably contributed to it.

He didn't particularly like being lectured on the finer points of happiness, because he didn't want a life like Dave's. It wasn't just the job and the hours, but the fact that he told Nick so many things he didn't dare tell Rachel, and when she'd gone to bed, if they were watching TV, Dave would start scanning the satellite channel for porn. At midnight, he'd flick between the Adult Channel and something German, where you got five free minutes of soft porn.

Dave loved Dish of the Day, which consisted of a tame striptease by women who were on the ugly side of plain. Nick reckoned that at least half of them were transsexuals.

'It's a bloke. Look at his hands.'

'It's not a bloke.'

'Have you ever met a woman with a nose like that?'

'Well, I'd shag him.'

If Nick told him he was a sad bastard for doing this so frequently, he'd say, 'I don't subscribe, do I?' It was better not to argue with a defence like that.

There was only one other day, some time in January, when

he spent much time thinking about Wendy. It was too cold to go into uni, so he busied himself by tidying the house and rearranging the furniture, but spent more time looking through old books and letters.

He found his old map book, the one he and Wendy had used on their world tour of Britain that first year. They hadn't marked their journey, but by looking at the more damaged pages it was easy to remember the places they'd been. He hadn't realised until then that they'd passed through Ludlow and never recognised it as the same place when they stayed there years later.

So many of the roads were routes he'd escaped by, or places they'd been to avoid Laurence. The map of Devon was the most difficult, because those names – Slapton Sands, East Prawle, Dartington – every one reminded him of being in the car with Linda, smelling nothing but her perfume, in the air and on his skin.

Other places were familiar because he could remember Wendy's voice saying them. Longframlington. Arnside. Houghton. He followed the journey up to Skye. Broadford. Elgol. Every name made him wince.

It was horrible to think of the place Wendy was living in now. Since he'd abandoned her that New Year, she'd spent all her time up at the commune, sharing a van with Ian. Nick had imagined some sort of VW camper, but it was on old BT van with no windows and less space than any bedsit. To use their heater they had to sit on the bed. They'd spend their days collecting wood for the burner, sorting out their dole and talking to the others. In the evenings they'd read by candlelight and smoke dope while Ian played guitar.

It sounded so boring, but when he'd said that in November Wendy had said boredom was almost welcome, given the alternative. She hadn't elaborated, but he'd known what she'd meant. Life had been interesting enough when they were together, but too harmful.

Wendy rang in February, just after Valentine's Day. She was on her way from Newtown and said she didn't know where else to go.

'What's the problem?'

'Things don't seem as real as when I was with you.' Before he could question that, she said, 'I'm running out of money.'

'You mean the phone or . . . ?'

'I only have a minute. I want to come round. You know. For sex.'

'*What?*'

'To get back at the bastard. You want to, don't you?'

Her money ran out, and although he masturbated every ten minutes until she arrived he was still hoping to sleep with her when she knocked at the door.

Her hair had been cut off, almost shaved, but that surprised him less than the change in her face. Her cheeks looked fat, but bony. She looked puffed up at the same time as being withered. Sores widened her mouth, like badly done lipstick. There was so little of her hair left that it looked brown, being nothing more than spiky roots.

'Jesus, Wendy.'

She smiled, running her hand through it. 'I know,' she said, wrinkling her nose. 'I'm going to grow it again.'

'What did you do that for?'

'To get back at Ian. He loved my hair.'

'What did he do to you?'

She didn't answer but asked if she could have something to drink. He brought tea, and they sat on the floor in the front room.

Nick couldn't help saying, 'Did you really want to have sex?'

'I just wanted to see you.'

She admitted that she was angry with Ian and wanted to get back at him, but wouldn't say for what. Changing the subject, she asked about his drawing, and he had to admit he was doing less these days. Sarah thought he'd been too obsessed with it at first, and they'd argued frequently about having their own lives. She'd said he could have his own life, but he had to make some time for her. Gradually, he'd begun to feel guilty whenever he took a day off to draw.

'She sounds like a bitch.'

'Well, no, and in a way I prefer it. When we go out, I experience the day. And I can remember that, use it later.'

'Don't you remember the times you were with me?'

'Of course. I remember everything.'

He asked if she'd seen her dad recently, because it was a subject they'd steered clear of in November.

'Once or twice this year. He hasn't changed. But he's given up on Mum. He's too selfish to be a martyr, so he found another wife. We thought she was a gold-digger, but she's more loaded than he is.'

'He just gave up?'

'He moved on.'

'Well, I wish we could have. He put us through all that for nothing.'

'Would you prefer it if he'd won Mum back then?'

'No, but there's a lesson there, isn't there? If life's shit, just ditch it and move on. You should do the same. Leave Ian and live with me.' He said it as a joke, as well as a flirtation, but Wendy's face was serious.

'It's not that easy,' she said. 'I had a baby.'

He couldn't work out how that was possible, considering that she hadn't appeared pregnant when he'd seen her a few months ago. While he tried to work out the details, he felt his eyes close, tears filling the lashes.

'But I saw you in November.'

'That was the first time I left her. She was born a year ago.'

'Why didn't you tell me?'

'I thought you might be upset.'

For the first time he felt as though it was really over. It occurred to him that even after the gap of years, he'd always assumed they'd be together again one day. Despite his affair with Linda, and the trauma caused by Laurence, time would see them reunited. Now that she was tied to another life, he realised how ridiculous that assumption had been. He felt more loss now than when they'd parted three years ago.

'I looked after myself,' she continued. 'I didn't drink or smoke. And I kept fit afterwards. We used to go swimming, because we couldn't have a bath. We got into the leisure centre free by signing on. So I got my stomach flat. But it's gone again now,' she said, pulling at it as though she was picking at fluff. 'The council finally got us a flat, but it hasn't helped.'

'They didn't get you a flat any sooner?' His voice was thin, because he was close to crying.

'They could have got us a place years ago, but Ian wouldn't have it. He wanted to stay up at Tessa's.'

'The wanker.'

'But it was impossible after she was born. I was cracking up. I mean it,' she said, as though he wouldn't have believed her. 'So we got this flat. Ian still goes back to the van for space. I thought I'd be happy in the flat, but I can't cope. I don't know what's wrong with me.'

'I'm sure it seems overwhelming,' he said, 'but everybody says it gets easier.'

Wendy looked younger than he'd ever known her. Not pleasantly so, but like a sick child. He couldn't imagine her holding a baby.

'Do you want to go to India?' she asked.

He laughed, 'Well, yes, but . . .'

'Sometimes I just feel like going. Letting her go. I'm meant to be in court tomorrow. Ian's trying to keep me away from her.'

'Then what are you doing here?'

'Letting him win.'

With that, her mood switched, and before Nick had time to take all this in, she'd decided to go back, and asked him to walk her to the station.

'Not India then?'

'I'd never forgive myself if I let her go.'

'What are his grounds for keeping you away, when he's the druggie?'

'He thinks I'm irresponsible.'

As they walked it kept going over in his mind that life didn't have to be this complicated. There must be easier ways to cope, but he couldn't think what advice to give her. It seemed the best idea was to encourage her to fight, to make sure she had access to the baby. If it wasn't for that, he could ask her to stay with him, just dump Sarah and commit himself to Wendy. It made him feel slightly drunk to think he could do that, just transform his life in a second. But it kept coming back to him how agonising it had been towards the end in Ludlow. And even before that they'd never found much calm, except at the very beginning. With these new problems and his guilt, they'd probably drive each other mad. And seeing the state she was in, he didn't want to get involved with that sort of problem in case it started having the same effect on him.

There was a bitter wind on the platform, made bearable by sunlight coming through the crossbeams of the station roof. They stood on the platform, as far from anyone else as they could. She hugged him, and he'd forgotten how small she felt. It was beautiful holding her, and he wished he could take her home again.

'You'll always be my friend, won't you?'

'Of course. Whatever you do.'

'You wouldn't if you knew me.'

He kissed her head, holding the back of her neck, and waited for a while before asking if she'd hurt the baby.

'I didn't, but I could have,' she said, sobbing and gripping harder. 'I really could have. You can see how it happens. My own baby.' When she'd calmed down she said, 'So I took her for help and Ian's never forgiven me. He says I'm a risk.'

'You did the right thing,' he said. 'Getting help. And you probably need more.'

Her train arrived and set off again before she'd found a seat, so they didn't get to wave goodbye.

It was a week later that Linda rang. Nick hadn't spoken to her for three years, but she didn't even ask how he was.

'I'm sorry to call like this, but I know you've been seeing Wendy.'

'Yes,' he said sternly, wondering if she was going to reprimand him.

'Then you probably want to know what's happened. She took an overdose, and just lost it. She's not dead, but they've sectioned her, and they can't get her to calm down. She's been trying to escape from the place they're keeping her. She actually got away yesterday and ran nine miles until they caught her. So now she has a nurse looking after her the whole time. One on one care. But she's just frantic.'

'She escaped?' he asked, finding it difficult to keep up with Linda's story. Having seen her so recently, it sounded ridiculous that she was having to escape from anything.

'They had those windows that open just a short way. They couldn't believe she fitted through, but she's so thin now. They've put her in a more secure ward.'

'I can't believe this.'

'It's not surprising, Nick. She's been going downhill, especially since the baby. And that bastard Ian does nothing for her. Nothing.'

He found it difficult to listen as she went on, because a pleading tone came into her voice as she said that Wendy still loved him. But he couldn't stop thinking about Wendy running nine miles. It was strange, because he imagined her running through a summer landscape of wheat fields and blue sky. She looked beautiful, her hair long again, moving in slow motion. But then he saw her standing on a cold lane, fingers gripping her scalp through short hair and her limbs convulsing as they dragged her away.

Chapter Sixteen

He put off going to see her until March, because Linda warned him that Wendy probably wouldn't respond at all until her medication started to take effect. Besides, it wasn't something he was looking forward to. The arrangements were complicated, because Caryn was short of time, so Nick had to drive as far as Worcester to pick her up, and then headed into Wales. They both felt guilty because it was such a pleasant day. If they had been out for any other reason, it would have been the first time in ages they'd enjoyed themselves together. She tried to lighten the mood when they were driving through a village. There were crowds of Girl Guides in freshly ironed blue uniforms, and Caryn leaned out of the window shouting 'Phworr'.

She slumped back into her seat, saying, 'That'll give them something to think about, realising they're desirable.'

They relaxed more after that, but in the last half-hour they talked about nothing but directions. Neither could find the word they wanted to describe the place they were looking for: mental hospital, asylum, loony bin. None of them seemed fair on Wendy.

From a distance it looked like a concentration camp. In front of the three-storey brick buildings was a huge chimney that gave off heat haze rather than smoke. It looked like an old prison, converted for the job. More than half the wards appeared to be closed down, and a number of windows in the upper floors were broken.

'What is it about disused buildings that makes the glass fall out?' he asked. 'It doesn't happen in rooms where there's lots going on, but the minute you abandon a building the windows let go.'

It was nervous chatter, and they carried on like that as they looked for the reception area. There were no patients walking around, and they both voiced their doubts about the value of such a place. It was enough to make you go mental.

'Don't you think it would be better if we just took her on holiday for six months?' Caryn said.

'I've often thought the same thing. Being stuck here can't help much. But it's most likely they'll wait until she isn't a risk and then dump her back in the community.'

He said the last word snidely. Care in the Community could have been a good thing, except that the Tories had come up with it. Nobody liked the idea of imprisoning people just because they were upset, so it was easy to sell to the public. But rather than being a system for reintegrating people, it was a cheap way of closing down hospitals to free up land for development. Nick had been out with a woman who'd lived next to one of the hostels on Vincent Street, and every night you'd hear screaming. In the street below he'd seen a wheelie bin on its side, litter in a circle around it, and a little man with black hair standing over it, his hands in fists, stepping backwards then leaning forwards to scream at it again.

'But you can't do *nothing*. It's an illness,' Caryn said.

'That's Western medicine for you. Treat pain as chemical imbalance.'

'Hasn't that been proved, though, that the chemicals do get out of balance?'

'Yes. But those imbalances are a response to being upset, not the cause of it. If you get pissed off, your brain makes pissed-off chemicals. That doesn't mean the chemicals are the cause. I think for these people something happened and they never got over it. Wendy wouldn't have ended up like this if her life had been all right.'

He'd intended to read loads on the subject but had only skimmed through two books. The upshot seemed to be that drugs were a bad idea but were the only option. You can't cure the past, so you have to numb the present. In other cultures they'd take somebody who was suffering and let them run wild, then nurture them in a big extended family. In the west, the best they've come up with is occupational therapy. Employment is worshipped as the ultimate norm, so the best cure for sadness is to get somebody basket-weaving.

They had to sign in at reception, explain their relationship and then wait for a nurse. She was quite old, but calmly concerned, and asked if they knew what had happened. She said that as well as possible schizophrenia, Wendy was suffering from amphetamine psychosis. With her overdose she'd taken a load of speed, and it hadn't left her system. Even when it did, her brain might have difficulty slowing down. She told them that no matter how prepared they were it would be upsetting.

The ward was reached through a series of wire doors, like an airlock. It looked like an old school corridor with beds hidden behind wooden screens. There were almost as many nurses and security guards as patients. The middle section was the day-room, where old sofas and armchairs had been gathered. The air was thick with smoke and the smell of coffee. The ceiling was far too high, and the windows were frosted so you couldn't see out. On the walls were drawings and paintings. In a corner there was a surprising number of toys, card decks and teddy bears. An unseen radio was hissing quiet jazz. Wendy was sitting in a huge armchair wearing a jumper Nick hadn't seen before, which was far too big for her. And she was smoking. He'd seen her smoke dope before, but she was holding a cigarette up to her mouth, hardly moving it away as she exhaled. Her hair hadn't grown at all.

Wendy recognised them and started crying. The nurse sitting with her just shrugged. He pulled up a couple of chairs, but Caryn sat on the armchair and hugged her. When she pulled away Wendy started fidgeting, saying she needed to smoke again. She got up and headed down the ward. The nurse had to follow her, and she sighed, making it obvious she'd rather not bother. She tried talking Wendy into sitting down again.

'Come and see your friends.'

When she sat down, they asked how she was feeling, and she said she wanted to get out.

'If I could just get away from here. They won't even let me outside. That's what's driving me mad.' Her mouth was twitching, perhaps because of the drugs she was on.

Caryn tried reasoning with her, saying why it was probably a good idea to sit it out and let people help her, but she kept crying, saying it didn't help.

'Please help me. Please.'

'We can't,' Nick said.

'Nobody talks to me, nothing happens. All they do is drug me.'

Nick wanted to take her away, thinking he could probably do a better job than these people. But he felt obliged to tell her that the medication might help and that it was better to trust them for a while.

She said she wanted to go to bed and walked away, but the nurse told them to stay where they were. A minute later Wendy came back, unable to sleep.

'I'm aching all over. Everything's tense.'

'Can't you just try relaxing?' he asked.

'Nothing works.'

Two men in overalls walked through with measuring tapes, and Caryn made a joke about them turning the place into a rest home. Nick didn't know how close to the truth that might be but asked Wendy if she knew who they were.

'Friends of my dad's,' she said, and for a second he believed her, his heart beating faster. Wendy looked at them again and said she didn't know them after all. They made some measurements, wrote in their books and left without making eye contact with anybody.

Caryn asked a few more questions, but all Wendy could tell them was that nothing happened. She wasn't getting any counselling or advice; she was only ever told to calm down.

After a long silence Wendy said, 'You don't know what to say, do you?'

They'd planned on staying for the afternoon, but after three-quarters of an hour they left. She begged them to take her with them and had to be held back while the nurses ushered them out.

Sarah made him feel that it would have been easier if he'd forgotten about Wendy years ago. At first he defended his right to see her and phone her up, but she made such huge arguments out of it that he found it was better to contact Wendy in secret. To Sarah's face he said he barely even thought about her. It was partly because Sarah made him so nervous that Wendy stayed on his mind. He found himself worrying when he used words that sounded like her name, or even that began with the same letter, in case he said Wendy by accident. The irony was that he never mentioned her name, but in every argument Sarah would bring her up. She'd say something about being damaged, that every argument chipped something of her away. Which made him worry that he was doing to Sarah what he'd done to Wendy. It was that, more than anything, that made him stay. The regrets he felt about Wendy made him realise that it's important to be kind.

'Maybe not to her,' Dave said. They were driving back from Birmingham, having been to look at a new car for Dave, and he wanted to keep talking to stay awake. And Dave's idea of talking was to argue.

'Imagine if I'd said that about Rachel.'

'You did.'

'Don't you think it's better that I commit to somebody than just flit from one relationship to the next? You were the one always pushing me to settle down.'

'All right, but can you speak your mind to her?'

'Oh, in your perfect patriarchy, a man should be allowed to say what he wants.'

'Don't be a tit, Nick. I just mean you shouldn't be afraid of talking about Wendy or seeing her.'

'Whatever.'

'I have no sympathy. Sarah's too young. And mental. And you should dump her.'

'Very mature. Look what happened last time I did that.'

'Wendy was half-gone anyway.' Dave listed all the stories Nick had told about times when she'd nearly cracked up. 'She was losing it long before you left her. You can't blame yourself for that.'

'Well, it depends how far back you look.'

'And Sarah's worse than her. I think you bring it on yourself, to justify your hatred of women. If you go out with mental children, you can feel hard done to.'

Nick was finding it difficult to keep up. Although he and Dave were always swapping insults, he'd never been attacked for his choice of girlfriends before. Dave had made the occasional criticism of Sarah, but this was the first time he'd spoken his mind.

'Ask yourself, how happy are you?' Dave said.

'That's not the issue. If there's one thing I've learnt, it's that relationships aren't about what you get.'

'So you let her walk all over you. Your life as a service to hers.'

'And what's the alternative at my age? Starting again? Meeting somebody else and going through the same fucking questions, the same fake excitement, the same enthralling discoveries? Everybody's the same, and it bores me.'

Dave snorted. 'You're the one who used to say we should all wait for the right person. I can't believe you're saying we should make do.'

'Well, I already met the right person and fucked it up.'

Evidence of Wendy began to vanish. It started with small things, physical objects that Wendy had left. A watch, several white pebbles from Arnside, a picture she'd drawn of the canal bridge. The same happened with a pen Wendy had given him, and even one of her jumpers; not just mementos, but things he used. They weren't misplaced so much as removed.

What is it about being close to somebody that means you'll believe the most outrageous lies? It took months before Nick confronted Sarah directly, and with a serene face she denied any knowledge. When he asked who else could be taking the objects, she shook her head, saying, 'It wasn't me.' The look also suggested that he shouldn't be so bothered. It was only stuff *she* had left anyway. The name Wendy was never mentioned.

He finally accepted that Sarah was to blame when looking through his books. None were missing, but on the inside cover of the books Wendy had given him, handwritten words had been wet (spat on perhaps) and rubbed into an illegible smudge. He wondered why she hadn't just thrown the books away. It was as though she wanted him to know she was taking his past apart.

If it had stopped there, with physical things, he could have tolerated it, but Sarah wasn't satisfied with that. She didn't even want him to think about Wendy.

Linda rang on a Saturday afternoon just to chat about Wendy. Although Sarah had no idea who had called, she must have sensed Nick's discomfort and sat on his bed, watching him as he talked. She'd never been told what had happened with Linda, but she was Wendy's mother and that was enough to cause trouble.

'Who was that?' she asked when he got off the phone.

'Wendy's mum.'

'Don't mention the bitch's name.'

'Sarah, you shouldn't call her a bitch. I know you're a jealous little girl. And I know you can't handle the fact that I have a history, but she isn't a bitch, and neither is her mother. If I want to talk to them or visit them, it's up to me.'

She leapt up quickly enough to slap him and then pulled him to the floor by his hair. She backed off immediately, pushing her face into the pillow and screaming. He had to threaten her to make her shut up, and he was shaking so much that he could hardly talk.

'I've done nothing wrong,' he said. 'Nothing. I'm trying to keep everybody sane, and all I get is blame.'

'Then leave her alone.'

'Just because I'm with you doesn't mean I can't have female friends. You never let me see anybody.'

It was the last valid point he made, because she started screaming so loudly that he had to calm her, worried that the neighbours would call the police.

She managed to calm down, eventually saying she was sorry, wishing he could understand. Yes, it was just jealousy, but he was unfair for ramming it down her throat. He dared to use the sense of compromise to say Wendy's name. It was an opportunity to normalise things again.

'Do you still love her?' she asked.

'As a friend.'

'And you expect me not to be hurt.'

'I'm only trying to do the right thing. I can't just abandon everybody because it upsets you.'

'Imagine if I did that to you. Imagine if I was traipsing off to see some ex-boyfriend and nursing him and caring for him. How would you feel?'

'I'd trust you, no matter what I felt. And I'd understand.'

'Well, aren't you perfect.'

'No, but I'm doing what feels right.'

'You're doing it to look good.'

She stayed on that theme for the next hour. He couldn't say when it happened, but at some point he weakened. He was so sick of her accusations and of making her upset that he chose damage limitation. He admitted that he'd done it to look good, that he thought people would be impressed if he looked after his ex-girlfriend.

'So you don't really care?'

'No.'

He felt guilty for saying it but also a small sense of relief that the argument was over.

'So you'll stop seeing her?'

'I didn't say that. I can't do that.'

'You could if you loved me.'

'Sarah, I can't.'

She stood up, threw the pillow down and said, 'It's no wonder your girlfriends try to kill themselves.'

He must have moved towards her because she ran to the side, then into the hall, yelling at him to leave her alone. In the bathroom he hit her, one hard-fisted thump on the temple. It was over before he knew what he'd done, with Sarah falling on to the floor, her hair suddenly a mess, wet with tears, face redder than it had ever been, her eyes wide, then creasing as she cried.

She slammed the door and locked herself in the bathroom. He heard her throat filling with mucus, so that she sounded unable to breathe. Despite all his pleading, begging and promises, she stayed there until dawn. When she came out in the morning, she said, 'I hope you're proud of yourself now.'

In June Wendy had been moved to a new hospital, closer to Ludlow. It wasn't going to be open much longer but was said to be less oppressive. Linda raved about it and said Nick would see a big improvement if he went to visit her. It was on a quiet Tuesday when Sarah was out of town that he managed to get away.

This building was set in wheat fields, with hills in the distance, and it was only two storeys high, which seemed much less threatening. There was no chimney, and it felt more like a large house than a hospital.

'She's in the chapel,' a male nurse told him. 'We'll send somebody for her.'

He waited in a public area near the tuck shop. This was obviously more like Butlins than the last place she'd been, which had to be better. The inmates, however, looked just as barmy. There was one man, with more beard than face, eyes pointing in different directions. He was fat, with a set of tiny brown teeth like fragments of bone, eyes so glazed he appeared to have cataracts. He stepped from foot to foot, as though cold, trying to get cigarettes and coffee from anybody who passed. He was edgy and sweating, and whenever he managed to buy a cup of coffee he'd down it in one before hunting for more.

Wendy's hair had grown, and she smiled.

'Having fun?' she asked.

'Well, it's an education. You seem better.'

She raised her eyebrows and nodded. 'I'm trying not to focus on myself too much. It was that obsession with me, me, me that made things so unbearable.'

'Well, you're doing better than this guy,' he said, pointing at the man who was trying to get coffee money from everybody who passed.

'Oh, yeah, this place is a fine example of natural capitalism. We barter and trade and steal. Just like the real world.'

'You sound so much better. I thought you'd really lost it.'

'Oh, God, Nick, I can't tell you. I was so far gone. They've changed my medication, I don't know how many times, but I'm beginning to feel better. And they let me out now for walks. I don't even get followed.'

'So you wouldn't try to escape?'

'I know I'm in for the long haul. We could go for a walk now. I'll show you around.'

She took him straight back to the chapel, checked to make sure nobody was there, and led him in. It was cool and smelt of plaster. She went to kneel in front of the cross, her face flushed by the red of the stained glass.

'I get something out of this now.'

'Good, that's good.'

'You don't really think that,' she said. They used to spend hours dismantling the myths of religion, both admitting they felt something must be out there but feeling dull for being such typical 1990s agnostics.

'Well, it is good. I wish I was a believer. Or at least an atheist.'

'It's calming. When you need to be sorry.'

'You've nothing to be sorry for, Wendy.'

'I'll show you the rest.'

As she walked, she kept pointing out different rooms – the laundry, the office, the kitchens – which were of no interest, but he had to say, 'Oh, right,' at everything she showed him. Even though it wasn't really normal, it was an improvement on last time.

'I wish Caryn could see you.'

'She writes,' Wendy said, then she stopped at a junction in the corridor. 'Does this place remind you of anywhere?'

'Not really. Perhaps my old school, a bit.'

'What about the mansion?'

'At Ludlow?'

'I sometimes think it's the same place. My room? Upstairs? I used to think it was that room with the snow in. When I first got here I kept thinking I was in there with you. Don't you think it's just like that place?'

'Yeah. We always said we should have used that building for something.' He knew what he'd said didn't make sense but didn't know how else to deal with her peculiar observation.

Outside, she walked him to the edge of the fields and told him about the activities they kept her busy with. Nothing went on beyond seven in the evening because everybody was so drugged up.

'All those lectures about not taking dope, and then they knock us senseless with pills.'

'But, Wendy, you do know about dope, don't you?'

'I used it because it made life bearable.'

'But it just makes the anxiety grow, because it never gets expressed. It's like holding back from crying, and then it all comes out. That's partly what happened to you when you took the speed.'

'I know,' she said. 'But it's no good having regrets. I don't even smoke now.'

She explained that she'd joined the music therapy group, and they gathered together on Wednesday afternoons.

'You're learning an instrument?'

'No. It's mostly percussion.' She mimed playing something like a triangle, and he had to force himself to smile. The thought that she'd been reduced to this, getting excited over a bunch of loonies banging out rhythms, made him struggle to speak.

'It's good that you're getting involved.'

'They might let me out soon. I'll go back to Mum's.'

'Not to Newtown?'

'No. Nothing for them,' she said, her mouth twisting and her tongue pointing into its corner. 'We'd better get back,' she said.

Things had improved with Sarah. Wendy wasn't mentioned, and he was so busy at work that he didn't get much chance to see his other friends, so Sarah had nothing to be paranoid about. The only thing that bothered him was the way she watched when he was on the phone. And sometimes she'd insist on staying at his house even when he was going out with Dave. She said she trusted him; it was just that she wanted to be in his bed.

This seemed fair enough, but it meant that when he did want to see Wendy, or speak to her, he had to plan carefully.

By October she'd been allowed to go home, and was back in Ludlow with her mum. They'd made an agreement that he would ring them and that they mustn't call his house.

Wendy had been asking him to go for weeks, because she was so bored. She said there was a lot of sitting around to do before they'd declare her normal, and she needed the company. There was no chance of her seeing the baby yet, and she wasn't meant to even think about it. 'They just want me to enjoy myself. So come. Please.'

Ludlow in October smelt exactly as it had when they'd first arrived: wet leaves and grass. Wendy came out to meet him, grinning. She'd put on make-up, which immediately made him feel bad. It was so much effort being around her, because everything she did made him feel so sad. It wasn't that she looked beautiful, because the make-up made her look unwell if anything, but that she'd tried.

'How long can you stay?' was the first thing she asked.

'I'll have to go first thing.'

'Oh, Mum, he's going tomorrow,' she called as they went into the house. 'We thought you'd be here for the weekend.'

'I'm so sorry. I just can't. But I'll come again.'

Linda said 'Hi,' looking glad of new company, and there was less tension between them than he'd imagined. 'Thanks for coming,' she said. 'Sit down. I'll bring you both some tea.'

Wendy told him she'd been painting. It was as though she'd prepared a list of things to tell him in order to look normal.

'It's just wax painting, but it's a start. You melt candles on to paper and iron them.'

She showed him some of her efforts, rectangles of paper with swirls of coloured wax. They looked like those projections at hippie parties, except for the carbon scorching. He managed to point out one he liked, his eyes watering because the paintings were so bad.

Linda was quiet, sitting with her legs up on the chair, watching.

'Mum's been doing car boot sales. That's her job now. And we tried to sell some of these. Just a couple of pounds. But nobody wanted them. Can you believe that? I was sure students would want them at least. For their walls.'

'Yeah. Well, I'd have bought one.'

'That's what I said.'

He stood up and went to the window, controlling his crying with deep breaths, pretending to bend down to the budgie.

'It's about the only thing I do enjoy,' she said. 'I don't even get any pleasure from reading.'

'Not even *Lord of the Rings*? Remember that?'

'I remember enjoying it. But I can't remember what happened. It's the medication as much as anything.'

In the afternoon they walked up to the mansion as far as the doors, which had been padlocked and chained now so there was no way in. They were so busy talking they hardly noticed and walked around the perimeter.

'So when you tried to kill yourself, was it an infamous cry for help?'

'No. I meant it. I was so pissed off that they got me.'

'But now.'

'It's all I think about.'

'Doing it again?'

'Yep. It's only because people go on at me that I don't.'

'Please, Wendy. Please don't. If ever it gets that bad, call me. Talk to somebody. There's always something we can do.'

'But I don't enjoy being alive.' It was disturbing that she

could talk about it with so little emotion.

'Think about what you'd be doing. This is all you've got. Please. We could do anything.'

'But I've hurt so many people.'

'You'd hurt us more if you did that. And do you know what would have happened if they hadn't got to you in time? Paracetamol makes everything break down. Every hole bleeds and you die a hard, swollen, painful death.'

'I know all that. But it's nothing compared to what I was feeling.'

He held her, and she hugged back, but it felt forced.

'Will you promise me that you'll ring me? If nothing else.'

'I promise.'

After they'd eaten she lay with her head in his hands. He tried to calm her by stroking her scalp. She complained about feeling tired and went to bed early.

Being alone with Linda was more ordinary than he'd imagined. It felt no different from the afternoon when Laurence had taken Wendy away on Skye. They talked, they worried and then they went to bed, separately. Whatever excitement there had been between them was gone.

He felt the need to go home as soon as he got up. Wendy was awake early and sat drinking milky tea, looking out of the window, absently talking to the budgie. She looked tired and more nervous than she had the day before.

He packed his bag, said goodbye to Linda and all three went outside.

Wendy smiled again when he was in the car, and he said, 'I can't believe you're still glad to see me.'

'Always,' she said.

Linda rang at Christmas to see if he'd got his present from Wendy. It had arrived the day before, the best of her wax

paintings put into a Perspex clip frame with Merry Christmas
on the back. Linda also said they were going to the Lakes,
and he was invited. A few of them, friends from Ludlow and
people they'd known in Leicester, were sharing a big house in
Keswick. Nick said he'd planned a trip up there with Dave,
and although they probably weren't even stopping overnight
they could turn up.

'Well, you're both welcome. She misses you so much.'

'Really? I didn't think she did.'

'I'll send you a map. Just pop in.'

When they arrived in Keswick, two days before New Year,
it was raining so hard they had to make do with a low-level
walk. Dave was heavily into conquering mountains, so he
was unhappy and suggested going to the pub. 'Or we could
go to that party.'

'I don't think it's a party,' Nick said. 'Just a way of getting
Wendy into the real world.'

'Do you want to see her?'

'I don't know if I can face it now.'

'Just for an hour?'

'That would almost be worse.'

Dave suggested they go for a drink first, but by the time
they'd had a pint Nick was certain he wanted to leave.

'I'll try again in the New Year.'

It wasn't as easy as that, because Linda rang in early January
to say Wendy had gone back to Newtown. She'd sworn she
was calm enough, had taken her medication with her, and
was going to sort out her life. She was going to see Ian and
start reasoning with him about the baby.

'It's that place that sent her mental,' Linda said.

'It can't have helped. Do you want me to go?' he asked.

'Would you?'

He lied to Sarah, not directly, but by leaving a message on his machine, saying he'd gone away with Dave. He rang Dave briefly, to warn him that she would probably ring to check.

'So I'm not meant to answer the phone?'

'Not if you can avoid it.'

There was so much traffic on the A5 and the surrounding roads that every short cut failed. He hadn't even made it as far as Wales when he started looking for a B&B. There wasn't a problem with them being booked up, but there weren't many open at that time of year, which forced him to give up earlier than he would have wanted. He was only an hour from Newtown, but it was after nine and it wouldn't be a good idea to go prowling round the place in the dark. He must have needed the sleep, because even though he got an early night he slept right through.

In the morning it was raining heavily, so the clouds blended over the hills, making it difficult for him to find his way. When he got to the commune there were fewer residents than there had been in autumn three years ago, with half the vans gone. He parked by the BT van, presuming it was Ian's, hoping Wendy would be in there. It was unlocked, but stale and so dark he had to look for a minute while his eyes adjusted to be certain it was empty. Nobody had been in there for a while, and there was nothing he recognised of Wendy's. She must have moved everything down to the flat.

He hadn't wanted to see Tessa, but his journey through the commune buildings was fruitless, so he sought out her caravan. She opened the door, said hello brightly enough, but stood looking down at him and didn't offer to let him in. His hair was already soaked, so she probably thought there was no point.

'Looking for Wendy?'

'Has she been here?'

'She was here yesterday, looking for Ian. But he's not been here for months. Left his van as well.'

'Could she have gone to the flat?'

'I told her he wasn't there, but she went looking for him.'

'If she comes back, can you tell her I was here?'

'I'll tell her.'

Linda had given him the address, but finding the flats was difficult, because they weren't on a street but on an area of land between two roads. He had to cross what felt like a scrap yard to get to the main entrance. There was so much metal around, corrugated iron and old prams piled against an old garage wall, that it made a roaring sound where the rain sparked off it.

The corridor smelt new but damp, the overhead bulbs smashed so the only light came from small windows at either end. It sounded as though televisions were switched on in every flat. He found her door and knocked loudly enough to be heard, while trying not to draw attention from other residents. After five minutes there was still no answer.

A big man, wearing jeans and a vest, with a block-shaped head, came out from the flat next door.

'He's not at home, mate. Gone away.'

'I'm looking for Wendy. Did she go with him?'

'Dunno. But he took the baby.'

'Do you know if she's been here at all?'

A woman with a vest and tattoos, looking half his age, joined the man at the door.

'He's looking for the girl,' the man said, jabbing a finger at the door.

'She was here yesterday.'

'No,' the man said. 'She left months ago.'

'Somebody was there yesterday, because I heard them.

And it wasn't him, because there was no baby.'

'OK, thanks. Is there a phone nearby?'

They directed him to a yellow pay phone near the laundry-room, but it didn't work, so he went outside. On the main street he found a phone, but once he was in the box he stopped to think. With only a handful of 10ps it was important to consider who to call first. He tried Linda but there was no answer. He left it ringing, looking out at the main square, where a Christmas tree had blown down, its bulbs shattered on the pavement. He tried his parents and they said they'd been trying to get in touch.

'Wendy rang on Friday. She sounded upset.'

'Has she been trying my house?'

'I don't know. We wondered that. I don't know why she rang here.'

'Was she going back to Leicester or Ludlow?'

He could imagine her turning up at his flat and then breaking down because she'd gone all that way for nothing.

'Where was she when she called?'

'She didn't say. She just said to say she'd rung.'

'OK. I have to go.'

He put the phone down and called the police, explaining that it wasn't just a missing person but somebody who'd been suicidal, and that she'd come looking for her boyfriend, and he wasn't here.

'We can check the flat,' they said, 'but not much else.'

It took over an hour for them to sort it out, because they weren't willing to break the door down. The landlord had to be located so they could get a master key.

The police let Nick go upstairs with them, to show them the flat, making sure it was the right one. There were five of them, which made it feel more frightening than he'd wanted it to. Their radios hissed and their uniforms rustled like nylon and smelled of dry-cleaning. Nick had expected the corridor to fill with the other residents, but their doors remained closed.

The police knocked and called. It was strange hearing them say 'Wendy' because they didn't even know her. They waited, unlocked the door and called again. 'Wait here,' they said, pausing for him to nod agreement. They opened the door and two went in. A breeze came from the room with a smell like rotten wood, which was strange in such a new building. Almost immediately one of the policemen said, 'She's here.' When Nick moved towards the door, he felt the others grab him. He caught a glimpse of the police staring towards the floor before he was pulled away.

Epilogue

Sarah was no help after Wendy's death. When I first told her, she cried, saying, 'How can I compete with a dead girl?' We came close to blows again, but it ended with me sending her home. She'd made threats to kill herself, and I said I wished she would. But she came back the next day and pretended to be supportive. Nothing was said about Wendy, but she took me out to the pictures. She said nothing else about it until after the funeral, when she obligingly asked how it had been. When I said it was terrible, she said, 'Am I meant to be proud of you, just because you're upset?'

It was a couple of weeks after the funeral that I realised my photos of Wendy had been burned. After she'd died I'd gathered together all the pictures of her, which would have made it easy for Sarah to get rid of them in one compulsive action. But her destruction was more calculated, because she'd been through the negatives as well, snipping out every one that contained Wendy. The wax painting had been removed, and the books she'd already soiled were gone.

When I confronted her she set her jaw, eyes wide, and said I was wrong.

In an attempt to get a reaction I told her I was devastated.

'It was only *her* stuff.'

'But I loved her.'

'How *dare* you?'

'I loved her, and you can't make me forget.'

It was a relief to finally say it. She wouldn't confess, but I'd already made my decision by then and asked her to leave.

I rang Dave and told him I'd kicked her out.

'I don't want to sound too happy,' he said, 'but fucking great.'

I spent the next week at his house. He kept running baths for me, cooked all my meals and got out the videos I wanted. We watched *Star Wars* about five times.

I spoke to Linda only once more, and the thing I remember most from that conversation is the sound of Joey in the background, saying his name over and over. I almost laughed thinking about the first time we'd moved him, as calmly as possible so he wouldn't die of shock. I considered asking if I could keep him, but thought better of it.

Linda was so upset by what Sarah had done that she tried to make up for it by sending me a few of Wendy's things: a shirt she used to wear when we first met, some of her favourite books, and a necklace I'd bought her and forgotten about because she'd never worn it. She hadn't left a suicide note, but Linda sent me the last thing she'd written. It was found in her room, on a piece of lined A4. She'd drawn a tree in felt-tip, and next to that a list of things to do: *Ring Dad. Ring Mum. Ring Nick.*

You can't throw something like that away.

There are so many things I could have done differently. Everybody I've talked to tells me it's not my fault. Dave keeps going on about Laurence, and even Linda, saying that if anyone was to blame it was them. He went to the trouble of cutting out articles about genetic propensity and mental illness. But although you can make excuses, it doesn't change how you feel. I know there are things I could have done that would have kept her alive. I loved her, despite her faults, and I should have done more about it. When she said *Let's go to India*, I should have gone with her. Imagine that. I can't believe she'd have gone mad if we'd just thrown ourselves into each other and left the shit behind. Or we could have kidnapped the baby and set up in the mansion. Even when she was at her worst, we could have run away again and found some way of making her happy. Imagine if I'd put every hour into looking after her and bringing her back; I could have read to her, and massaged her, and told her stories; we could have gone travelling and drawing again. There were a thousand opportunities to make things better, but we kept holding back. It wasn't the damage that killed her, but that we did nothing about it.

For a long time after I left Wendy in Ludlow that New Year, I felt like I'd been a selfish shit, but that too much harm had been done for me to cure it. If I wanted to make amends, it had to be with somebody new. Love, I decided, has nothing to do with feelings but is about how you treat people. Which is why I wanted to make Sarah's life perfect; it was a fresh start, with no blame or history. But that made me so cautious about hurting her feelings I didn't realise she was cauterising mine. By the time I'd kicked her out, I'd realised the truth. Feelings give us clues about who we should be kind to.

   That doesn't mean it's about getting married and settling down. Wendy and I would both have gone mad if we'd tried that. But we should have taken our feelings more seriously. For all that lecturing I used to do about painting and having a big life, none of it matters as much as looking after each other.

I can remember so much about our time together, but it's difficult to recall the pain. When I remember the funeral I can picture certain details – the bell ringing, the tiny coffin, Linda's unnatural howling as it went into the ground – but I feel nothing. Even when I remember Laurence, unflinching, coming over to shake my hand and thank me, I feel nothing. But sometimes, when I least expect it, the feelings catch me out. I can't go anywhere without being reminded of her. But even that is less of a problem than seeing new things and wishing we could have shared them.

There was a day in spring when I went to see Caryn in London. On Old Compton Street the air was filled with a light like sunset, which made everybody appear tanned. It was probably pollution, but it made the buildings like sandstone, and the sky was as blue as winter. I know it isn't healthy, but I tried to imagine what it would have been like if Wendy had been there.

I have a problem with imagination, because I've never been able to separate fantasies from intentions. If I picture something, it's because I want it to come true. So when I picture Wendy it's as though I'm making plans for the future, and I almost believe it will happen. I imagine us together, spending an afternoon in my room while it's raining, staring at the weather and harping on about the light.